BLOCKED

GOLD HOCKEY #1

ELISE FABER

BLOCKED

BY ELISE FABER

Newsletter sign-up

BLOCKED

Print ISBN-13: 978-1-946140-14-2

Ebook ISBN-13: 978-1-946140-08-1

Cover Art by Jena Brignola

ACKNOWLEDGMENTS

AUTHOR'S NOTE

I started playing hockey when I was fourteen and still play several nights a week with my husband in recreational leagues. It's a fun, fast-paced sport, and I get to see the occasional good-looking guy with his shirt off. Okay, that may be my husband, but you know what I mean. ;)

The sport has brought a lot to my life: competition, discipline, and, nowadays, lots of good exercise. If it's ever been something you've been interested in, I would encourage you to check out USAHockey.com. There are many programs for women and men to start at any age and any skill level.

I hope Brit and Stefan's story brought you some laughs and lots of heat. (I can state truthfully that their locker room is a lot cleaner than the ones I usually use!) Backhand, Gold Hockey #2 will be coming September 6th (preorder here) and Boarding, Gold Hockey #3 is slated for later this year. More novels will be coming soon, and each standalone will feature a different couple who fit into the larger Gold timeline.

Thanks again for reading and please feel free to find me on

Facebook (facebook.com/elisefaberauthor) or in my street team (facebook.com/groups/fabinators) or Instagram (@elisefaber). I welcome all questions, comments, and hilarious viral videos.

And remember, when in doubt, just puck it.

—XOXO, E

GOLD HOCKEY SERIES

Blocked

Backhand

Boarding

Benched

Breakaway

Breakout

Checked

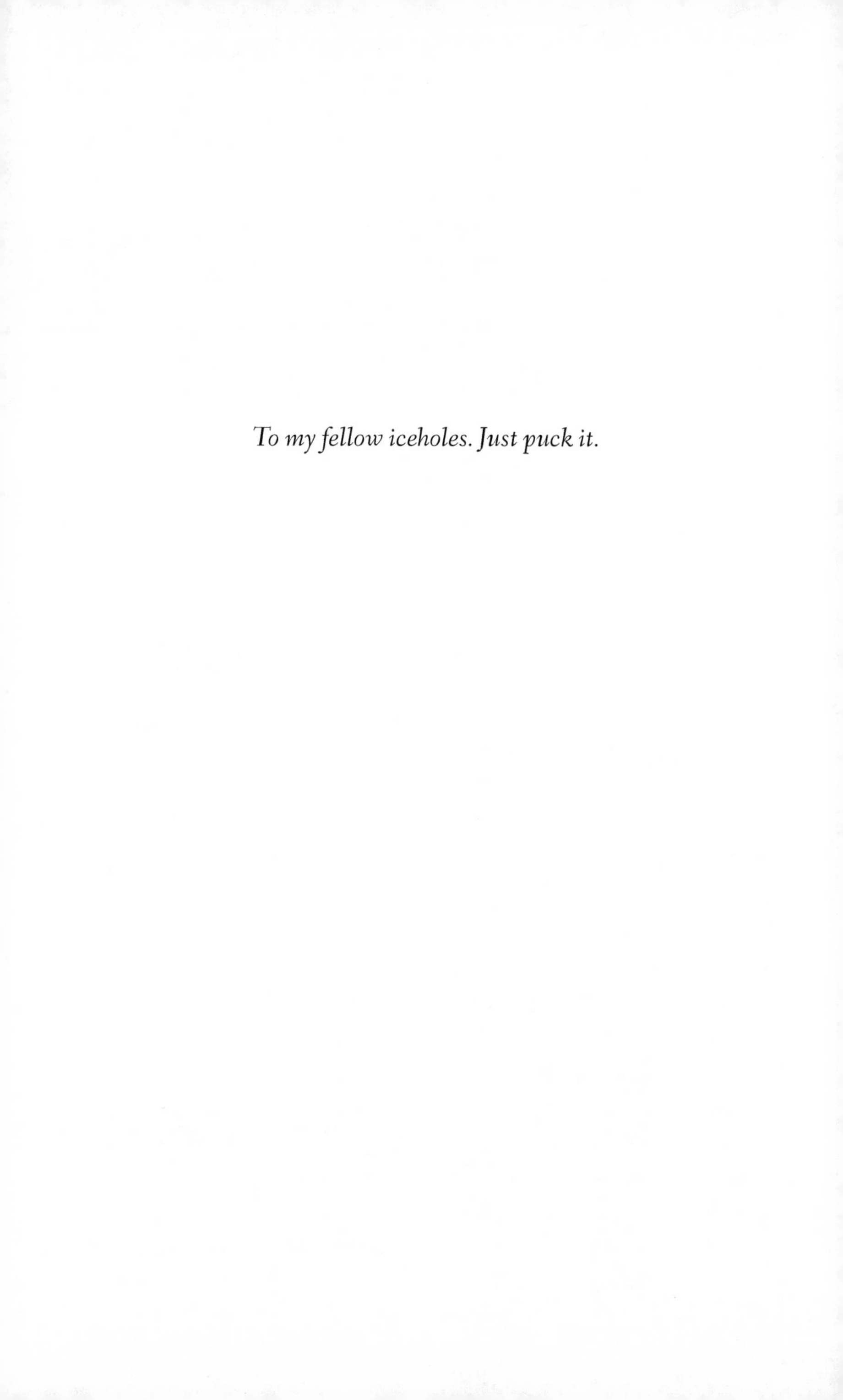

To my fellow iceholes. Just puck it.

ONE

Brit

THE FIRST QUESTION Brit always got when people found out she played ice hockey was *"Do you have all of your teeth?"*

The second was *"Do you, you know, look at the guys in the locker room?"*

The first she could deal with easily—flash a smile of her full set of chompers, no gaps in sight. The second was more problematic. Especially since it was typically accompanied by a smug smile or a coy wink.

Of course she looked. *Everybody* looked once. Everyone snuck a glance, made a judgment that was quickly filed away and shoved deep down into the recesses of their mind.

And she meant *way* down.

Because, dammit, she was there to play hockey, not assess her teammates' six packs. If she wanted to get her man candy fix, she could just go on social media. There were shirtless guys for days filling her feed.

But that wasn't the answer the media wanted.

Who cared about locker room dynamics? Who gave a damn

whether or not she, as a typical heterosexual woman, found her fellow players attractive?

Yet for some inane reason, it *did* matter to people.

Brit wasn't stupid. The press wanted a story. A scandal. They were desperate for her to fall for one of her teammates—or better yet the captain from their rival team—and have an affair that was worthy of a romantic comedy.

She'd just gotten very good at keeping her love life—as nonexistent as it was—to herself, gotten very good at not reacting in any perceptible way to the insinuations.

So when the reporter asked her the same set of questions for the thousandth time in her twenty-six years, she grinned—showing off those teeth—and commented with a sweetly innocent "Could've sworn you were going to ask me about the coed showers." She waited for the room-at-large to laugh then said, "Next question, please."

TWO

THIS WAS IT, the call up of her life.

And Brit was sitting in the parking lot of the arena, unable to force her fingers off the steering wheel.

"Get it together," she muttered. "Or you will suck on the ice."

Harsh, probably. But the truth.

Still, the words were enough. Enough to get her body in motion, to pop her door, and walk around to the trunk of her ten-year-old Corolla.

Her gear was shoved inside the small space like a sausage threatening to burst from its casing. Brit grabbed the strap and hauled out her bag before slinging it across her shoulder.

"You know they have guys for that."

The voice made her jump, and her gaze shot up, then up some more until she stared directly into the eyes of the captain of the San Francisco Gold, Stefan Barie.

The slight tinge of a Minnesotan accent made her shiver.

Uh-oh.

And seriously, only a hockey fan would find a Minnesotan accent sexy.

He smiled. "It's the coldest-winter-is-summer-in-San-Francisco thing." When she frowned, he cocked his head. "The wind chill."

What?

"You know? Mark Twain?"

Her brows pulled together. "I know who Mark Twain is, and I'm familiar with the quote. Though it's a common misnomer, and Twain didn't actually say it. Still, it is windy in the city . . . I just don't know why you think I'm cold, and it's not —" She shook herself. What was the point in her rambling? "Never mind."

This was what her mind did.

Every single time.

It drifted, focused on mundane details she then couldn't prevent from bursting free.

No surprise that once they *were* free, her conversations were punctuated with awkward pauses.

Like the one happening now.

Brit sighed. Give her an interview any time. Let her spout off sound bites to the camera and no problem. It was the real life human interactions that were terrible.

"No," Stefan said. "Tell me. What is it?"

It was only because he seemed genuinely interested that she answered.

"It's not summer."

"What?"

Another sigh. *Yep. Way to go, genius.* "It's technically fall. Summer has been over for six-and-a-half days."

There was a moment of quiet, a long, uncomfortable pause during which neither of them spoke.

Then surprisingly—*shockingly*—Stefan laughed. Her heart gave a little squeeze, her brain said, *Uh-oh*, but then before she could really panic, he spoke, "You're absolutely right. Now come on." Snagging her sticks, he nodded toward the arena. "I'll show you the ropes."

THREE

OH NO, this wouldn't do.

This. Would. Not. Do.

Brit stared up at the obviously hastily created sign—black squiggles of Sharpie and crumpled computer paper tended to highlight that fact.

This would not do.

"Okay then. See you on the ice," Stefan said, handing over her sticks and walking down the hall.

Brit dropped her bag to the black skate mat laid across the concrete floor, pushed open the door, and peered inside the room, just to make sure it wasn't full of her teammates, that this wasn't a lame joke for the new girl.

It wasn't.

Hot rage slid through her that she tried to swallow. She needed to be on her A-game. Needed to focus.

And this wasn't the players' fault. Apparently, management had decided to go for this little endeavor on their own. Likely, they were trying to keep things PC in order to avoid a potential lawsuit.

But this was Brit's future.

She fumbled for the switch and flipped on the light. Her heart sank further as a wave of disappointment welled up.

It was exactly as she'd feared.

A single bench. One equipment rack.

Yup. Getting dressed by herself was sure going to help her integrate into the team.

The locker room was the heart of any hockey team, where joking and ribbing and plenty of cursing took place. It was where she'd always felt most comfortable, and where she'd been able to find at least a few allies.

How was she supposed to receive coaching sequestered by herself? Should she just watch the team bond and draw up plays without her? Miss the talk about D-pairs or changes in the system?

She wasn't the first woman to sign a contract with a professional men's hockey team, but she was damn sure the first to have earned a chance at the backup goaltending spot.

Which might someday lead to a starting position.

A major step of which was connecting with her teammates.

Brit let the door slam closed, shouldered her bag, and walked down the hall.

She heard them before she saw them.

"Chin up," she murmured and pushed into the room.

It took a few moments for the guys to notice her. Silence fell, stifling, hot, embarrassing.

Not that a little embarrassment would stop her.

Spotting an empty bench and rack, she walked across the room. Her bag hit the floor with a thud; her sticks clacked together as she set them against the wall.

She could have heard a pin drop, could practically smell the smoke coming out of her teammates' ears.

Not about to let them get the drop on her and having been

through this more than her fair share of times, Brit knew it was best to get the awkwardness over.

She unzipped her bag, hung up her gear, then toed off her shoes and stripped down.

All the way down.

"Everyone get that good look," she said into the quiet locker room.

Her gaze slid around, meeting each of the guys' in turn. Some were obviously confused or shocked, a couple were irritated by her or her interruption, and some were typical men—if their eyes glued to her breasts were any indication.

Others—like Blane, her teammate now three times over—were familiar with her methods. He didn't even blink at her nakedness, just kept his eyes on hers and nodded in greeting.

"Get it out of your system," she told the interested ones, "and get over it," she said to the irritated section. She was here to stay, and if they had a problem . . . well, they could suck it.

To the rest, she said, "Now let's play some fucking hockey."

With that, she snagged her sports bra and underwear and started getting dressed.

"Style points, sweet— I mean, Brit."

She grinned up at Blane, who was half-dressed and standing in front of her, and feigned indifference, even though her heart was pumping with jitters. This may not be her first professional hockey rodeo, but it was still the NHL, where the best came to play.

No way she wanted to screw that up.

"You know how it is," she told him. Her anxiety eased when he stepped closer and gave her a quick hug. It was nice to have him there, especially since the two of them went *way* back, having played together in juniors.

"Ten points out of ten." His voice dropped. "You okay?"

"*Now* I'm fine." She was. And as soon as she got onto the

ice, she'd be even better.

"Good."

Her lips twitched. "Good for *you* to catch that *sweetheart*."

Blane grimaced, tapped his nose. "Hasn't been the same since the first time I made the mistake of using it."

She'd been young with a chip on her shoulder the size of a redwood. Blane had made the mistake of trying to prove to his friends he could get in her pants.

The result had been a broken nose for him and a month-long grounding for her.

But they'd gotten that nonsense out of the way, had settled into a warm and easy friendship.

"I'd say sorry—" she began.

"But I wouldn't believe you anyway." He grinned. "Glad you're here," he said and crossed back to his spot to finish getting dressed.

Brit grabbed her pelvis protector, pulled it on, then snagged the black and gold striped socks that had been in the other dressing room. Just as she was about to slip one over her foot, a soft voice interrupted her.

"Well done," Stefan said.

She turned to look at him, not having noticed he was in the stall next to hers, and her heart gave a little tremble.

Which she ignored. Obviously.

He raised two fingers in silent salute before continuing to get dressed.

Slowly, noise filtered back in through the room, lewd jokes punctuated by awkward pauses as the guys glanced toward her for her reaction.

"You'll have to do better than that," she called after a particularly bad one. "I've heard that lame excuse for a joke before."

Stefan snorted, and her eyes flashed to his. Was it pride in his gaze? Annoyance? She couldn't tell a damned thing.

She'd just knelt atop her pads and begun strapping them on when Coach Bernard came in. He hesitated for the briefest moment, as though surprised to see her, then plugged an iPad into a cord in the corner of the room.

The image on the tablet's screen was projected onto the far wall, and he ran through each of the drills in turn.

"Move it," he told them. "Ten minutes."

On the way out, he paused near Brit, glared, then inclined his head to an open door just off the main part of the locker room. "When you're finished."

She nodded, tied the last couple of straps, and stood. Leaving her chest protector and helmet on the shelf above the bench, she walked to Bernard's office. Her pulse raced, and her palms were sweaty.

His expression had said this chat wouldn't be concerning her welcome party.

The buckles on her leg pads clinked when she hesitated on the threshold. Bernard glanced up from a stack of papers on his desk and waved at her. "Come in."

Brit shuffled her way inside, waited.

Bernard studied her, his face completely impassive, and yet there was something under the surface. It wasn't dislike exactly, but she got the feeling he hadn't been one hundred percent on board with her being there.

Well, tough. She'd prove herself to him as well.

Just as soon as she figured out a way to end this god-awful silence.

A minute went by. He stared at her as she stood there, half-dressed and awkwardly taciturn.

Eventually, she cleared her throat and asked, "You wanted to see me?"

"Yes, Brittany—"

"Brit," she interrupted automatically.

Bernard didn't say anything for another long moment, only regarded at her with a raised brow.

Her gut went tight as she stared back. Last thing she wanted to do was get on the wrong foot with management and, between her locker room striptease and interrupting the coach, she had the feeling she was off to a very bad start.

"Brit," he finally said, "I think you're a good player, don't doubt that. But I'm not sure you being here is the best thing for the Gold."

Ouch.

The Gold were the NHL's newest expansion team, a controversial addition—and an unnecessary one at that, some thought—in the already professionally crowded, but hockey-hungry Bay Area.

As with most expansion teams, they weren't very good, which wasn't unusual, but the owners were running out of patience, and the team had gotten some bad press last season: carousing, the odd DUI, then a scandal involving one of their top players and a rape allegation. Couple that with losing the majority of games . . .

Rumor had it, if the team didn't improve this season, the owners might sell.

"You think I'm a publicity stunt." A way to clean up the Gold's image rather than a valuable addition to the team.

It wasn't something she hadn't already thought of.

Bottom line, though, was it didn't matter what management's motivations were. This was her chance to play at the highest level possible. To be the first woman to do so.

It was a really big deal, no matter the pushback she would have to withstand.

God knew, she'd already endured plenty of it from the media, from other players in the league, from her own mother, who worried she might be in over her head.

Outwardly, she held onto a shield of confidence, pretended all of the naysayers had no freaking clue.

But inside? She *did* wonder if she was good enough.

Only time would tell.

Still, Brit knew one thing. And it was a big one.

She knew she could deal with pretty much anything if it meant she could play hockey.

The sport was in her heart, in every single nerve ending and cell. She *never* felt more at home than when she was on the ice.

"Maybe you're a publicity stunt. And maybe it'll work out." He shrugged, like it wasn't her future he was so casually dismissing. "But my experience tells me not."

"Well, thanks for the vote of confidence." She didn't bother trying to keep the sarcasm from her voice. Any bridges she might have worried about conserving had been burned long before she'd even set foot in the locker room.

Bernard sighed. "You're talented. I'll give you that much. Your glove hand is one of the fastest I've ever seen. But you're shorter than the male goalies and weak on your upper blocker side. That will need improvement if you want a chance at a start."

"Noted," she said. "I'll work on it." And she would.

"Good." A beat of quiet. "See you on the ice."

With a nod, she left the office, knowing that despite Bernard's lack of confidence in her abilities, he had spoken the truth.

She *was* shorter. Her blocker side—the hand that held her goalie stick and was protected by a large rectangular pad—*was* her biggest weakness.

It wasn't as if she could grow six inches on the spot, but . . . she could work on her technique, bust her ass, and practice hard.

Harder than she ever had before.

FOUR

A MAN STOOD next to Brit's stall when she came out of Bernard's office. Mid-fifties with close-cropped white hair, he wore a black tracksuit with the Gold's logo and skates. A pair of gloves and a stick were propped next to her gear.

"Brit," he said, putting out his hand for her to shake. "I'm Frank, but the boys call me Frankie, so feel free."

Call him Frankie?

Words literally would not form on her tongue.

Because she already knew who the man was. Had researched each member of the Gold's coaching staff before she'd signed her contract.

But that didn't stop her from being starstruck.

Frank wasn't just Frankie. He was Franklin Todd, renowned goalie coach and former professional player, and just about as close as she got to a hockey orgasm.

Meeting him, *talking* to him was better than shutting down a cocky forward on a breakaway, better than stacking the pads and stealing an almost-guaranteed goal.

He was her idol.

Except . . .

Her heart sank because he probably felt the same way as Bernard. She was an annoyance, a not-quite-good-enough player.

Worse. She was a girl.

Well, fuck that.

Straightening her shoulders, Brit glanced up and forced herself to witness the derision in Frankie's eyes firsthand.

Except it wasn't there.

She stumbled for a moment before settling on "H-hi, Frankie."

He grinned, grabbed up his stick and gloves. "Hi, yourself. Don't let Bernard get to you. He's a hardass to every new player, and he especially doesn't like rookies."

She shrugged into her chest protector and began securing it in place. It was strange to be considered a rookie at her ripe old age. In hockey, rookies tended to be in their teens, or sometimes their early twenties. Definitely not well on their way to their third decade.

But that aside, she decided to ask the bigger question. "Why'd he agree to have me on the team?"

If she'd been expecting a platitude about Bernard really liking her on the inside or some crap, she'd have been wrong.

"He had no choice."

Okay then.

"I wanted you and threatened to walk if management didn't give you a contract."

Brit was dumbfounded for a long moment before she found her voice. "But . . . why?"

She'd had her fair share of supporters through the years, her brother, some coaches and players, a small—*very small*—segment of fans who knew who she was.

But why would someone she'd never met—someone she didn't know—put his neck out for her?

"I saw you in Buffalo."

She frowned, thought back to all the times she'd played in Buffalo. Only one game stood out. And not because they'd dominated. "But we got creamed."

Her team had lost 8-1, and she remembered each of the four goals that she'd let in with crystal-clear accuracy. The two periods she'd played had been some of her worst hockey ever.

"I know."

Confused, she just stared at him.

"You let in some soft ones."

Was that supposed to make her feel better?

"But after you were pulled"—after the coach had taken her out of the game and let the other goalie play—"you stayed on the bench instead of going to the locker room."

Brit remembered sitting there, at first because she hadn't wanted to make the walk of shame past her teammates, and then in sympathy when the score continued to rise.

"Yeah, I did."

Frankie watched her for a long moment, his eyes fixed on hers, as though willing her to understand.

She didn't.

Big deal. She sat on the bench. It isn't like she'd done it for unselfish reasons.

Frankie sighed, clapped her on the shoulder, and turned toward the hall that led to the ice.

"Five minutes."

FIVE

THERE WAS nothing like those first few moments of stepping on the ice.

The crisp, dry air coating her lungs, the slight tingle as the cold hit her cheeks. The smell—part sweat, part residual gas fumes from the Zamboni, part the cool, clean scent that had been present in every, single rink Brit had ever been in.

She bobbed her head toward her chest, sliding her helmet from where it rested at her hairline down over her face without using her hands. It wasn't repainted yet and still had flames of red and gold interspersed with the Kansas City Panthers' logo—the AHL, or minor league, team she'd been playing with only four days before.

Her contract had been freshly modified to allow her to play with the Gold, but it did possess a clause that enabled management to bump her back down to the Panthers if she didn't perform well enough. The clause sucked, but her position as a *rookie* meant they hadn't been able to negotiate much better than a standard, entry-level NHL agreement.

Though, if she performed well enough during training camp and the preseason games, her agent had managed a section that would enable her to secure a one-way contract—meaning she couldn't be demoted back to the AHL without being paid at the NHL rate.

The boost in pay was both a perk to her and a deterrent for management to get rid of her. It wouldn't guarantee Brit's position with the Gold, but it was the best she or any other new player could hope to get.

For now, Brit's goal was to prove herself good enough to stay in the big leagues.

She hoped—

No, dammit. She would do it.

Shrugging her shoulders, she tugged at her jersey. It was black, her pads white . . . and none of that mattered because . . .

She was delaying.

Enough already. One tap of her stick against her leg pads, one against the right side of the open door—she was nothing if not superstitious, just like every other goalie she'd ever known—then out onto the ice.

Normal people had bad dreams of being late or giving a speech naked.

Brit wasn't normal, not by a long shot.

Her worst nightmare was eating shit on that first step. But today, just like 99.99 percent of other days, she was fine.

Still, skating into a new rink, for a new team, in a new city meant Brit was stripped bare and vulnerable.

Which really, *really* sucked.

She despised vulnerable. Hated weakness—

A puck glanced off the glass less than six inches from her head.

It may have been an accident, but she doubted it. These guys had too much control to miss the net by a good ten feet.

No doubt, the shot had originated from the irritated section of the locker room.

Awesome. She stifled a curse and continued warming up.

Brit had spent way too much time having pucks shot at her to flinch. In fact, she was much too desensitized to the high-pitched clang to react in any noticeable sort of way. But inside she noted the action for what it was.

A warning.

SIX

Stefan

HOCKEY WAS IN HIS BLOOD, in his gut. His soul.

Vulcanized rubber smelled like ambrosia. Hockey tape could fix anything. And there was no better feeling than skating every, *single* day.

Stefan wasn't the best player in the league, not by a long shot. But he worked hard, maybe harder than anyone else.

He also wasn't an asshole.

Which was how he'd ended up as captain midway through last season.

After Devon Carter—the General Manager or GM for the Gold—had made the disastrous decision of choosing Peter Gordaine at the beginning of the previous year, management had decided to let the team vote.

For some reason, they had chosen him.

Of course, it was probably because Gordaine had very nearly destroyed the team—a team of professionals, who were paid to do a job, and typically didn't bring bullshit to the table.

He'd done it with a streak of meanness that burned

everyone in his path—player or employee alike. It had been Stefan's most miserable season of hockey ever, which was saying something, because he'd had his fair share of jerky coaches and prima donna teammates.

But, at least, Gordaine was gone, with Stefan in his place.

Being captain was both a blessing and curse.

It was a pretty special thing to have the team look up to him, the notion humbling and a little daunting, especially with the added pressure to both perform and set a good example.

The curse part came from dealing with the fallout from last season's scandal and now with Brit rocking the boat—

He heard the distinctive *pop* of puck meets glass and turned, watching as one collided with the boards less than a foot from Brit's head.

"Son of a bitch," he muttered and started to skate over.

Brit met his eyes, and he stopped mid-stride when she shook her head.

"Ignore it," that shake seemed to say, before she adjusted the grip on her stick and skated to the empty net.

Stefan bit back a curse. Had he just been thinking the team was special? Nope. Special was definitely not the right word.

Idiotic was more like it.

He was dealing with a bunch of *idiotic*, teenaged-boys.

SEVEN

THIS WAS GOING to end badly.

It was less than ten minutes into practice, and Stefan was stretching along the boards.

Which wasn't the problem, though the fact that he felt a little stiff and sore from his early-morning workout was concerning. Namely, because it showed that he was getting old.

Thirty years on the planet, and he was on the downward side of his career. Not that he wasn't going to be hanging around for the next five or six seasons—hopefully—but hockey was truly a young man's sport.

Stefan had already been in the NHL for nine seasons: six with the Calgary Flames, one with the Ducks, and the last two with the Gold.

He was lucky in that he hadn't had to fight his way up from the AHL.

It had been *dumb* luck, really, paired with a couple of unfortunate injuries for some teammates that Stefan's opportunity to play in the NHL had come at the beginning of his first professional season.

But after that, it had been his work ethic that had secured the position.

He'd taken the opening and worked like hell to fit right into the Flames' lineup. Then the Ducks'.

He'd been happy in Anaheim. Secure. Figured he'd hang around there until his retirement. But the Gold were located in San Francisco—a place his mother had always wanted to live—so he'd requested a trade.

Ducks' management had understood, obliging his request and allowing him to be traded to the Gold. He'd moved his mother out from Minnesota, jumped into forging a new place on a new team . . . upon which he'd been thrust into a shit-show of epic proportions.

Backstabbing. Laziness. Poor coaching.

The switch had become instant regret.

But that wasn't the current problem, or at least not the one that was troubling him at the moment. The Gold were on a better track this season and had a real chance at redeeming themselves to the general public. What was making tension shoot down his spine was the fact that the guys were taking it easy on Brit, and that with every soft wrist shot slung her way, Stefan could see her frustration level rising.

He was surprised there wasn't smoke coming out of the ear holes in her helmet.

It was his duty as captain to make sure everyone came together, worked as a unit. To that effect, he couldn't help but wonder if he should go over there and rip a shot, just to set the tone, to let the guys know it was okay.

But would that cross the line with her? Step on her toes? Or—

He agreed with Brit's decision to come into the locker room. Female or not, she was a teammate and deserved a space with the team. Further than that, the team wouldn't take it easy on a male goalie in practice, so they shouldn't do any different by her.

But . . . what if he hurt her?

Which was probably a stupid thought, because it wasn't like Stefan's shot was that hard, not by NHL standards.

Still, it went against his vein to even chance hurting a woman, and he knew that most of the guys—with the sole exceptions being Stewart and a few other idiots—felt the same.

There might as well have been a tightrope strung across the ice.

On one side was how they would normally react. The other was what they were doing now. How were they supposed to navigate it?

Turned out he—*they*—didn't need to.

Another shot fluttered toward the net, barely making a sound as it hit Brit's leg pads.

She chucked her glove, blocker, and stick on top of the net then yanked back her helmet.

Her strides were rapid but quiet as she skated toward the top of the circles. Her words, when she got there, were not.

"What the fuck do you think you're doing?" Brit shoved the player hard in the chest. Chad was one of their forwards, a second line right-winger, and the push meant he had to scramble to stay on his feet, barely escaping a fall straight back onto his ass. "I can shoot harder than that in my sleep. How the fuck am I supposed to get some fucking practice if you won't shoot the fucking puck with any-fucking-power? Are we in peewee fucking hockey or the fucking NHL?"

The string of f-bombs unleashed impressed Stefan—and a few others on the team, judging by the bemused expressions emerging on their faces. She was well-versed in using hockey's favorite curse word as both adjective and verb.

Chad, for his part, appeared equally shocked and awestruck.

When Brit paused for breath, he nodded, said, "Okay."

Man of few words . . . that was Chad.

Brit narrowed her eyes at him, and he nodded again. She whipped her glare to a few of the others before skating back to her crease—the blue half circle directly in front of each goal.

Helmet down. Blocker and glove on. Stick in hand as she reached for the water bottle on top of the net.

Stefan saw what was going to happen before anyone else did. He burst to his feet and—

"Watch—"

Too late.

Crack. A stick collided with the ice. The puck flew through the air and collided . . . with Brit's back. It hit with a sick *thunk* —the noise akin to a pumpkin cracking in half—and she went down to one knee.

Here was the thing about goalies. All their padding was in the front. Their backs had basically no protection. Players knew that, which was why rule number one in hockey was never shoot the puck when the goalie wasn't looking.

Fucking five-year-olds knew it. Dumbass, twelve-year-old boys knew it. And certainly professional NHL players knew it.

Mike Stewart knew it.

He was also a giant bastard.

Stefan was just about to launch himself at the no good son of a bitch who was wearing a smirk the size of Mona Lisa's, when there was the sharp *trill* of a whistle.

"Take five!" Frankie hollered as he skated toward Brit.

Before Frankie reached her, Brit shoved to her skates and picked up her stick. She pointed it at Stefan and nodded.

He hesitated midstride. Did she want him to—?

She banged her stick on the ice, a sharp tap that caught his attention. Nodded again.

Okay then, Brit wanted him to shoot. And . . . *what?* He shouldn't? He should?

After a moment, he figured he'd at least better make it count.

Stefan wound up and ripped a shot at the net. Not a simple one either. A far side, lower-corner slap shot that . . . she stopped easily.

He grinned.

"I'll be damned," Max, his defense partner and one of his best friends muttered. "She's good."

"Of course she's good, you moron," Frankie said, with a whack of his stick to back of Max's calves. "Now show the rest of the team that."

Max took a slap shot. His was one of the fastest on the team, and it bounced off Brit's pads with a *thud* that reverberated through Stefan's stomach and the empty arena.

One of the guys whistled in surprise, and then they were off, the break forgotten, more shots, more surprise . . . more respect gained for Brit's ability.

By the time Bernard called them all into a mid-ice huddle before dispersing them into their individual groups, Brit looked to have earned more than half of his teammates' approval.

Including his.

He watched her out of the corner of his eye: her helmet propped back onto her head, her cheeks slightly rosy from exertion, one tendril of blond hair having escaped her ponytail to curl around one cheek.

She looked like an angel.

Stefan almost snorted. Okay, no angel. She looked tough and serious and fierce and . . . like every single one of his hockey wet dreams come to life.

She was also his teammate. And he was captain.

So he needed to forget that she had smelled like roses when he'd walked into the arena next to her, forget the way her pale brown eyes had flashed with hurt when she'd seen the room management had wanted to stick her in.

He also really needed to forget the sight of her naked breasts. Forget they were just the right size to fit in his palms—

Bernard gave a puff on his whistle, and the team stood, skating to their assigned locations.

Stefan hadn't heard a single word his coach had said.

Good thing he always studied the drills for the next day's practice the night before.

He joined Max and sent a small but fervent prayer to the hockey gods that Coach hadn't changed anything up on him.

EIGHT

STEFAN LUCKED out with respect to the drills.

Everything else was a clusterfuck.

The team wasn't coming together. At all.

Their former captain, Gordaine, had been a great hockey player, despite his complete failure at possessing any of the morals a normal human being might have. But Mike Stewart was a cancer to the team, eating away at every single bond Stefan had managed to erect.

It would have been annoying, or maybe just a little sad—the way Stewart so effectively tore people apart—if not for the impact it was having on Stefan's, and every other person on the Gold's payroll, livelihood.

If the Gold were sold, chances were the team and staff would be dismantled, parceled off to other teams or maybe just let go altogether.

Which was the nature of hockey, he supposed. Players were traded all the time. Families were moved or separated. But ninety-five percent of the team and coaching staff were good, hardworking people.

He didn't want the Gold reduced to pieces under his watch.

Yet Mike was almost certainly ensuring that would happen.

He'd been bumped to third-line defense when Bernard had joined the coaching staff this season and seemed to think it was his personal duty to show everyone how unhappy he was with the decision.

If the drill called for no contact, Mike used his stick, elbows, and fists instead of his shoulders and body. If it called for light contact . . . you'd better watch it. Your ass was getting laid out.

After the third time Mike drilled their rookie, Blue Robertson, into the boards, Stefan had had enough.

It was unnecessary, and someone was going to get hurt.

He skated over and got into Mike's face, yelling at him to back off. Surprisingly, Mike nodded, muttered an apology, and got back into line.

Alternate universe. Clearly Stefan had just stumbled into one.

He turned to Blue. "You okay?"

"I'm fine," the nineteen-year-old snapped. "I can handle myself. I don't—" He broke off, peeled himself up from the ice. "Mind your own fucking business."

Stefan watched Blue skate away and tried to figure out where in the hell that conversation had gone wrong.

When he turned and saw Mike with a smirk on his ugly mug, Stefan knew.

The cancer was spreading.

USUALLY STEFAN STAYED LATE and did off-ice conditioning—stairs, squats, wind sprints, that sort of thing.

It was comfort and training all in one short forty-five-minute workout, doing the exercises he'd learned as a kid when he and his mom hadn't had any extra money for a professional off-ice coach. And it probably said strange things about him that one of his happiest childhood memories was running through the routine with his mom.

But then again his mother had always been his rock. Add in hockey? No question why it had become so important.

Typically a few of the guys joined Stefan for the workout, but today he undressed, hung his gear, and showered as quickly as possible.

"Stairs?" Max asked, mid-sock removal.

Stefan shook his head. "Not today."

"Everything okay?"

That was the proverbial question, wasn't it? Part of the reason he was so concerned about the Gold disbanding.

His mom's doctors were in San Francisco.

"Everything's good," he forced himself to answer in a neutral voice. "Just have a meeting."

"This about the restaurant?"

Stefan's lips twitched. "You know there's no way I'm investing in your restaurant, right?"

"The food will be incredible."

"Half of restaurants fail in the first year."

"*Pff*. Minor detail," Max said as he straightened and stripped out of his jock. He stood there for a long moment, dick flopping, completely naked, then his eyes flashed over Stefan's shoulder.

To where Brit sat, unbuckling her pads.

Max's eyes widened, and he sank to the bench, covering his groin with a black-and-gold hockey sock.

"Nothing I haven't seen before," Brit said, in a voice slightly louder than stage whisper. Her gaze was focused on her pads as she fussed with one of the straps. "Don't let your balls smell on my account."

Max's cheeks went a little pink, but he pushed off the

bench, dropped the sock, and hit the showers. He snagged a towel along the way—probably the first time in history he'd done so. Max was one of those guys who didn't mind being naked.

"Air drying," he always said, *"is the way to go."*

Stefan thought it more likely that Max's mouth was moving so fast his brain didn't have a chance to remember pesky things like public nudity.

Still, he glanced toward Brit. "Shh-wetty balls?"

Her lips twitched. "You quoting SNL on me?"

"Those were the better days."

Stefan had meant the show, but a wave of nostalgia rolled over him, softened his words until they had taken on a completely different meaning.

One he really didn't want to discuss with anyone.

Son of a bitch.

He bent, tied his shoe. He just wanted to get out of there as quickly as—

"Everything okay?"

Brit's question was gentle, way more so than anything he'd heard come out of her mouth in the last couple of hours.

Dammit.

"I'm good."

"You su—"

"I'm sure." He shouldered his small workout bag, pushed his wallet into his pocket. The equipment guys would take care of the rest. "You've got enough to deal with. Why don't you worry about yourself?"

Stefan hadn't meant to sound like a dick.

He had anyway.

Brit's expression locked shut, all the softness disappearing as her face went completely smooth. She held his eyes for another second, scalding russet depths that seemed to pierce right through him.

Then she turned back to her equipment without another word.

It was a dismissal, plain and simple. One he'd facilitated, but damned if he didn't hate it.

Not the time, Barie. Not. The. Time.

"See you tomorrow," he told her.

Brit nodded.

With a sigh, and feeling like he'd just blown a *Gold*en—no pun intended—opportunity to bond with Brit, Stefan turned and left the room.

He couldn't worry about hurt feelings, about dickwad defensemen, or investing in a Gold-themed restaurant that was probably going to sink and sink fast.

His mom needed him.

NINE

Brit

HER SHOULDER HURT LIKE A MOTHERFUCKER.

Every motion as she pulled off her gear was a knife-prick of pain that had Brit gritting her teeth. It wasn't as bad as when she'd dislocated the joint there, but it wasn't comfortable by any means, and she'd have a hell of a hard time lifting her arm in the morning.

Just what she needed when Bernard had basically told her she needed to improve a hell of a lot if she wanted a chance at playing. Dammit. But this wasn't helping so she allowed one more moment of fury before forcing herself to get it together. It wasn't like she hadn't dealt with this her whole life.

With the men it was always the same, always making her jump through a hundred hoops to feel welcome.

And, she remembered with a shudder, sometimes those hoops left scars.

Every women's team she'd ever played on had been different. Still competitive as hell, but supportive . . . at least in terms of her teammates not peppering her with slap shots when her back was turned.

If she found out who'd taken that shot—

No. It didn't matter.

"How's the shoulder?" Frankie asked.

Brit hadn't heard him come up, but that wasn't exactly a surprise, considering how deep she'd been in her thoughts.

She needed to pull free of the anger and the past and focus.

"Fine," she said. She was. Really. And her shoulder would be too—after a gallon of ibuprofen and a bottle of wine.

Frankie snorted. "Sure you are. PT after you shower. Then we're going to talk." When she opened her mouth to protest, he narrowed his eyes. "Hustle up, I don't want to be here all day."

Well, then.

She nodded and went back to work on her gear. Less than a minute later, she pulled the remaining pad off and set it down before crossing to the showers. It was tempting to stay and fuss with the buckles, straightening, checking her clasps.

But that was her version of a security blanket, and she knew she needed to respect the equipment staff's ability to do their job.

So Brit shoved the nervous habit to the back of her mind and snagged a towel.

She peered inside, checked the showers. They were mostly clear. Or at least most of the guys were on one side—whether that was in deference to her or just chance, she didn't know.

Or care.

Okay, care *much*. Her heart pounded, and a fine sheen of sweat coated her skin as she made herself step inside.

This part had become okay: the stepping inside and getting clean. So long as there were others showering, too. So long as she wasn't alone.

And Blane was in the other room. Brit knew he'd have her back.

Suck it up.

With a few quick movements, she stripped down and dunked her face under the water.

A long slow whistle made her roll her eyes. "*Damn,* girl."

Seriously?

She'd thought her not-so-sexy striptease would have done the job. She flicked a gaze over her shoulder, ready to loose a retort, and saw Max staring at her.

Or *not*?

Because his eyes were locked on her back, not her butt, not trying to sneak a peek at her breasts.

"What?" she asked.

Max flicked his gaze up to hers as he tucked the edges of a towel around his waist. When it was secure, he took a few steps closer, just near enough to make those old feelings inside of her well up. For the fear she normally kept locked tight to slither free.

This was why she changed with the team. Why she *didn't* shower alone anymore.

Because there was strength in numbers.

Max stopped immediately, freezing a couple of feet away, and Brit felt a wave of shame wash over her. How much had shown on her face?

The honest truth was that she really should be over this by now, over the fear, over glancing around every corner for the monster to come out again.

But she wasn't. No matter how much she tried to convince herself differently, she wasn't.

"You okay?" Max asked, all teasing lost from his expression.

So he was sweet in addition to really good-looking.

Which really wasn't what she should be thinking about. But

it was a relief to grasp onto the inane thought, to get lost in something stupid and superficial.

Her heart slowed enough that she was able to shove the fear down.

So deep she could almost fake normal.

Max was tall, strong, and built, a steam engine on two legs. Yet that wasn't what called to her. There was something soft about him, a kindness in his eyes, a teddy-bear-like quality that made her want to confide in him.

Brit wondered if she'd ever be able to open up to a man, especially one like Max.

He'd be protective, tough, and—

Crap. She didn't have time for this, for imaginings that would get her nothing but trouble.

Plus, she didn't need a man to protect her.

"That's one hell of a bruise," Max said when she didn't respond, and if his voice was carefully light, Brit was ignoring it.

No need to come across as a total basket case. At least not on her first day.

"I'm fine," she said, forcing her eyes away and stepping into the water. "It's just swelling and blood under the surface of the skin. You know, capillaries were ruptured with the impact of the puck and the blood pools under the skin. It looks bad, purple and. . ."

She was rambling again, introducing all sorts of unnecessary details to the conversation.

"Well . . . I'm glad you're okay," Max said when she managed to clamp her mouth shut.

"I bruise easily," she blurted. Or not. Word vomiting was her specialty.

Max paused. "Good to know. Hurt?"

He was throwing her a lifeline. Brit glanced back over her

shoulder and grimaced as she poured shampoo into her hand. "Like hell."

His eyes crinkled at the corners, his lips curved. "How about a beer tonight? Couple of the guys like to go to a place around the corner, Alberto's."

Her heart gave a little squeeze at the invitation, at the offer of inclusion. It felt good, but . . .

"Can't. Frankie wants me to hit up PT," she said, turning slightly so she didn't have to crane her neck to look at him. "Thanks for the invite, though. I'd rather that than spend an hour with some kooky sports therapist."

Max laughed. "I wouldn't let Mandy hear you say that."

A frown pulled down her brows. "Why?"

"You'll see." He started to walk out of the showers, paused, and called, "See you tomorrow."

Social skills. She still had a long way to go.

With a stifled sigh, she quickly finished her shower and dried. Unfortunately, her thoughts weren't so easy to stifle. Not about physical therapy, but about her inability to have a relationship. About walls and barriers and barbed wire strung tight around a person's heart in order to keep it safe.

Maybe Brit didn't *need* a man to protect her, but . . . sometimes she longed for one.

TEN

ICE BATHS WEREN'T ALL they were cracked up to be.

"Quite whining," Amanda—or Mandy, as the boys called her—said. She was the head of PT and took absolutely zero shit. "I swear, you're worse than the boys."

"It's really cold."

"That's kind of the point." The other woman, petite and brunette, vivacious with curves for days—basically everything Brit wasn't—glanced at the clock. "Two more minutes."

Brit wasn't sitting in a tub of ice, a la *Major League,* but with the combination of the cold stuff and some botanical version of IcyHot on her shoulder, she might as well have been.

Despite her discomfort, she had to admit the physical therapy suite was . . . well, sweet.

Pale grey walls were emblazoned with the Gold logo. White built-in cabinets held a variety of Mandy's torture instruments. There was a stim—or TENS machine—in one corner, an ultrasound unit in another, and all varieties of tape, bandages, and braces.

She sat on one of the three exam tables and thought her dad would have loved it.

But then again, he had loved anything that involved putting bodies back together. If it wasn't broken or bruised or sprained, he hadn't been interested.

Wow. Really?

Maybe all the pucks to her head over the years were finally catching up with her.

She'd been in the suite an hour, first filling out her medical background forms, even though Mandy appeared to know everything about her, from her distaste of mushrooms—they'd ordered in for dinner—to the three fractured fingers her senior year of high school. Then she'd undergone Mandy's prescribed treatment.

Which wasn't bad or anything Brit hadn't had experienced a hundred times over, but with all the memories cropping up and making her feel vulnerable, she was ready to get the heck out of there.

A couple-mile run would push the crap from her mind, and tomorrow she'd be able to function.

"I'd say you should probably take a day off—"

That cleared Brit's mind right up. She shot her gaze toward Mandy, who appeared amused.

"I didn't say you *had* to take the day off. Just that you *could*."

Brit snorted.

"Yeah. Didn't think that was likely." Mandy snagged a roll of KT tape—a special type of kinesiology bandage that reduced swelling and bruising. "I won't tell Bernard that you need a day off so long as you promise to tell me if the pain gets worse."

"Of course."

Mandy shot her a glare. "Seriously. Promise."

Irritation and humor coursed through Brit, and she put her hands up in surrender, not for the first time since she'd walked in.

In the sixty-plus minutes she had come to know Mandy,

she'd learned it was easier to accept defeat than argue with the therapist.

Clearly Max hadn't been exaggerating in the shower.

"I promise," Brit said.

"*Promise*," Mandy pressed. "For real."

"What are we, in second grade?" Brit rolled her eyes. "*I promise*. Or maybe I should say I *solemnly swear* to not overdo it?" She reached up with her good arm to hold her hair out of the way when Mandy bent to tape her shoulder.

"Yeah. Sure. You and every other professional athlete I know who pushes through injuries they shouldn't." The other woman huffed, finished the tape job, then leaned back and met Brit's eyes. "You know what this means, right?"

"Um. No?"

Had Mandy not realized she was joking? Was she really going to tell Bernard—

"You've just locked yourself into a *Harry Potter* marathon with me."

Relief coursed through Brit. She let out a breath, her heart settling. "*That* I can do. *Harry Potter* is everything."

Mandy laughed, a delicate tinkling sound that counteracted her tough-as-nails demeanor in the PT suite. "Agreed."

"Good. I'll bring the popcorn." Brit stood. "We done here?"

"Yup. Do those stretches, and we'll reevaluate after tomorrow's practice."

Argh. But it was better than being benched over a stupid bruise. "Okay."

She hightailed it for the door.

"Brit?" Mandy called.

Hand still on the knob, she turned. "Yeah?"

"Watch out for Mike Stewart," Mandy said. "He *always* goes for the cheap shot."

It didn't surprise Brit that Stewart had taken the shot. Or at least that was what she assumed Mandy had meant with her cryptic statement.

The professional hockey community was fairly small considering the amount of teams in its various leagues. But over time, rosters tended to overlap as players moved up the ranks.

Brit had played on her fair share of teams. Owing to that, she knew a lot of people.

And hardly anyone liked Mike Stewart. He was crass. He was arrogant. He'd gotten popped for two DUIs in the last few years and had even spent the night in jail for a bar fight the previous season.

If there was one person she needed to watch out for, it was Stewart.

Except there was nothing she could do but keep her guard up. With a sigh, she walked to her stall in the locker room to finish packing up her backpack.

Keys, dirty clothes, wallet, phone. Her gear would stay, now in the hands of the equipment guys.

The room was quiet, and half of the lights were off, bathing the room in shadow.

Something moved on the far side.

It was so similar to that night that Brit had to bite back a gasp. But it was early, she told herself. There were still plenty of people around.

This wasn't *that* night, and she was a lot more experienced now than three years before.

Multiple courses in self-defense, a can of pepper spray, and way too much money at a therapist would do that.

The shadow moved again, and speaking of spray, Brit reached into her backpack to grab the smooth metal can.

Frankie's voice both soothed and startled her. "How'd PT go?"

Brit had completely forgotten they were supposed to talk after her session with Mandy. "Good—"

Her eyes flicked to the corner again when the shadow rotated.

Frankie's gaze followed hers. "Eunice, could you come here?"

A woman in her mid-forties rose out of the darkness, walked toward them, and all the fear that had stiffened Brit's spine dissipated. She realized that the older woman must have been cleaning something, given the towel and spray bottle in her hands.

"Brit, meet Eunice," Frankie said.

"Pleasure to meet you, Ms. Plantain." Eunice extended her hand as though to shake before biting her lip and drawing it back.

Brit didn't know if it was because the other woman wore gloves or just didn't make a regular habit of shaking players' hands.

She didn't care about either.

Reaching across the space between them, she smiled and grasped Eunice's palm.

"Nice to meet you too," she said. "And Brit, please."

The other woman's smile lit up her face, settled the last of Brit's nerves.

"Eunice helps with cleaning on practice days. She never misses a shift." Frankie cocked his head, winked. "Unless her son is playing."

God, Brit loved this sport. Loved the way it put a look of pride on parents' faces, loved the way it lit up kids' lives.

Of course, there were assholes, and people who got hurt or had negative experiences.

But all in all, she'd never been part of anything better.

The three of them chatted for a few minutes more, Brit learning that Eunice's son was getting a shot at Junior As—a decent prospect for a California kid—and that he played center.

"She works in exchange for equipment," Frankie said quietly once Eunice had gone back to her cleaning. "Couldn't afford it otherwise. Bernard brought her on with the stipulation that she never work on a day her son plays."

"You're trying to soften me up to him."

"No need," Frankie said. "He's a good man. You'll see that soon enough. He's hard as hell but . . ."

Brit sighed, even though in her heart she already knew the truth—having seen him interact with the team at practice.

She'd had bad coaches. Bernard wasn't one of them.

"He's good," she said in agreement. Which really shouldn't be annoying, but somehow still was.

Frankie grinned. "Now, you're getting it." He nodded toward Eunice. "And her son is the best-outfitted kid on his team with his NHL *rejects*."

"Well, damn," she mock-griped, thoroughly charmed despite herself. "Why'd you have to go and tell me that?"

"Can't have you laboring under a misapprehension."

She blew out a breath and slung her backpack over her good shoulder. "I could have labored for a few more days."

"Better that you don't. Come on." Frankie gestured toward the hall. "I'll walk you to your car."

Brit felt relief at his words, which tempered some of her amusement. "I'm fine."

Frankie didn't reply, just started walking, and she had the feeling that even if she refused his offer, Frankie would still walk her to her car.

As Mandy had demonstrated, some battles weren't worth fighting.

Especially when the outcome was what she needed deep down anyway.

ELEVEN

Stefan

STEFAN PULLED up to his house, a decent-size older bungalow in a small suburb just south of the city. The lights were on, and he knew his mom was still awake.

She always waited up for him.

He pulled into the drive and got out, wondering how, at thirty years of age, he'd come full circle and was back living with his mother.

The move to San Francisco had been for her, to make her dream of living in the famous city come true. After she'd battled and beat cancer, Stefan had wanted to make that happen for her.

And somehow living with his mom had become okay.

She wasn't obtrusive. They got along. It had been just the two of them when he was growing up, and it hadn't taken much for them to get back in the groove.

Still, his intention had been to buy her a condo or house—whatever she'd wanted.

Then she'd gotten sick again, and everything had shifted.

Stefan hadn't been around for her first battle with cancer—no amount of begging would move his mom to Canada—and though he'd flown to Minnesota as often as possible, he'd still been in the middle of the season. His visits had been limited, and her care had been mostly regulated to health care professionals and the few friends she'd let help.

But things were different now. Even though the season was gearing up, she was close, and he would damn well be by her side.

Where she'd been for him countless times.

His road to playing professional hockey meant that he'd had to move a fair amount growing up. Some players stayed with host families, others boarding schools. *His* mom had always managed to find a new job in the new city and had moved with him, so they'd lived together. More than that, she'd always had an uncanny ability to make every place they'd ever lived feel like home.

Which was something his sixteen-year-old self had resented. His adult-self? Well, he understood how much of a sacrifice it must have been for her.

The garage door rumbled open, and he walked in, right past his mom's battered 1999 Honda Civic.

He shook his head as he walked past the old rust bucket, its license plate askew and the headlights stained yellow from age.

How many times had he offered to get her a new car?

With a sigh, he pushed into the kitchen. It was quiet, which was unusual, and there were no cooking smells, which was even stranger.

He frowned, glanced around, almost feeling like this was some sort of joke, like a cameraman would pop out and yell, "*Gotcha!*"

But of course, nobody did.

"Mom! I'm home."

There was no response. No hurried footsteps down the hall, no hum of the TV.

Stefan's heart stuttered. He slung his bag and keys onto the counter and took off running.

If something had happened to her while he was at work . . .

He didn't take note of the small framed photos she'd filled every corner of his house with or the bright purple throw pillows he'd given her such a hard time about buying.

No, he just sprinted down the hall toward her bedroom, his feet pounding against the hardwood floor.

Her bedroom door was ajar, and he pushed in without hesitation—

She was asleep.

Soft breaths punctuated the silence, soothed the frantic beating of his heart.

Carefully, he backed out of the room, shutting the door behind him. But he'd barely made it two steps before he had to sit down, his spine right there against the pale green wall his mom had repainted just after her diagnosis.

Stefan could do three-hundred-pound squats until his trainers were blue in the face. But the thought of something happening to his mom made his knees buckle.

Cancer.

Recurrent Stage 2 breast cancer.

When he'd heard the news six weeks before, Stefan had immediately flown back to Minnesota and packed his mom's belongings. She'd refused to come the previous year, not wanting to "cramp his style" in a new city, but he'd finally worn her down and she'd been planning on coming later in the season, after she'd found and trained her replacement at her job.

He hadn't cared about any of that.

No way could she manage her appointments through a Minnesotan winter—not to mention clearing the driveway of snow, brushing off her car, and the million other things that crept up when someone lived in a place with a shit-ton of the white fluffy stuff.

Stefan could have hired someone to take care of those things for her, like he'd done before, but that wasn't what the Baries did. That wasn't what was right.

His mother had taken care of him. So he would take care of her.

Even if he had to personally pound every cancer cell into submission.

After a few minutes, the adrenaline let down, leaving him shakier than a playoff game. He pushed to his feet and walked to the kitchen.

It only took a minute to throw together a turkey sandwich for himself then set out crackers and dish up some chicken noodle soup. He'd heat it for his mom when she woke.

Stefan wished she would eat more, gain back some of the weight she'd lost. But his mom had just finished her second round of chemo on Friday. And though she had this week off, residual nausea still made it tough for her to keep anything heavy down.

He ate his sandwich in a few bites, made another, and grabbed a beer and bottle of water—no one could say he didn't take hydration seriously—before sitting down in front of the TV and trying to push all of his fear for his mom to the side.

For once, it worked.

He watched random stories on ESPN, reveling in the way his mind went numb, not absorbing anything. For the first time in weeks, he actually relaxed.

Gradually, the sunlight coming in through the windows dwindled as day turned to night. His mom still slept, but that wasn't a bad thing. She needed her rest.

It was almost dark when he heard something that snapped his mind to razor-sharp focus.

" . . .trouble with the Gold already?" the female announcer said. "Notorious womanizer Barie is seen flirting with the first female slated to play for an NHL team, Brit Plantain."

A picture of him talking to Brit in the parking lot flashed on the TV. They were both leaning over the trunk of her car. It was a cozy shot. He and Brit close enough to touch and him smiling down at her.

If Stefan didn't know better—if he hadn't actually *lived* the scene—he might have believed the story the announcer was spinning.

But he *did* know better, and despite the rumors, he didn't actually sleep with every member of the opposite sex.

Not any longer anyway.

Hitting the bar, staying out too late, and screwing everything in sight had lost its appeal after just a few seasons.

Unfortunately for him and Brit, his reputation hadn't gone away quite as easily, and the press loved to regurgitate his so-called *conquests*.

One—*one!*—fucking date with a very popular celebrity had ensured that. They'd decided they weren't right for each other, and Stefan had been photographed out with someone else the next night. There was no bad blood between him and Kelsey, but that picture had cemented his place as a playboy.

Ah. The stupidity of youth. Especially since the second date hadn't been any better than the first.

The camera cut back to the anchor, who gave a coy smirk. "Is Brit going to fall just like every other female in Barie's path? Or will she be able to hold her own against those baby blues, and be the one to knock Stefan to his knees?"

"Christ," he muttered and switched off the TV, blinking

against the sudden lack of light. "This is why I watch *Sports-Focus* and not *Entertainment This Evening*."

Knock him to his knees? *Hell no*. But Stefan couldn't deny his surprise at how sweet Brit seemed. He'd expected there to be nothing feminine about her, and though she was fierce as a wildcat—as she'd demonstrated so clearly on the ice—she was also eager, a little anxious, and almost . . . soft.

Like there was a vulnerable core under that tough exterior.

Not to mention gorgeous—

"Brit, huh?" his mother asked. "Is she pretty?"

TWELVE

STEFAN NARROWED HIS EYES. "You promised not to pull out those ninja skills, Mom."

His mom's lips twitched as she sat onto the couch next to him. "I wasn't quiet. You were engrossed."

In Brit. In memories of her smile, her cute but awkward social skills, and . . . an ass he wanted to grab with both hands.

"Stevie?" she asked, making him jump like a guilty toddler.

"I'm not engrossed. Just have a lot on my mind." Yeah, like Brit. When he should really be worried about his mom. Plus, if he was thinking about the team at all, he should be coming up with ways to corral Mike Stewart before his presence did any more damage.

The man was a black hole. Stewart sucked a team down, and they were never seen or heard from again.

"I didn't know you'd gotten up." Stefan pushed to his feet, trying to not notice how fragile his mom looked. "How are you feeling?"

"Fine."

He bit back a groan. It was always *fine* with his mom, even when she was puking from the chemo or being jabbed with ten different needles. But instead of arguing with her, which would get him absolutely nowhere, he turned for the kitchen.

"Good. I'll heat you up some food. You've missed dinner."

"I'm not hungry," she said, even as she stood and followed him into the kitchen.

His eyes flicked to hers, and he glared. "You need to eat. And it's just soup and crackers."

"But—"

"Please, Mom." Realistically, he knew he couldn't fight the fucking cancer for her, but at the very least, he could make sure she ate and was well-rested.

She sighed, sinking into the kitchen chair like it was a torture rack.

"Want to cross your arms too?"

That earned him a smile. "I can't believe I raised such a stubborn son."

"Where do you think I got it?"

Her snort was familiar . . . and welcome. Any sign of his BS-spotting, tough-as-hell mother eased the vice around his heart.

The microwave dinged, and he put the bowl, a spoon, and crackers in front of her, not breathing until she actually began to eat.

Relief spread through him, loosened the muscles of his neck and shoulders. She would be okay.

She had to be.

"You going to tell me about Brit?" she asked between bites. "Or am I going to have to pull it out of you?"

Here we go. "Mom."

She tilted her head to the side, studied him intently. "Do you want to date her? I know inter-office relationships are frowned upon, but I think this situation could work with a little creativity . . ."

"Diane," he warned and shot her a look that would have made a rookie piss himself.

Did his mom have a similar reaction? No, of course not. She smiled beatifically and kept on talking. " . . .and you know you're getting older. Now's the time to start a family, when you're young. And virile."

He gagged. "Seriously. That word is never allowed to come out of your mouth again."

"What? Family? Or *virile*?" Her eyes glittered with amusement, and even though it was at his expense, Stefan laughed along with her.

Then he lied.

"I'm not interested in her, Mom," he said. "She's a teammate. That's all."

His mother glanced up at him, lips twitching. "That's not what *SportsFocus* said."

He sighed. "When have you begun believing anything the media says?"

"Since you haven't given me anything else."

"Today was her first day, and you were sleeping when I got home."

His mother took another bite, her appetite apparently restored by the fervor of her curiosity.

"So is she pretty?"

He groaned.

This was absolute agony, being questioned by his mother about Brit—who he absolutely couldn't be interested in, no matter how good she looked naked.

Stefan had more than appreciated the view, even if it had been in the middle of the locker room.

Grudging respect had joined with the attraction at that point. But then add in her attitude on the ice?

Well, that had cemented it for him.

In his book, tough as hell also happened to be sexy as hell.

But it didn't matter that his body had reacted to Brit's strip-down like a Mack truck hitting a brick wall, that it had been a fucking exercise in control just attempting to tamp those feelings down.

What was important was that he view Brit solely as a teammate, both for himself, as captain of the team, and for her.

This was her shot at the show, and she needed to grasp it with both hands.

Still he couldn't help but think his mom would like Brit's balls-out attitude.

"Yup, she's pretty," his mom said and took another bite.

For the first time, Stefan considered that this line of questioning might be worth it if his mother continued to eat.

"Pretty has nothing to do with it."

"It does where the media is concerned." She set her spoon down. "Pretty gets more ratings. So what were you doing talking to her in the parking lot?"

Son of a bitch. Just how much of that story had his mom seen?

"I got in at the same time as Brit, wanted to show her the locker room."

"She's changing with you boys?" she asked, wrinkling his nose. "Isn't it stinky?"

His mom still remembered the days when his gear would smell up whatever one-bedroom apartment they'd been staying in.

Not that his shit hadn't stunk something fierce, but these days the equipment staff for the Gold kept the team's gear smelling fresher than his laundry.

"Yes," Stefan said. "Brit was quite adamant about it." He shrugged when his mom's mouth dropped open. "Makes sense to me. She needs to bond with the team, not miss any system or lineup changes."

"But the showers? And changing? Doesn't she want privacy?"

He smiled. "I'm guessing she's used to changing with a bunch of dudes. Plus, the nudity thing is pretty much ignored. She's not going to be looking at anyone, and no one will look at her."

"Really?"

Maybe. "Really."

"Hmm. I wonder if she's gay."

Irritation filled him, and he had to work to keep his tone light. He'd already caught this question being posed about Brit more than was comfortable . . . which meant he'd heard it exactly more than zero times. What did it matter who she was attracted to, anyway? Plus, that wasn't the vibe he got from her. "She's not gay."

"How do you know?" his mom asked.

"*I know,*" he said.

He hoped. *No.* It didn't matter.

"I guess you'd know . . ." His mom hesitated. "So is she good enough to play with you guys? Or is this a publicity stunt?"

Stefan's head shot up in surprise, and that surprise deepened when his irritation tightened into a thread of anger.

It was a fair question. Maybe. But it still pissed him off that anyone was questioning Brit's skills.

He'd seen her on the ice. He'd watched tapes of her games. She'd earned her spot the old-fashioned way.

The problem was that the focus of his anger was his mother. His *cancer-stricken* mother.

Fuck.

Guess he'd bonded with Brit more today than he'd realized. Or . . . he was feeling a little caveman for another reason.

Like possessiveness. Like desire.

Nope. No way. He was defensive of his teammate. Just like any other captain would be.

"She's good enough."

But as he told his mom about practice, about the cheap shot Stewart had taken and the way Brit had handled it like a boss, his mind wasn't quite convinced.

Especially as it conjured up a replay of Brit stepping from the showers, her skin glistening, her towel wrapped snugly above those fabulous breasts.

The season had just gotten a hell of a lot more complicated.

THIRTEEN

Brit

THE BLARING of the alarm on her phone was both unwelcome and unsurprising.

With a groan, Brit turned it off then shoved the covers back and pushed to her feet. Her body was still on East Coast time, but five a.m. came early, no matter where she was.

Plus, blackout shades weren't exactly conducive for waking up, especially when she hadn't gotten much sleep the night before.

Her shoulder had bothered her a fair amount, but that ache —bruised skin, irritated nerves and muscles—was familiar. The anxiety plaguing her had been much worse.

Usually, after her first practice with a new team, all of her nerves disappeared.

The Gold were different.

Bernard was against her being there. Stewart was going to try to stir the pot.

And for the first time in her life, it was hard for Brit to shake off the notion that she *was* nothing more than a stunt, a cute little story about a girl who liked to dabble in a man's sport.

That she would never be good enough in Bernard's eyes to earn a start—

Wow. That was way too much self-pity for five a.m.

Grabbing her workout clothes from where she'd laid them out the night before, Brit surveyed the room that would be her home for the next little while.

The team had put her up in a decent hotel just three miles from the rink. She'd be able to run to the arena most days. Though on game nights, she expected that she'd need to drive so as to not encounter post-game rowdy fans.

If she was even around that long—

Stop it.

Shoving the annoying little pity party to the back of her brain, Brit pulled on her clothes, tied her shoes, and slung her backpack over her shoulders.

The city was surprisingly quiet as she pushed through the lobby doors and turned in the direction of the arena. She'd memorized the route the night before and immediately took off at a slow jog, just fast enough to warm her tight muscles. When everything began to loosen, she picked up the pace.

San Francisco was different than any place she'd ever lived. Though summer was barely over, a thick blanket of fog shrouded the lightening sky. It made everything feel quiet and otherworldly, almost as if that layer of gas and water in the sky was actually a buffer between reality and fantasy.

Brit's footsteps echoed on the pavement as she ran, a quickening pace that chased her rising pulse.

By the time she arrived at the arena and had pulled out her identification badge, she was breathing hard, sweaty, but feeling about a million-and-a-half times better.

"Morning," she told the guard at the gate and held up her badge.

He blinked at her, glanced at the ID then back at her. "Ms. Plantain?"

"Call me Brit," she said. "And you are?"

"Richie."

She smiled at the man, skinny as a pole with bright red hair. "Nice to meet you." They stared at each other until she finally took a step forward. "Not too many of the guys run in, huh?"

"Um, nope."

Brit shrugged. "Different is good, sometimes."

Richie's lips twitched, and he nodded, his eyes sweeping down and up appreciatively. "That it is."

She couldn't help it. She laughed.

Richie flushed. "That came out really bad, didn't it?"

"Yup."

"Well, damn." He shook his head. "Way too early for this. I'll write you on the list so you don't have to check in every day, Ms. Plantain. Will this be your typical time?"

She nodded. "It's Brit. And thanks."

"You're welcome." He gestured to the gate. "Go on with you."

Brit nodded and ran forward.

The locker room was quiet but not empty. A few of the players, including Blane and Max were already there. They looked up as she walked through the door and murmured quiet hellos.

"Morning," she said and walked to her stall, which she was pleased to see actually held a nameplate with her name.

Her equipment was laid out, exactly as she preferred, pads to the left, chest protector hung up.

But it wasn't time to get her gear on.

She walked down the hall that led to the ice, waving at Mandy through the window of the PT suite as she went. Mandy gestured at her to come in, but Brit mouthed "later" and kept moving.

Past the therapy room, past the gym. All the way into the arena.

It was impossible to hold back the awe that washed over her.

This was her dream.

Brit could picture the stadium full to the brim, filled with 17,000-plus fans, screaming and shouting. The *crash* of players into the boards, the *crack* of sticks against the ice, the sting of the puck hitting her glove.

She shook herself, dislodged the image.

That wouldn't happen unless she worked as hard as she could.

Starting now. Continuing for the indefinite future.

After sliding in her headphones, she cranked the volume and turned for the stairs.

Not that she'd tell anyone, but her kryptonite was boy bands. In any form, shape, or number. If they sang catchy pop music, she was sold.

Backstreet Boys, N'Sync, One Direction, 5 Seconds of Summer. Heck, even BTS. It didn't matter. Brit loved them all.

She grinned as one of her favorite songs blared to life in her headphones, snorting as the guys sang about being one of a kind. *Yup.* That she was. But maybe according to Bernard, not in a good way.

"Move it," she muttered, blinking away the previous day and focusing on the present.

And so she ran.

Up one section, over, and down the next. She kept it strictly to the lower bowl for today, not wanting to overwork her legs before practice.

Left. Right. Left. Right.

The rhythm was so ingrained within her that she could have almost run blindfolded.

Except she wasn't.

A fact which Brit was abruptly glad for when the *pat pat* of footsteps very close behind her permeated the music blaring through her ears.

FOURTEEN

IT WAS DARK, only a few of the lights on inside the arena.

Brit was on the far side of the ice, as physically distanced from the locker room as she could possibly be.

Glancing behind her, she saw a tall, shadowed masculine form. He seemed to fill the space, to loom over her as he worked his way up and down the stairs.

Following her.

Her.

Some logical part of her mind recognized that the man must be a Gold player, that he was probably doing the same thing she was.

The rest of her—the piece that had been damaged three years before—was stronger.

It took over her mind.

She picked up the pace, cutting across rows as quickly as she could.

If she could just get back to the locker room, she would be safe.

The footsteps behind her sped up.

Brit's heart pounded, breath whistled in and out of her mouth. Her feet were a blur as she watched them carry her body through the sections.

Only two more to go.

But the man was gaining. Closing the distance as effectively as a great white to a seal.

She put every last bit of energy into her feet. So close. Her eyes flicked behind her, desperate now to get away.

What she saw didn't help. The man wore a grey sweatshirt, its hood pulled up and over his head. It was just like—

She stumbled. Saw a row of steps coming straight for her face. One arm came up, an attempt to shield the inevitable fall.

Which didn't come.

Instead warm hands caught her and pulled her back. She collided with a strong, hard chest, and they went down in a heap.

The man grunted as she landed hard on his stomach, but her mind had shut down. She struggled, her only thought to get as far away as humanly possible.

Next they'd grab her ankles, shackle her wrists. Fear was an icy blade down her spine. It spurred her to fight, even as part of her registered the chest beneath her rumbling as the man spoke.

The words didn't penetrate.

"No," she said, thrusting her elbow back, fighting to get free with everything she had.

The man held tight.

Then her earbuds were plucked out—not that she'd really heard the song over the *whoosh* of blood in her ears, the rapid pounding of her heart. But with the music not blaring, she was finally able to comprehend the voice.

"Hey. *Hey*! It's okay."

Stefan.

One beat of her heart to understand. Another for her panic to fade. One last one for embarrassment course through her.

Except it wasn't the typical hot, scalding version. This was frigid, a blanket of frost settling over her skin, burning, but only because it was so cold.

It was heavy. Stifling.

And full of shame.

"Are you all right?" Stefan asked.

A single jerky nod was as much answer as she could muster.

Silence stretched. It was awkward and filled with the expectation. He was anticipating, *waiting* for an explanation she couldn't provide.

She'd just been intimidated, cornered . . . scared.

Really scared.

And the fear leftover from the assault—that something *could* have happened, that she could have been so easily overpowered—had fractured something inside of her.

It was a lot harder to regain confidence than to possess it in the first place.

"Let—let me go," she managed.

"Okay." Stefan slid to the side, depositing her on the step next to him.

For a moment, she actually missed the warmth of his chest, the security of his arms—which was absolutely insane because Brit hadn't found comfort in a man's embrace in so long that she'd actually begun to believe she no longer possessed the capability to do so.

Which wasn't the point, but the stray thought helped the last dredges of panic fade from her system.

Stefan hadn't said anything further, just sat next to her in silence as she focused on getting her breaths to slow to a more reasonable rhythm.

"I'm sorry," she murmured, not willing to talk about it and

totally unable to put into words the abrupt terror that had gripped her when he'd approached her from behind.

"I—" He thrust a hand through his hair, and unconsciously Brit flinched back. Stefan froze, looked at her, a wealth of emotions in his expression. "What . . . what happened to you? Did—"

Brit swallowed hard, was ready to laugh off the whole scenario as staying up too late the previous night, watching scary movies or some other such nonsense.

Except . . . there was a flash of something in those baby blues—not quite pity, not quite remorse—and it pissed her off.

She *shouldn't* be mad, not when he'd stopped her from breaking her ass on the row of stairs, not when he was trying to be kind now.

But he was looking at her like she might be broken.

"I'm not weak," she spat. "I just—"

Just *what*?

Freaked the heck out.

Because she *was* a little broken.

But she didn't show that side to the world, and definitely not to Stefan Barie, who never went out with a girl more than once, who'd dated half the city's available—and not so available—females between the ages of eighteen and eighty, according to the tabloids.

For *him*, she needed walls of steel, coated in barbed wire. Hell, she could use a couple of those pots of boiling oil at the top, ready to pour down and burn the tendrils of whatever she was feeling—attraction? gratitude?—to ashes.

For the love of pucks, she was a freaking wreck.

With a shove at his chest, Brit struggled to her feet, her legs like Jell-O.

Stefan didn't say anything, just studied her with an intensity that made her heart beat faster—and not from nerves this time . .

. or at least not entirely. He stared as though he could see inside of her, view the very depths of her soul.

The arena was quiet, the crisp coolness of the ice creeping up to coat her sweat-laden skin. She shivered. Stefan stood, took off his hoodie, and slung it around her shoulders.

And just like that, her anger dissipated, was wrapped in a layer of cotton, traded for the scent of sandalwood and spice that crept into her nostrils and loosened the iron grip on her emotions.

Her eyes burned.

Hell no. Just no. She didn't cry. Not ever.

"It's okay if you don't want to talk about it."

Stefan's voice was gentle, not demanding in any way. But that almost made it worse.

She could deal with someone barking at her, cursing at her to move faster, to stop the fucking puck.

What she couldn't deal with was sympathy.

"It's nothing."

"Okay," he said after a moment and when he reached for her hand it took everything inside of her to not flinch back.

If the expression on Stefan's face said anything, it was that he knew exactly how much of a struggle it had been for her not to move.

Still, his touch was light, a careful brush of calloused fingers against calloused fingers. He tilted his head in the direction of the aisle. "How about we finish these stairs then?"

Disbelief he wasn't going to press or demand an explanation coursed through her. The relief that chased it was a powerful thing, one that loosened the stranglehold of the past and allowed her to extract herself from its oppressive force.

"Yup," she said. "Last one done buys the beer tonight."

As Brit stood, she thought she saw a flicker of something—of *blond*—out of the corner of her eye. But when she turned to look fully, nothing was there.

Stefan started to get up, and, not wanting to lose, she took off, smiling at the shock on his face, at the surprise *she* felt for having made the invitation at all.

It was better than the past.

And that was all she could ask.

FIFTEEN

Stefan

STEFAN HANDED a twenty to the bartender, thinking he was a sucker, through and through. They hadn't been able to go out for drinks that night a week ago. Brit had gotten sucked into an extended physical therapy session with Mandy, but he'd challenged her to a rematch on the stairs just before practice that morning.

The result being that he'd somehow ended up buying beer for four.

"Only two pitchers?" Max asked when he returned to the table.

Brit laughed.

"Do I need to remind you that we have practice tomorrow?" Stefan set the pitchers down then went back to the bar to retrieve glasses for him, Max, Blane, and Brit. When he returned, he sat in the only open spot, which was in the booth next to Max, and tried to push aside the bizarre sensation that he was on an episode of *The Bachelor*.

Max huffed. "The day I couldn't handle two pitchers—"

"Would be like every other time we come here," Stefan said dryly.

Brit snorted, and his eyes flashed up, studying hers. There was no trace of fear, not like the terror that had dominated her expression the other morning on the stairs.

Max continued to act like his usual annoying self. "That's not true—"

"Shut up, and drink your two and-a-half beers," Stefan said as he poured the first round.

They all picked up their cups and took a drink. Their gazes met over the rims of the frosted glasses, and awkward silence fell.

Surprisingly, Brit was the one to break it.

"So . . . you guys come here often?" she asked.

Though—since their responding laughter made her eyes widen in shock—Stefan didn't think the attempt was intentional.

"You're just the same as you were five years ago, Brit. Promise me you won't change." Blane punched her in the arm.

Stefan wondered if he was the only one who saw her wince.

Was it because of the punch or Blane's words?

Blane wouldn't hurt Brit intentionally. He was a good guy and Stefan hadn't missed the longing glances coming from the first-line forward when Brit wasn't looking.

Blane watched Brit like she was *a woman*.

Not a teammate.

Which was a familiar feeling, Stefan knew. There was something about her—fragility mixed with strength, drive, and confidence. It was impossible to not want some of that essence.

His thoughts drifted to her shoulder, to the monster bruise she'd been sporting in the locker room. He hadn't *wanted* to notice it . . . or the creamy white skin dotted with a pattern of freckles he wanted to trace with his tongue. Or the ass he could bounce a dime off—

It took Stefan's groin tightening for him to cut off the image. For fuck's sake. He needed to get his shit together.

Brit had been solid in practice, so a casual observer might think her shoulder was fully recovered. But they were professional athletes.

Playing through the pain was nothing new.

"Let's hope I'm a little bit better," she said, soft enough that Stefan thought he might have been the only one who heard it. Especially since Max and Blane had moved on to laughing about some video on YouTube.

The words, laced with a hint of sadness, made his heart squeeze tight.

"You've gotta see this," Max said, leaning diagonally across the table to thrust his phone in Blane's face.

"I can't—" Blane got out of the booth, came around the table, and shoved Stefan's shoulder. "Move."

Normally, Stefan would have snapped at his teammate—ever heard of the word *please*?—but since the end result was him sitting next to Brit, he got up and crossed to the other side.

"You good?" he asked softly. Her eyes flew to his, questioning. "After that—" He shrugged, searching for the right words and failing miserably. "The fall didn't hurt you, right?" It was the first time he'd brought anything to do with that morning up, but Stefan found that he needed to reassure himself. Brit had been beyond frightened—*of him*—and though he knew it wasn't his fault she'd been so scared, being the cause of someone's fear wasn't a normal occurrence for him.

"Fine," she said, her tone a little tart. His words clearly hadn't found the right mark and he almost let it go. Probably *would have* if not for her hand. The one nearest him was clenched into a fist and trembled where she rested it on her thigh.

Stefan couldn't stop himself. He reached across the six inches of space separating them, took that shaking hand into his, and carefully separated her fingers. The skin wasn't smooth like most of the girls he'd been with. There were callouses, scars.

They were capable fingers, strong, and yet somehow still feminine.

Perhaps just a different version than many would expect.

Brit had jumped almost a foot at the contact, her lips parting in surprise. But when he gave her hand a light squeeze, she relaxed.

Words weren't necessary in that moment. It was simple. Comfort freely given then received.

The action was instinctive in the way he consoled a teammate after a bad shift or tapped Julian's—the Gold's starting goaltender—pads with his stick after a goal. Small gestures that taken alone meant nothing, but could be pieced together into a larger expression of camaraderie.

But unlike the others, *this* comfort was laced with something else. Heat licking up his arm, coiling in his stomach . . . and lower.

Which was why he forced himself to pull back.

Even though what he really wanted to do was lace his fingers with hers and tug her close.

He knew the thought was wrong but it didn't stop him from wanting. And while normally he might have been able to shrug off his desire as a stupid male thing, this need tempered with tenderness made the situation extra complicated.

He couldn't cross the line between teammate and woman and him getting in her space was probably the last thing she needed after what had happened in the arena.

So he returned his fingers back to his own lap, even laughed when Blane turned the phone to them and played the video of some idiot attempting to use a roof as a diving board.

Still, when Brit glanced at him, a small smile on her lips, her eyes soft, Stefan couldn't suppress the notion that he'd just . . . somehow become tied to the woman next to him.

SIXTEEN

STEFAN CALLED his mom the moment he was in his car.

"Hi." It was perfunctory because the more important thing was "How are you feeling?"

Diane sighed. "I told you to stay out and have a good time. You don't need to worry about me."

Impossible. But he couldn't tell her that. Didn't want to add to her stress.

"We have practice tomorrow. A late night isn't in the cards."

"Stefan, really?" she said. "You're worried. I understand that. But you need to live your life."

Not surprising that his mom would see through him. She always had. But the excuse had worked with the guys, a finite end to the evening, allowing him to get home without anyone knowing the one person who'd been his steady throughout his life might not survive her battle.

It was too soon to talk to anyone about what his mom was going through. Too soon to know her prognosis and be able to confide his fears to his friends.

Besides that, his mom had asked that he not let Max know, the one person he might have actually told. Their mothers were friends, and she'd said, *"I don't want Betty fussing over me for nothing."*

Nothing being recurrent Stage 2 cancer. Surgery and chemo. Bloodwork and fatigue.

"Have you heard anything from the lab?" he asked, setting the phone in the cup holder as the Bluetooth kicked on. He put the car into gear and pulled out of the parking lot.

"No." She paused. "But you know the initial report came back okay. It's smaller this time and less aggressive. I'm going to be fine."

"So why don't you want Betty to know?"

"Stefan." His mom was rolling her eyes; he could practically hear it through the airwaves. "You know she would fly out, and Max's sister just had her baby. They need Betty's help more than I do. You're not going to ruin her first experience as a grandmother, are you?"

Stefan wasn't sure he believed that, but he also wasn't about to verbalize any of his fears. His mom was going through enough without him needing to dump those on her—no matter how much he would have liked to have steady, capable Betty at his mom's side.

"Fine." He sighed, though having his mom manipulate him was much better than the pallid, civilized version of herself she'd been since the surgery. "I won't destroy the sacred bond between grandchild and grandmother. But you're going to have to tell her eventually."

"I know."

There was a moment of quiet, a pause where it seemed as though they were both thinking of the possibilities of what *could* happen but were unwilling to say them aloud. Then he shoved that garbage away.

"Milkshake?"

His mom laughed. "When have I ever said no to milkshakes?"

"Never." Which was why he'd asked. Empty calories at this stage weren't a bad thing. "And done. I'll be home in twenty."

Stefan drove to the all-night dairy, got out, and ordered his mom's milkshake—a vanilla malt with chocolate sandwich cookies mixed in. A few fans came up to him as he waited for the shake, but no one got out of hand.

That was the thing about the Bay Area.

People were huge sports fans and, though hockey's popularity was on the rise, Stefan wasn't so recognizable that he couldn't just go hang out somewhere.

For the most part.

Just as the worker handed over his mom's milkshake, Jessica approached him.

He mentally groaned.

She was a puck bunny—which was a not-so-nice term for hockey groupies—who also happened to be a local reporter who'd been around the locker room so many times that he actually remembered her name. He'd yet to ride her particular bicycle and had no foreseeable plans too. His taste had evolved past easy lays.

Hell, that was when he'd even *had* a sexual appetite—which hadn't been often over the last season and a half. He'd poured every last bit of his energy into the team and helping the Gold recover from last season's scandal.

Not to mention, since Brit's appearance, his fantasies had been less about buxom brunettes with a pound of makeup on their face and more about lithe, unmarred femininity.

Which was very, very dangerous for the team he'd been working so hard to rebuild.

"A picture with my favorite hockey star?" Jessica all but purred.

Fake breasts pushed into his side, and lips, obviously injected with something that made them look as though they would explode, pursed in the idiotic fishy pout that was so popular nowadays.

Stefan figured the best course was to take the stupid picture and get the hell out.

"Sure." He grabbed the phone, used his long arms to his advantage, and took the photograph. It a quick move he'd learned over the last couple of seasons: ignore the advances, mitigate any potential unhappiness, then get as far away as possible.

"Gotta go," he said and started toward his car.

She followed him.

Shit.

Unlocking the driver's door—and only the driver's door, a lesson learned after another fan had jumped into the passenger's seat when he'd been trying to make a quick getaway very similar to this one—Stefan stowed the shake inside and started to fold his body into the very narrow frame of his Mercedes.

The hand on his arm stopped him, at least for a moment. Then he brushed it off and started to close the door.

"I can—" she began.

"Thank you, but I'm not interested." Had never been. Would never be.

Jessica's beady blue eyes narrowed . . . or maybe it was just the result of all the black crap outlining them. "You don't even know what I'm offering."

He actually *did* know what she was offering, had heard about it five times over.

She gives the best head, dude. And then when you actually hit it . . .

Yeah. Sloppy ninths or tenths didn't appeal to him.

"Goodnight, Jessica."

"Who's the milkshake for?" she asked, a hardness coating her expression. It gave Stefan a moment of pause. She *was* a reporter after all. "I know you wouldn't drink that crap during the season."

The lie was easy. "Doesn't everyone deserve a cheat day?"

With that, he shut the door and drove away, a sick feeling in the pit of his stomach. It was common knowledge that, aside from Jessica's bedroom antics, she could spin a story into a tangle of half-truths and sensationalism like no one's business.

Damn. He was probably screwed. They'd have him paired off with some visiting actress just because she'd been in the city.

But he also couldn't worry about that now. There was a milkshake to be delivered, tapes to be studied, and drills to memorize.

His mom practically snatched the shake from his hand the moment he walked through the door then oohed and moaned about how good it tasted. So far, the treat was the single guaranteed thing she could keep down.

Hopefully that lasted.

It wasn't until he'd finished his prep for tomorrow's practice and lay down to go to sleep several hours later that he remembered Jessica's cold look.

Stefan had clearly overreacted, his worry was unfounded. He'd been getting a damn milkshake after all. There was nothing there. Nothing to spin.

What could she possibly say?

It wasn't until he woke early the next morning and turned on the news that he realized Jessica could say a whole, whole lot.

SEVENTEEN

Brit

SHOES TIED. Phone tucked in her pocket. Earbuds in. Or one this time. After her freak-out with Stefan, Brit wasn't about to make the same mistake of not being totally aware of her surroundings.

Therapy had helped after the *incident*.

But it hadn't cured all. She still hadn't been able to tell anyone else what happened. Not her brother, not her parents.

Of course, one had to actually *talk* to their parents in order for that to occur.

And that wasn't her reality.

The best that someone could have said was that her parents were detached.

Her father had been so wrapped up in his career as an orthopedic surgeon, until he'd died eighteen months before, that, as an adult, she had only spoken to him on Father's Day, his birthday, and Christmas.

He'd never taken time off when she went home to visit, never turned down a surgery.

Brit's mother wasn't a bad person, but she'd made an art out of creating excuses for Brit's dad not being, well . . . a dad. Worse was that she had never supported Brit playing a *man's sport* like hockey.

Needless to say, it made things tense at home.

Luckily, she had her brother. And when he was in the country, however infrequently that ended up being, they always got together.

He didn't know about the incident either. There was nothing Dan could have done, and it would have only made him feel guilty.

Brit hadn't wanted that, so she'd talked to a therapist who'd agreed with her assessment. What had happened to her was sexual assault, no matter that the team had tried to play it off as good-natured team building, or at worst hazing because *all* the rookies got the same treatment.

Hazing was a word she had barely known before the incident, and something she'd never spent more than ten seconds thinking about until after she'd seen a random news story about it occurring at a college fraternity and realized *that* was what the guys had tried to claim happened to her.

The news story had been her catalyst for therapy.

Because it *hadn't* been hazing. It was assault.

Brit hadn't gone to college, had always felt safe with men. She'd grown up in locker rooms with them, had never had an issue until then, and while she knew that it wasn't her fault, that her lingering fear and anxiety were a normal part of the healing process, it still really fucking sucked.

She didn't like feeling weak or broken.

But she did.

And so she continued to deal with the normal part of recovering

A totally shitty part, but not abnormal.

Which didn't necessarily make it easy to get over.

Especially when she was by herself in a strange city or quiet arena.

Being in a new place wasn't a unique experience for her; she was used to the moving and upheaval. Especially early on, it had been exciting to see so much of the world, to be in a different place every night.

It was unfortunate that one of those nights had managed to cast so large a shadow on her life.

THREE YEARS ago

THE HAND on her shoulder made her jump.

She turned and saw it was Sergei, her captain. He wore his trademark grey sweatshirt, the hood pulled up over his head like some idiotic version of Rocky.

"Hey," she said, gripping her towel tight to her breasts. She'd been about to jump in the shower. "What's up?"

"Strip."

Brit blinked. "What? No," she said, not liking the gleam in Sergei's eyes. Two of the biggest players on the team stood behind him. The rest of the guys looked on. "Back off. Now, Sergei."

The room went suddenly and utterly quiet. Brit could have heard a pin drop, let alone the collective sucking in a breath.

"You don't get to make that call."

The air frosted with malice, and shivering, Brit took a step back.

Sergei and the two players behind him moved as a unit.

Fingers manacled her wrists, strong arms immobilized her

kicking legs. And faster than she would have thought possible, the towel was torn away.

She fought. Struggled.

It was only when Sergei bent over her that real fear settled in.

"I knew your body would be fucking hot," he said once she was pinned. He trailed a finger down her throat, between her breasts. Then he gripped her nipple, twisted it hard enough to make her cry out in pain.

Bile burned her throat when his hand slid lower.

This was actually going to happen. She was going to be a statistic, one of the twenty-five percent of woman who were sexually assaulted in their lifetimes.

But just as the hand reached the apex of her thighs and her eyes slid closed, her mind desperately attempting to grasp onto some sort of numbness, to find a dark, empty place in her mind, Brit was tossed through the air.

She collided with a slick, tiled surface. Hit her face hard against the floor. Blood exploded in her mouth, and icy cold water hit like bullets against her back.

There was laughter. The sound of skin against skin as palms met for high fives all around.

Then the locker room went silent.

Brit didn't know how long she stayed in the shower, the cold water pounding against her back before she managed to shove to her feet and stumble into the adjoining locker room.

Her clothes were nowhere to be found. But her equipment was in its normal spot. She grabbed the shorts she always wore under her gear, wrestled them on, and threw her jersey over her head.

Shivers wracked her body. She had never been colder in her entire life.

Somehow, she made it to her apartment without wrecking

her car and stumbled into her bedroom. She didn't bother to change, just huddled under a mass of blankets until morning light had begun filtering in through her windows.

It took everything she possessed to get up and walk into the locker room the next morning.

"Sorry about the fat lip," was the first thing Sergei said when she walked through the door. "You were fighting us so hard that you slipped from my hands."

One of the defensemen who'd held her in place laughed. "You're fucking strong, Brit. I almost got dunked."

"Dude," someone called, whose face Brit was way too shocked to register, "the water is the worst part."

"At least you got cold," another player had chimed in. "My ass got roasted."

Brit struggled to grasp the invasive memories, wanting to shove them back into the recesses of her mind, but it didn't matter she was three years in the future and playing for a different team in a different city. The dark thoughts didn't want to be shut away.

She rested her head against the smooth wood of her hotel room's door and, run temporarily forgotten, she breathed. Just breathed.

Her teammates had been so cavalier about the violation. They'd done it to others. They would do it to more.

If she didn't do something stop them.

So Brit had reported the incident to her head coach . . . and found herself cut from the team a matter of days later.

It was all history now, part of a past that was painful and usually buried deep in her mind.

But the assault was also another reason she'd done her little stripper stunt on day one of joining the Gold. Let the guys see whatever they wanted to see. Remove the notion of forbidden fruit for some, and, at the same time, diffuse the awkwardness of having a member of the opposite sex in the room.

Because there was strength in numbers. Usually.

For the rest of it, she would be aware of her surroundings, and she'd had a shit ton of self-defense training since then.

She just needed to remember to use it.

With that thought, Brit opened the door to the hotel room, jogged down the stairs, and was out the front door in less than a minute.

She would be fine. She was *always* fine.

Except, when she arrived at the arena twenty minutes later, *nothing* was fine.

Insanity had been unleashed on the front gate.

EIGHTEEN

REPORTERS WERE LINED up along both sides of the road like some sort of loud and very obnoxious receiving line at a wedding.

When they spotted her, it instantly felt much more like a gauntlet. The questions were loud, vicious blows to her senses.

"Is it true?"

"Did the Gold pick you up because you're sleeping with Barie?"

"What does Bernard think of your relationship?"

Her feet slowed, the single earbud she had in place falling from her ear, the music blaring in short staccato bursts of vibration against her chest.

That single moment of surprise—of hesitation—cost her. The reporters closed in, encroaching on her personal space. Pushing. Yelling.

It was too much. Her heart pounded and cold sweat took the place of the exercise-related version.

"Back up! Make a path, people!"

A few seconds later, Richie was by her side, his cheerful, smiling façade she'd come to know over the last week closed down and dark. He slung an arm around her shoulder, tucked her against his side, and started to pull her through the crowd.

"Stay close," he said directly into her ear.

She nodded and lifted her chin. Despite the nerves and assault on her senses, she wasn't going to let anyone see her as weak.

He pushed them forward, and when they neared the gate, another security guard she'd never seen before let them pass.

Richie dropped his arm but stayed close.

"What the hell was that?" she asked.

"*That* is the media on a scandal." He rolled his eyes.

"What kind of scandal warrants that?" She waved a hand over her shoulder, encompassing the myriad of news trucks, of shouting men and women with microphones and black handheld news cameras.

"A good old-fashion Gold scandal. Not that I believe anything that reporter says, Ms.—"

"Brit," she interrupted. "Is this because of the whole first female thing?"

Richie laughed then sobered rapidly when he glanced down and found her frowning. "No. Not that."

"Then what—"

The side door he was leading her to opened abruptly.

"Bye, Ms. Plantain." Richie stepped back and gestured her inside.

"Brit," she reminded him again, stepping through.

He just waved as the door swung shut.

Bernard stood on the other side of the plank of metal, and he wasn't happy.

The man wasn't appealing even on a good day, but the frown pulling his bushy grey brows together at the moment—hello, unibrow—was ferocious.

He didn't say a word, just pointed down the hall.

Which was when Brit's stomach sank pretty much to her toes.

She followed Bernard past his office, past the locker room, and into a conference room she hadn't known existed.

Inside were a bunch of suits—five men, one woman—and all looking very serious. They sat around a large mahogany conference table, which was empty, save a pitcher of water and a handful of glasses.

"Sit," Bernard told her, pointing toward an empty chair.

Brit sat even as Bernard remained standing, taking up a position behind her left shoulder. She would rather be facing a breakaway in sudden-death overtime than the six people in front of her.

The addition of Bernard at her back made her feel as though she had two enemies, one coming at her from the front and one from the rear.

"Would you care to explain this?" Devon Carter, the general manager, asked. He was dressed in an expensive-looking suit, and his face was handsome, though, like most former hockey players, he hadn't escaped his career completely unscathed. A scar bisected one brow, and his nose sported a few bumps from the times it had been broken over the years.

Devon slid an honest-to-God manila folder across the table, and Brit had a flash of one of those interrogation scenes from a cable police show.

Good cop. Bad cop.

She almost snorted to herself. Then she saw the picture inside the folder.

Her gasp was loud in the silent room.

"What is that?"

"Why don't you tell us?"

The photo was clear, despite the limited light, and it showed . . . oh God. Her eyes slid closed in embarrassment. In the shot, she was sprawled on top of Stefan, their faces very close, their bodies pressed together.

It was from the arena. From the week before, when Stefan had accidentally scared her and—

And what? She felt violated? Exposed? Vulnerable?

Yes to all of those things.

She swallowed against the rise of tears in her throat, struggled to put her face back into an expression of calm.

Because she also looked to be very close to losing her job.

"I don't know what that is—" she started.

The woman, mid-sixties, with a severe bun of grey hair and more diamonds around her neck than the crown jewels, snorted.

"I was running stairs, didn't hear him come up behind me because I had my headphones on." She shrugged, tried to push away the fear that had crept back into her at the memory of being chased, the sick heaviness that had sunk into her limbs. "I startled, and we both went down."

"Then didn't get back up?" the grey-haired woman asked with a sneer.

"A photograph only takes a second."

Bernard's voice surprised her. Especially since it sounded as though he were standing up for her.

"Why are you asking me this?" Bernard's support—as trivial as it might turn out to be—gave her the strength to set aside the memory and focus on the present. "I've done nothing wrong."

"You're here because of these pictures. Because of the news stories," the older woman said. "And because the sheer volume of attention this picture has wrought presents us with a particularly unique opportunity."

"Susan is right," Devon said. "We know there is nothing going on with Barie. He told us as much just a half an hour ago. But that doesn't mean we can't turn the rumor to our advantage."

The nerves Brit had managed to bank were suddenly back and battering her insides like hell. She had an inkling of where this might be going.

Devon and the others were waiting for her to speak, waiting for her to ask the obvious question. Her mind recoiled . . . and yet she plunged ahead anyway. "What kind of opportunity?"

Susan's lips curved slightly, not quite a smile, but enough to make the older woman look more than a little possessed.

Perhaps she was. Because Susan's words turned Brit's inkling into her worst nightmare.

"You're going to seduce Barie, and then you're going to take your relationship public. Dates. Hand-holding. PDA," Susan stated, her voice calm, as though she hadn't just asked Brit to prostitute herself for the team. "You'll give the press what they want."

"I—" Brit scrambled for a moment, trying to figure out what the hell she wanted to say. The fury and disgust she felt were obvious reactions, but ultimately, she ended up blurting the most persistent question that was bouncing around her skull. "Why?"

"Public opinion," Susan said. "After the unfortunate situation with Peter Gordaine and Rhonda Campbell, we need good press. The team barely got the necessary tax breaks from the city to return this season, and unless we make a significant dent in our public image, they've told us we won't receive them next year."

Devon nodded. "And we need money. Filled seats. Merchandise sales. Think of the marketing opportunities from a relationship like this."

Brit dropped her gaze to the table, her mind spinning as she tried to find a way to talk them out of this. It couldn't be real. *This* couldn't be her reality.

"You never wanted me on the team to play did you?" she asked softly.

Devon snorted. "Women don't belong in the NHL. Still, when Frankie wanted you, we agreed because your presence presented us with an opportunity." He paused and she glanced up, saw the cold calculation there. "Feminism sells. You'll make sure of it."

Fuck. She hadn't expected her run with the Gold to be rainbows and puppy dogs. She'd expected reactions like Bernard's, expected some pushback from the other players.

But this?

Playing for a team with a board that wanted to openly manipulate their players and lie to their fans?

It was tempting—so damned tempting—to turn and walk out. Except . . .

This was her shot at the NHL.

Her gaze swiveled around the room, attempted to find an ally. But Devon and Susan were the only two who would make eye contact; the rest kept their gazes on the table, their expressions vaguely uncomfortable.

"This is bullshit." Bernard's voice was gruff.

Her jaw wanted to fall open in surprise at the show of support, but she clenched her teeth together, unwilling to let it drop. She turned, saw her coach's expression had gone thunderous, and was relieved the depth of anger wasn't directed at her.

"This is *fucking* bullshit," he said. "Come on, Brit. Leave these morons to their own devices. You're not doing this."

"Clear your office."

The three words from Susan were quiet, but crystal clear and laced with steel.

"What?" he asked.

"You're fired," she said. "You're still on probation, and we can let you go at will."

"I know what my contract says," Bernard snapped. "And it doesn't matter. If this gets out—"

"It won't." Susan's expression was shrewd. "Because you know what will happen if it does."

Bernard's face paled. "You can't make that decision. The board—"

Devon chose that moment to speak up. "Well, I can speak for the board. We're all in agreement, correct?" The nods were small, but they were there. The rest of the board wouldn't interfere. "Bernard, you block this in any way, and your job is forfeit."

There was a moment of terse silence then Bernard spoke, "Do what you will, but I won't go along with it." He touched Brit's shoulder, startled her into motion. "Let's go. You're not doing this."

She stood, started following her coach to the door.

Susan's voice caused her feet to hesitate at the threshold.

"Do you really want that man's job on your conscience? Did you know his wife is sick? Apparently she has very rare form of blood disease." A twist of an old wrinkled mouth shrouded in pink lipstick. "Tragic, really."

Bernard cursed. "That's enough."

Brit turned. She would have thought Susan to be a sweet, older woman if not for the calculation in those cold blue eyes.

"Do you really want her to lose her health insurance?" Susan pressed.

Brit's eyes flicked to Bernard's hoping, wanting . . . to *what*? See Susan was lying? That it was all just a ploy to get her to go along with the truth?

Except when she looked at Bernard, the truth was there.

His wife *was* ill, and if the tortured expression on her coach's face was any indication, the illness was a serious one.

Fuck. Her gut clenched. Her heart squeezed hard. She couldn't do this . . . but dammit, how could she *not*?

Bernard blinked, and his face went blank, a calm, clear slate that was an epic sort of mask. One she didn't buy for a moment. His words, when they came, were laced with such tension that he might as well have just agreed with Susan.

"Don't listen to her," he said. "My wife is fine."

She wanted to believe him. Desperately. But—

"His wife is *sick*. And he's up to his eyeballs in debt." She clucked. "Gambling is such a hard habit to kick."

"You're a conniving bitch," Bernard gritted out.

"At. Will," Susan countered.

The room fell silent for one long, slow breath before the scheming resumed.

"We also received a very interesting delivery the other day." Susan's gaze locked with Brit's. "Some pictures from three years ago that were quite . . . *revealing*."

Panic swelled.

Hands grabbing. Laughter. Cold water. Biting back tears until her heart bled.

Bernard slammed his hand against the doorframe, a sharp *crack* the made everyone in the room jump, except for Susan and Devon. "Shut your goddamned mouth—"

"I'll do it," Brit interrupted, forcing her gaze from Bernard and meeting Susan's frosty indigo depths. "But once the press is on the Gold's side, I'm done. We'll break up, and everything will go back to normal." She was quiet for a beat. "And I won't fuck him."

She could do this, could manipulate and save in equal terms. But only if she didn't feel, only if she could convince herself that Stefan wouldn't get hurt. She'd keep things innocent and light, protect them both.

Otherwise . . . it would be too difficult to bear the person she'd become by agreeing to such an act in the first place.

"The relationship will be in name only," she told the plethora of blank faces surrounding the large conference table. "And you'll take the 'at will' clause out of Bernard's contract, plus provide health insurance for him and his wife for the remainder of their lives."

Susan hesitated only the barest of a second. "Fine."

"I want my lawyer to look at and approve Bernard's contract before I do anything."

"Fine," Susan repeated. "But you breathe a word of this to Barie, and the deal's off the table. Your contract as well as Bernard's will both be void. Stefan is too moral for his own good and—"

Brit interrupted with a wave of her hand, having had enough of the other woman. "I agree. Send me the contract, and let's get this over with."

"Stop." Fingers gripped her arm tight, halting Brit when she would have swept from the room.

Her stomach sank. What more could the woman possibly want? Wasn't it already bad enough?

Susan's words were a hiss. "Don't think you're dictating anything else. I've abided by your terms because they're easy to allow and you're going to give me what I want. But if you sabotage this opportunity in any way, understand that those pictures will be splashed over every market within the hour." A squeeze of those bony fingers. "I know what they're worth. Right now, you and Barie are a bigger cash cow. Don't make me changed my mind. Understood?"

"You—"

Another squeeze. "I asked if you understood. Is that too much for your puck-addled brain to comprehend?"

She saw red but . . . Bernard, his sick wife, and her throat tightened, *the pictures.* Brit needed to keep a calm head and remember why she'd agreed to this.

"I understand," she said from between clenched teeth.

"Good," Susan said. "Now run along and give the press a good show."

Anger raged inside her as she left the room. This wasn't Hollywood. There wasn't a freaking casting couch to sleep her way across.

Which apparently didn't matter because, regardless of how violently her body and mind protested, she was still going along with it.

What kind of person did that make her?

Her eyes slid shut on one slow, controlled exhale.

A person who didn't want to examine herself too closely, that was what.

She slid past Bernard—whose expression was one of utter shock—then went into the locker room to gear up.

It was time to play some goddamned hockey.

NINETEEN

Stefan

STEFAN KNEW something was wrong the moment Brit stepped onto the ice.

Her fury was a tangible thing, a heavy fog that spread across the rink, inundated the team with tension.

Practice was typically a noisy affair with pucks colliding against the boards, ringing off the glass, curse words and ribbing mixed liberally amongst the sounds of good ole hockey.

Today, twenty-four skaters went quiet. Even Julian Beausoleil, the starting goalie who was usually completely oblivious to any and all social cues, stopped fussing with his crease and stared at Brit.

Crunch. Scrape. Crunch. Scrape.

Brit rasped her skates across the front of the net she'd claimed, scuffing the ice so that when she dropped into butterfly —the best position for a goalie to make a save when the puck was on the ice—and scrambled from post to post, she wouldn't slide too far out of the crease.

Max skated up to Stefan and murmured quietly in his ear. "Is this about the news story?"

"No." Stefan sighed. "Well, partly, I guess. I'm assuming management pulled her in too. They tore into me, and I imagine they weren't any nicer to her." He shrugged. "I told them nothing happened, but you know how they get when it comes to the media."

Max raised a brow. "That didn't exactly look like nothing. I mean, come on, man. She's one of us now. You need to leave her be."

Stefan fixed his friend with a look, hostility boiling his blood at the implication, even as his brain mercilessly reminded him that Max was right. He *was* attracted to Brit in a very inappropriate way.

But that was the physical only.

The rest of it—the respect, the confidence in her abilities—was acceptable. He was good at compartmentalizing, and he'd shoved her very firmly into the teammate zone of his mind.

Plus, this was nothing more than instant chemistry. Or at least nothing more than insta-*lust,* and lust he could deal with.

No problem.

So he glared at Max and said, "You of all people should know that pictures don't always tell the full truth."

It was a low blow. Max had felt the brunt of a particularly brutal and untruthful media campaign over the summer. It had cost him everything—his wife, his kid—all because of some falsified pictures and a forged paternity test. The truth had come out. Eventually. But the damage had been done.

They locked eyes for a long moment, Max's past a corporal and uncomfortable presence.

The tension broke when Max grimaced. "You're right. I'm sorry."

Stefan nodded, acknowledging the apology even while

trying to communicate his own. He shouldn't have brought it up . . . but then again, he shouldn't have done a lot of things.

"There's nothing between us," he told Max. "She had her headphones in, I startled her, we got tangled up and fell."

"Gotcha." A pause. "You both okay?"

"Besides the bruise on my ass the size of a fucking elephant?"

Max laughed but went abruptly silent when Brit's gaze whipped toward them. "Fuck. She's scary."

"Naw. She's just like us."

"What do you mean?"

Stefan grasped onto the sudden bit of clarity with two fists. "She's pissed, maybe a little hurt. And she's needs a way to work off some of that frustration."

"How?"

"Dude. She's a *hockey* player."

"Oh."

He waited. Wasn't disappointed. Max could be seriously dense sometimes.

"I don't get it."

"Come on, man! Go take some fucking shots on her. That's how she gets rid of her frustration. *She plays hockey*."

"Oh." Max glanced at him. "Are you sure?" But his friend's lips were twitching.

"Oh my God," Stefan said. "You're an idiot. Go."

Max grabbed a puck, skated to the top of the circles, and waited for Brit's attention.

When she nodded, he ripped a slap shot that collided with Brit's pads in a resounding *thud*.

More of the guys joined in. More shots. More saves. And the tension in the rink began to dissipate.

Frankie came out and began running the drills about five

minutes later. Stefan joined in, skated his ass off. Sweated. Rushed. Shot. Defended.

It was a typical practice.

Except for the fact that Bernard never appeared.

And Brit didn't smile. Not once.

In the small amount of time he'd known Brit, one of his favorite things about her was the giant grin adorning her face every time she stepped on the ice, made a save, or hell, took a sip of water. He'd even seen it in the scouting videos and in her interviews.

Her enjoyment in the game was palpable and inspiring . . . and somehow in the last twelve hours, that joy had disappeared.

WHAT DID an idiotic male say to the fuming female next to him?

Stefan sucked in a breath, reminded himself to man up. "Are you—?"

"No," Brit said. "I'm not okay or fine or on my fucking period. *Okay*?"

His fingers froze on the laces of his skates. Was that a rhetorical question, or did she want an answer?

"Jesus Christ," she muttered, tossing her chest protector to the floor and kneeling to remove her leg pads. "I'm fine."

"I just thought—"

"That's your problem," she snapped. "Thinking."

Well, fuck that. He might respect Brit a whole lot, might think she was hot as hell, and a damn good goalie, but fuck her pushing him around. He wasn't a weak-ass rookie. He was the captain. And more than that, he was a man who wouldn't tolerate someone giving him bullshit.

Didn't matter if the mouth the crap came from was male or female.

Carefully, *oh so carefully*, so he didn't step on her fingers, didn't slice through any of that gorgeous porcelain skin with the sharp blades still strapped to his feet, Stefan knelt beside her.

He brushed her fingers aside, said, "Let me get that."

Then he pretended to help her untangle a particularly bad knot on the lace holding her pad to the underside of one skate.

"Let's get one thing straight," he told her, gripping her ankle tight, his tone mild, but his words no less fierce. "I will not be pushed. I will not be snapped at. I'm the captain of this team—"

She shoved his hand away. "Get the hell away from me. You don't know shit, Barie."

He caught her wrist when she would have shoved him again. "I know enough." A squeeze. A warning. "I know more than enough." His tone was laced with steel.

Brit's eyes widened, but she let him reach forward to untie the bottom lace on her pad.

When it was loose, he stood then sank back down onto the bench in front of his cubby. His skates were off seconds later, the rest of his equipment and sweaty clothes following suit.

The locker room had quieted during the exchange with Brit, but Stefan was beyond giving a shit.

He strode naked into the showers.

Living the dream. He was living the fucking dream.

TWENTY

STEFAN HAD a moment of fuck-the-record-breaking-California-drought and stayed in the shower long past the recommended three minutes.

Unfortunately, the lukewarm water did nothing to temper his . . . temper. Frustration rode him hard and mixed with confusion to create a lethal combination.

He wanted to punch something. He wanted to fuck someone.

In one abrupt moment that made the pipes groan in protest, Stefan cranked the water off, wrapped a towel around his waist, and walked back into the locker room.

The lights were partially off, but the space wasn't empty.

Or at least not entirely.

Brit was still at her station, still half-dressed in her gear.

Her face was so forlorn that all the anger twisting him up inside faded.

"What's up?" he asked, kneeling next to her.

She jumped and big brown eyes flashed to his. "Nothing." Fingers pushed her blond hair back from her forehead, but several short wispy pieces didn't cooperate. They slid forward, curled around her temples, her ears. She gave an irritated sigh. "We already went over this."

Hands up, Stefan rose and began getting dressed. "Whatever, Brit. Keep it to yourself or don't. But cut the bitch act. It doesn't suit you."

She sucked in a breath, and he tried not to feel guilty. He really tried.

Dammit. He would not apologize.

Underwear on. Then slacks and his button down. He was bending to put on his shoes when the fucking guilt got to him anyway.

But just as he opened his mouth to apologize, Brit spoke. "I'm sorry."

Stefan shook his head. "No. That was a shitty thing to say. I shouldn't—"

"It's not you," she said and peeled down the black and gold hockey socks she wore. Her legs were bare underneath, and he worked really hard to not notice how sexy they were.

They were muscular, maybe a little hard—not unlike Brit—but her skin held a soft glow to that made him want to press a kiss to her ankle . . . then lick all the way up.

His hands clenched, and he shoved the image away.

Teammate. She was his teammate.

Shit. That wasn't working.

"I've got some stuff going on in my life. Complications, I guess," she said. "Then with the pictures." She shook her head, but met his gaze straight on. "I took it out on you, and I'm sorry."

Those eyes—he suddenly had a craving for milk chocolate—left his and focused on removing the rest of her equipment.

"What's going on?" he asked. "Maybe I can help?"

It was an offer born of the man in him, the piece of him that wanted to fix, to do something to remove the sadness in her.

He had no business making such a proposal, not with his

own life in shambles—the team, his mother's illness, the goddamned media—but he found himself unable to take it back.

Her hockey pants and girdle dropped to the floor with a soft *thunk*. She released a breath. "Thanks for the offer, but I'm the one who needs to sort this out."

Somehow, he doubted that was the truth. But he figured he'd pushed her far enough.

For now.

"You want me to turn on the lights or get out of here so you can shower?"

"No, thanks." She shook her head, the gesture casual, except there was something in her tone—too abrupt, too quick to answer—that made his hackles rise.

Questions. This woman filled him with so many damned questions.

"I'll just shower back at the hotel."

He frowned. "You haven't found a place to stay yet?"

She rolled her eyes, turned her back, and stripped off her sports bra.

Creamy skin. Delicate muscles on her back. Stefan's mouth watered. His fingers tingled with the urge to touch, to stroke. To kiss the giant bruise that still marred her skin and make it all better.

He almost groaned. He was so fucking screwed.

Gripping his thighs hard enough to cut off circulation north of the border, he forced himself to appreciate the workmanship of the large Gold logo on the far side of the room.

"No," Brit said, her tone just acerbic enough to make him grin. "I haven't found a place to stay here. I've been in San Francisco for less than two weeks. Between training camp and practices, I've been too tired to look." She paused. "Plus, I don't know that I'll still be here in a month. Makes no sense to look until I'm sure."

Stefan's position on the team had been so safe over the last few years that he'd forgotten what it was like to be a rookie . . . or at least a rookie on an NHL team.

First was the call up. Then the hurdles of training camp and preseason games. Brit had showed well at the first, but that didn't necessarily mean her place on the team was cemented. The preseason games would be her next biggest obstacle.

He'd assumed management bringing her in meant her spot was locked, but now he realized that had been ridiculous. *Everyone* had to earn a place on the first go-around. Hell, if he hadn't had excellent seasons the last few years, he would have been just as stressed about earning his own position.

But Stefan didn't give voice to any of that. "I know a good real estate agent for when you officially make the team."

A moment passed where neither of them said anything, and Stefan wondered if he'd overstepped his bounds.

"Thanks."

There was something strained in Brit's tone, so he flicked his eyes over, was surprised to find her in the same position, back to him and topless.

Except, her hands were wrapped behind her back in an impersonation of a pretzel as they scrabbled up toward her shoulders.

"You okay?"

"No." She sighed and dropped her arms then leaned forward to rest her head against the wall.

"What is it?" he asked.

"Mm shmpf," she said, her voice muffled and completely indecipherable.

"Was that English?"

Her head tipped back, and she stared up at the ceiling. Half the recessed lights were off, bathing the usually stark white and black room in soft golden light. It gilded her skin, and the beauty of it took his breath away.

"I said I'm stuck."

"Stuck?"

Brit was standing, free and clear, a few feet away from her locker. A little shriek of frustration escaped her. "Oh my God. This seriously isn't happening." She turned, arms crossed over her breasts.

He tried to not notice the way the action pressed them together, the way his mouth watered with the urge to bury his face there.

"I'm stuck," she said. "I'm sweaty, and my shoulder hurts, and this fucking bra is all twisted, and I'm stuck!"

Her chin wobbled, and for one awful second, Stefan thought she was going to cry.

Then her eyes slid closed, and she sucked in a breath. "Can you help me?"

"Um—"

"Never mind," she snapped and turned again.

Reaching up—for the first time, he noticed the strip of black fabric twisted over her neck and shoulders—to grab at the back of her bra. But though her fingers could touch the bunched-up band, they couldn't get enough purchase to untangle it.

His brain finally began working again. "Here." He closed the distance between them, tried to ignore the way she smelled —floral, like roses, with a slight tinge of salt from the exertion of practice—as he slipped his fingers under the edge of her bra and pulled down.

It came. Partway.

The sides were still twisted, and he couldn't stop himself from running his fingers around to the front, under her arms, unwinding the bra and brushing the sides of her breasts in the process.

She sucked in a breath. So did he.

Forward. His fingers moved forward, tugging the bra down.

Stefan's chest pressed close to her back, and he looked over her shoulder as he carefully worked the Lycra over her breasts.

He totally looked. He shouldn't have.

But, damn, was he glad he'd done so.

He tugged the soft black material down, covering the rosy tips, even though all he wanted was to see how well her breasts fit in his palms.

Instead, he forced his hands to slide down her ribs. They came to a stop on her waist, unable to completely break the contact.

Especially when she sighed, and her head tilted, exposing her neck. It was screaming for a kiss, a lick, a *nip*.

He leaned down, inhaled the soft scent of her, and she shuddered. His groin went impossibly hard.

"Thanks," she murmured, her posture tensing just the slightest bit. Brit didn't pull away, but she wasn't fully in the moment any longer.

Stefan stepped back, dropped his hands. "Anytime." His voice sounded like he'd spent some quality time with a flamethrower. He swallowed, tried to clear away the desire.

Lush lips quirked. Chocolate eyes twinkled. "Somehow I knew you were going to say that." She was laughing at him, and he found he didn't give a damn. He'd take the brunt of any humor if it meant she smiled at him like that.

"Yeah?" His amusement surged to match hers.

She shrugged. "It's the Y chromosome."

Laughter burst out of him, and he slipped on his suit jacket. "Are we that easy to read?"

Brit pulled on her t-shirt and sweats. "Yup." Sneakers in hand, she sank onto the bench and stepped into them. "What's with the monkey suit? Bernard only requires them on game days, I thought."

"That's true. Just got used to wearing them, I guess."

"Suits you. No pun intended." She stood. "See you tomorrow."

Her footsteps were quiet, her stride determined, as she crossed the industrial carpeting—except Stefan was watching her so intently that he saw her slight hesitation at the door.

"Barie?" She turned.

"Yeah?"

"Thanks"—she waved a hand at her breasts—"for this. And . . . I'll get my shit together by tomorrow."

He nodded, but when she would have walked out, he hurried to close the distance between them and put a staying hand on her arm. "There's nothing to get together. You're doing fine."

Brit seemed as though she would protest. Then she shook her head and forced a smile. "Thanks."

He released her. "See you later."

"Bye." The word was chipper, but it didn't hide the undertone in her expression. Brit didn't think she was doing fine at all.

Both the man and the captain in him were aligned for the first time in recent history.

He wouldn't let Brit self-destruct.

No matter what it took.

TWENTY-ONE

Brit

FINE.

Brit was doing fine.

She snorted. Yeah, sure. Ordered to all-but-screw the captain of her team in front of the entire populace of the United States and Canada, and she was fine.

Son of a puckhole.

With a sigh, she picked up the pace until she was practically sprinting through the city streets. Security had offered her a ride from the arena back to the hotel, and she'd taken it . . . for a couple of blocks.

Until her frustration had boiled over, and she'd had them pull over so she could run the rest of the way.

Thankfully, there were no news vans, no shouting reporters or smartphones pointed in her direction.

Brit could run.

Though, she couldn't quite escape the fact that she and her teenage-boy-esque-hormonal body weren't going to be able to keep their distance from Stefan.

She wanted him. Which she could have endured, if not for—

"Stupid," she muttered with sigh.

The problem—or *problems,* rather—were her brain and her heart. Those traitorous organs liked Stefan's wit, appreciated his concern and sensitivity.

Unfortunately, management had taken her chance away of actually pursuing something with him along natural channels. They'd ruined the might-have-been.

Which sucked. But she had to put on her big girl skates and deal.

She'd agreed. That was that. She would wait for the contract to be approved by her lawyer, and then she would jump headfirst into a relationship with Stefan. Get the shots and coverage and get the hell out.

There wouldn't be anything real. There was no potential for a future.

Hell, they were teammates, a future wasn't realistic anyway.

The trick was keeping Stefan interested for more than a date or two. Although, she only had to frame it to the public as though they were dating, so perhaps that would help.

Despite all of the plans bouncing around her skull, Brit still had the notion that she was in way over her head.

She thought of how Stefan had behaved in the locker room. He'd been sweet, understanding . . . at least until she'd pissed him off.

Then he'd been fierce and hot as hell.

If management hadn't ordered her to pursue him, if he wasn't her teammate, Brit thought that Stefan might be the man to help her put all of her anxieties aside. He might be a man she could just be *herself* with.

Which didn't exactly help the *in over her head* feeling.

Warm, calloused fingers on her back, her breasts . . . the

spice of masculine aftershave teasing her nose . . . a muscled chest right against her spine—

The door came out of nowhere.

Well, not *nowhere,* since Brit had noticed the SUV parked on the sidewalk. She just hadn't expected the door to slam open six inches from her nose.

She jumped out of the way.

Nice to see her reflexes were intact, in spite of the crap swirling around in her head.

"Oh! I'm so sorry!" The voice was feminine and apologetic but didn't quite ring true. "I didn't see you there. Wait! You're Brit Plantain!" The woman—dressed in a skin-tight red suit—turned her head. "OMG, honey! It's Brit Plantain!"

Forcing a smile while trying not to step back, Brit nodded. "Hi," she said. "Nice to meet you."

"I'm Jessica," she said and stepped even closer, encroaching uncomfortably into Brit's space. "I almost hit you with my door! What if I'd injured you?" Heavily lined eyes narrowed. "Do you really think it's safe to be running by yourself after all the money the Gold spent on your contract?"

If Brit's smile had been forced two seconds before, now it was tortured. And *all* the money? Since when was the league minimum a lot? By the time her agent took her cut, it wasn't much more than the dot-commers populating this part of the city made.

"I'm fine, thank you," she said. "But it's been a long day. I'm going to—"

Brit started to move off, and the woman stopped her, long talons—okay, long red varnished *nails*—gripping her arm.

"Wait! Could you sign something for my niece?" She fumbled in her jacket pocket and produced a notepad. "She's only nine and just started playing."

Brit relaxed. Now that she could get behind. Supporting

girls in sports, fostering their confidence, improving their discipline, their teamwork?

Hell yeah.

"Sure. What's her name?"

"Umm . . . Sophie."

Again that weird intonation in the woman's voice. But at this point, all Brit wanted to do was get the hell back to her hotel room and soak in the tub. She scrawled a quick note of encouragement then signed her name and handed over the paper.

"Here you go. Nice to meet you, Jessica."

"Likewise!" A toothy grin. "Hope to see you again, Brit!"

The words made the hairs on her nape stand up, especially when she glanced over at the car and noticed the driver's seat was empty.

Who had the woman been talking to?

Shaking herself—she'd probably just been on Bluetooth—Brit forced herself to give another smile before waving and jogging away.

Tomorrow she was driving.

THE NEXT DAY dawned cloudy and cold, but Brit didn't care.

Because it was game day.

She sat in the back of a car—after having to call security for a ride because her hotel was absolutely inundated with press. It had been scary enough running through the gauntlet the previous day, let alone trying to navigate through a mess of news vans and cameras in her little beater.

Nope. This was better. The car had swept up to a side door, and they were zipping right over to the arena.

Her life had gotten really freaking weird.

She wished she could run to the arena because nerves were

making her antsy as a mother. Her foot tapped against the grey carpet lining the floor of the black sedan, a rapid *tap-tap* that annoyed the crap out of her. And if it was bothering her, the poor driver had to be—

"Nervous?" he asked, his eyes meeting hers in the mirror. There was amusement in their depths.

"Nope," she lied with a rueful smile.

Josh had also driven her the previous night—at least before she'd jumped ship—and couldn't be older than twenty-two. He seemed nice enough, despite the terrible indie grunge music trickling through the speakers.

"Just ready to be on the ice." That part was true at least.

"There's nothing like it," he agreed.

"You play?" she asked, surprised. He was maybe a buck-forty soaking wet. *She* outweighed him and had a good six inches on his five-feet-nothing frame.

"Yup."

"Grow up on the East Coast?"

Another look in the mirror. More amusement. "Nope. Grew up here, but I like the sport. Started as an adult." He focused on the road. "I suck, and there's *still* nothing better than those first couple of strides on the ice." He paused. "Well, when you manage to stay on your feet, that is."

Brit always forgot that Northern California had such a large contingent of hockey players. In fact, they had some of the largest recreational leagues in the states. It was great for the sport . . . but still weird to think of beach babes and surfer dudes strapping on skates and picking up sticks.

Total misconception, of course. Especially in the Bay Area.

For her, growing up in Maine meant winters outdoors, skating on frozen lakes, white puffs of condensed breaths, and trying to not bust her ass on divots the size of the Grand Canyon.

Winter in California was more like occasional rain and a light jacket.

But there were some things that were true for all players. "I agree."

"Is it true you're getting the start?" he asked. "I heard it on the radio." His eyes flicked to hers then back to the road. "That's big."

It *was* big. Hence the anxious foot tapping. "As far as I know, I'm starting. Julian's knee is bothering him a bit." Which meant this was her shot to show her stuff.

The nerves were eating at her. They always did. Right up until she strapped her pads on.

Then the nerves disappeared, were replaced with calm, laser focus.

"That sucks." The car stopped at a red light, and Josh tossed a grin over his shoulder. "But I just know you're going to stone the Ducks."

She grinned back, felt the first twinges of excitement rather than nausea. "Damn right."

The light turned green, and Josh navigated the sedan through the crowd of journalists at the front gate of the arena. Security waved them on, and a moment later, they were safely ensconced in the lot.

Josh parked as close to the side door of the arena as possible. "Let me get that door."

"I got it," she said, popping the handle. "Thanks for the ride."

He nodded. "I'll meet you right here after the game. And Brit?"

She paused, halfway out of the car.

"Kick some avian ass."

TWENTY-TWO

TWO MINUTES LEFT in the game and the Gold were up three to one.

A two-goal advantage was considered to be the most dangerous lead in hockey. And the Gold were demonstrating perfectly why that was true.

Her team was getting complacent.

Sure it was preseason, but that didn't mean they should be letting up on the boards or giving the Ducks' players so much space as they carried the puck into the zone.

It also meant she was taking more shots than she should have this late in the game when she was already tired, and her team was slow to clear any rebounds.

She sighed, bolstered her strength, and crouched into ready position just as the ref dropped the puck for a face-off in their own zone.

Winning this game was going to have to come from her.

Her center lost the draw, and a Ducks' defenseman shot from up high. Hard.

Brit watched it come, saw the slight deflection off her own player, and had to move quickly. But instinct guided her, and she had made the necessary adjustment before her next heartbeat.

The crowd gasped before cheering loud enough to make her ears ring when she caught the puck in her glove. She held tight until the ref blew his whistle.

Her eyes flashed to the scoreboard.

A minute fifteen left.

The next faceoff was to her right, her strong side. Stefan lined up at the hash marks in front of her—the short red lines at 3 and 9 o'clock on each of the circles—and Max took the space directly on her blocker side.

At the whistle, she raised her glove, and the ref dropped the puck. Brit heard nothing but the beat of her own pulse as the Ducks' center won the draw back to his player for the second time. She was ready for the shot when it came screaming through Stefan's legs.

Except it didn't go straight through.

The puck hit his shin pad, and this time she wasn't prepared for the deflection. The shot went from being six inches off the ice to rising rapidly and screaming toward the far side.

She lunged.

There wouldn't be anything graceful about this save. It was desperation, brute strength. And she might not make it.

Stretching. Reaching out. Then her glove was . . . *there!*

Clenching the puck so hard her hand was cramping, Brit collapsed to the ice in a heap. The stick that made contact with her head then stomach wasn't a surprise—the opposing team had free reign until the whistle was blown.

That was the reason she was closing her glove so tightly.

But that also didn't mean it hadn't hurt.

What *did* surprise her was Stefan's reaction.

"Don't fucking touch her!" he yelled.

A runaway train had nothing on him. He launched himself

at the Ducks' player, taking them both to the ice. His gloves and stick went flying, and then his fists were colliding with the opposing player's face.

The refs pulled him off, hauled him to his feet, and shoved him in the direction of the box.

"Four minutes for roughing, Barie," the head referee said before skating toward the scorekeeper and reporting the necessary information. The normal penalty length had been doubled because Stefan had drawn blood on the Duck with the punches he'd landed.

Brit's frustration was a boiling, writhing mass under her skin. Why had he done that?

The contact had been normal, easily discouraged by Stefan giving the other guy a shove or warning tap with his stick.

What he'd done instead had crossed the line from being protective of his goalie to bat-shit crazy.

And now she had a minute to kill, one player down, with a team that was lethargic at best.

Mike Stewart blew her a kiss as he skated by to take up position in Stefan's former spot. "Don't screw up now," he said with a smirk.

So that was how it was going to be.

Down not one, but two players.

The ref blew his whistle. Brit took note of the angle of the players, got herself set in her net.

She raised her glove, shored up her spine.

The puck dropped.

Brit came out of the showers to find a package on her bench. There was a Post-it on the outside.

. . .

As requested. Impressive results so far. Keep it up.
—Susan

She unfolded the brad and opened the flap on the manila envelope. Inside was the revised contract for Bernard.

"Yeah. Not until my lawyer looks at it," she muttered under her breath as she shoved it in her messenger bag.

"You showered," Barie said from his spot next to her.

Brit stifled a sigh, still pissed he'd lost his cool during the game and still wholly unable to understand what the hell he'd been thinking.

That frustration loosened her lips. "Strength in numbers."

Stefan got very quiet, so much so that she heard the rustle of his pants against the wooden bench of his locker space.

He was going to ask her to explain and, damn, she had to come up with something innocuous, an excuse that had nothing to do with years-old scars about an assault she should really be over.

Her eyes locked on the Gold logo in the center of the room. The miner—pick ax over one shoulder—looked almost demonic as it clutched a large gold nugget in his palm.

Someone really should do something about that. Make it look less creepy.

"Sorry about losing my cool."

"What?" Her mouth dropped open.

That was pretty much the last thing she would have expected Stefan to say. Apologizing didn't come naturally for men in general, and definitely not in this sport.

She glanced over, saw his face appeared genuinely contrite.

"I'm pissed at you," she told him.

"You should be." His gaze connected with hers. "I took it too far."

Five words, and her anger drained. "Don't let it happen again."

Stefan nodded before his expression darkened. "But I won't apologize for protecting you in the crease. It's my job."

She felt her brows pull together. "I can handle my—"

"*It's my job,*" he repeated, and her face went hot. She opened her mouth to snap back, but he went on, "Look, I get it. This isn't some alpha bullshit—"

She snorted.

"It isn't," he insisted. "Okay fine. Maybe it was. But it won't be anymore. I went a little nuts, but I won't take it too far again."

Tucking her towel tighter around her, she fixed him with a look. "You do realize they're going to poke at me more now to try and get a reaction from you."

He grimaced. "I know. But"—his lips twitched—"what you did to Stewart with ten seconds left will have anyone second guessing that course."

A shrug. "He was in my way."

"Stewart was being an asshole."

"True."

He'd hung in front of the goal, blocking her view, not going after the puck even when it was clearly his to take. At one point he'd fumbled *accidentally,* and Brit had needed to scramble forward and launch herself on top of the puck.

It was in that scramble she had committed an *accident* of her own.

Seeing a six-foot-six, two-hundred-and-twenty pound piece of shit flying ass-over-teakettle into the net had been pretty amusing.

Plus, she'd managed to hold onto the lead, so Stewart and his shenanigans could suck it.

"So . . . are we cool?"

Brit rolled her eyes. "We're cool." They were going to be a

lot more than cool if this contract checked out, at least according to media.

"Just keep it on the level next time, 'kay?" she said.

"Noted."

She finished dressing, packed up her gear, and left, the manila envelope burning a hole in her bag.

TWENTY-THREE

Stefan

STEFAN WALKED into the arena the next day, feeling as though the weight of the world was resting on his shoulders.

Between his mom and her treatment and the media camped on his doorstep, the cheap shot on Brit had been bad timing. A coincidence that had pushed him past his breaking point. But Stefan had meant it when he'd told Brit he wouldn't go crazy again. He was a professional, and that meant keeping it locked up.

No matter that the press was insinuating they were in a relationship—pictures of them having beers had surfaced . . . without the inclusion of Max and Blane, of course.

No matter that his mom was exhausted from the chemo, had another week to go, and still wouldn't let him call any of her friends.

He understood his mother's health was her secret to keep. But it was eating at him, being so helpless. He wanted to have someone with her. A nurse, her friends. *Someone.*

But she'd refused, and unless he wanted to go against her wishes, his hands were tied.

Hence the frustration and going off on Dimitri Petrokov the night before. The Ducks' forward had left with a swollen lip and black eye, but no hard feelings, especially after Stefan had taken him out for a beer.

They'd played together before Stefan had been traded to the Gold.

"You're going to have to let her handle it herself," Petrokov had said as they shared that pitcher.

Stefan knew Dimitri had been talking about Brit—and his former teammate was right—but it also applied to the situation with his mother.

The trouble was, he didn't want either of the women to have to handle things on her own.

Which made him a total chauvinistic asshole.

He found he didn't care.

Crease versus cancer—remarkably different and yet similar all the same.

At least Brit's position gave him an outlet. He could punch someone . . . so long as he didn't take it too far and jeopardize the game.

Like he'd done the previous night.

Like a fucking rookie. *Jesus.*

He walked down the hallway leading to the locker room, its walls bare-white with black trim and bright fluorescent lighting shining down from the ceiling.

Stefan had come in early, just like every other morning. It didn't matter that by the time he'd finished his post-game cool-down routine—thirty minutes on the bike, stretching, then the beer with Petrokov, it had been almost one.

Now it was barely eight, and the arena was empty.

But Stefan got antsy when he wasn't here, didn't do his normal routine. Especially since they had another game tonight.

Brit wouldn't be starting this one. Not because of her performance. She'd played like a champ, had held the team together when they looked flat.

But because Julian was still the starting goalie. He had maybe one more year of professional hockey in him, and he wouldn't give it up.

Stefan didn't blame him.

Hockey was all he'd known, and to not have it was unthinkable. And yet . . . a human body could only endure so much. Julian had a history of injuries—to his shoulder, his knee, his groin. It made this season precarious, but it also meant that Brit might get more of a chance to play at the Gold than she would have gotten on another team.

She'd made a very smart career decision coming here.

As he neared the locker room, he heard voices. Bernard's office light was on, the door cracked open.

He would have walked by . . . if he hadn't heard his name.

"I'll talk to Barie," Bernard said. "Make sure he doesn't do it again."

"He won't." Brit's voice made Stefan's feet skitter to a stop.

"What makes you so sure?"

She chuckled. "Because he apologized to me in the locker room. And it was a genuine one."

"Bet it sounded like he'd swallowed glass."

Stefan smiled—it was true, after all—but he did believe in owning up to his mistakes. He started to move past the office.

"My lawyer is going to look at this." There was a *crinkle* of paper, and Stefan's feet stalled again.

"Brit, I told you," Bernard said, "you don't need—"

"I *do* need to do this . . ."

Do what?

A few seconds later, Bernard's rumbling voice drifted into the hall. "I still don't feel right about it."

"It doesn't matter if you do or not. This is what management wants, and . . . your wife—" Her voice went firm. "It's important."

Tense silence filled the office, slid into the hall.

"Plus, Susan sent a note last night," Brit said. "Said she was happy with my progress with Barie."

Stefan's heart gave a jerk. Her *progress?*

"It's bullshit." Bernard sounded both fierce and contrite. Stefan had never heard that particular combination from his coach before. Tough as nails? Yes. But remorseful? No. Definitely not.

"Look," Brit said. "They've got your balls in a vice. My metaphorical ones as well. We just need to ride this out. Let me handle Stefan."

Handle? Fuck that.

"I—" Bernard began.

The sound of a chair scraping against concrete echoed into the hall. "I need to get on the ice."

"Brit."

"Yeah?" Her voice was very close to the open door, but Stefan didn't move. He didn't care if she knew he'd overheard. He was going to find out what the hell was going on. How it involved him and management and *handling* things.

"You played good last night."

Stefan wondered if Bernard heard Brit's soft inhale, or if she was too far away. He'd have bet his right arm that her eyes had gone wide, her expression surprised for one long moment.

Outright compliments didn't come often from professional coaches.

"Thanks," she said, a little hesitant.

He imagined her dutifully wiping the expression away, nodding, and walking out.

Which was exactly what she did.

Straight into his chest.

TWENTY-FOUR

STEFAN GRABBED Brit's arm to steady her then quickly stepped back, remembering how she'd reacted to his being in her space on the arena stairs.

Though she hadn't seemed to mind when he'd helped her with her bra, which he really shouldn't be thinking about—not if he wanted to discover what was going on with her and management and Bernard.

A phone rang, Bernard's "Hello?" as he picked up clearly audible.

"Keeping secrets?" Stefan asked, rough—*too rough*—but the best he could manage, considering the frustration coursing through him. "Or maybe you're going to *handle* me some more?"

"I—uh—"

Her eyes flicked to the slightly ajar door, Bernard's voice pouring out the opening.

"What?" Stefan snapped. "Afraid he'll hear?" Anger won out, and his voice rose. "What kind of game are you playing?"

"Shh."

"I—"

She slapped a palm over his mouth and grabbed his arm

before tugging him away from Bernard's office. "Just wait a second."

Stefan let her pull him down the hall, both because he didn't want Bernard interrupting and . . . also because he had the sinking sensation it would be nearly impossible for him to deny this woman anything.

He ignored his inner voice telling him to man up.

Brit opened the first door they reached—which happened to be the temporary locker room management had wanted to stash her in—and flicked on the lights.

It was still nearly empty, just the single locker space taking up a third of one wall, and a trail of black skate mats placed on the concrete floor leading from the bench to the hall.

"It's not like you think," she said once they were inside, and Stefan had closed the door.

His rage was a potent thing. He crowded into her, forgetting his promise to give her space, to not exacerbate the fear she'd shown in the arena.

Stefan liked to think that if she had freaked, he would have backed up, but truthfully he *wasn't* sure. His draw to her, as both teammate *and* woman was already strong.

Add in a touch of secrets?

He fucking *hated* when people kept things from him, and hearing her discuss him like he was a problem child with Bernard . . .

Well, something inside him had snapped.

Rationality was toast and so he crowded her.

Brit didn't back down. In fact, something hot and dark flashed across her eyes that made his nerves alight.

"I think you're playing with me," he said.

"I'm not."

Another step toward her. Inches separated their chests, the clean scent of her inundated his senses.

"Then what?"

Brit must have recognized something in his tone—probably how the far fuck-gone he was—because now she stepped away from him.

He didn't care. He closed the distance, reveled in her sharp inhalation.

"What is it?" he demanded.

One more step backward. Stefan let her retreat, knew she had nowhere to go. The wall was just inches behind her.

"Tell me."

The order did something to Brit, shored up her spine, made sparks fill her eyes. Her chin lifted. "Don't pull that captain bullshit with me. This doesn't involve the team."

"Like hell it doesn't," he snapped. "It involves me and Bernard. The Gold is firmly entrenched in this."

"Fuck off."

"Fuck *this*." He stepped close, backed her against the wall until his chest was against hers, until the softness of her breasts pressed against him. He lowered his head, felt her breath against his lips. "Tell me."

Stefan searched her eyes. No fear there. Only heat . . . and regret.

She shook her head. "I can't."

"*Tell me.*" His hands dropped to her shoulders.

"No."

The anger boiled over. He released her, turned away, and slammed his fist against the wall.

Sheetrock gave way with a small puff of white powder, but he barely felt the sting of the impact.

"Why is every single goddamned woman out to fuck with my head?" he asked, slamming his fist into the wall a second time.

Twin fist-sized holes stared back at him, accusing.

Stefan hadn't punched an inanimate object—Ducks' forwards aside—since his teenager days, and no other action could have made him feel more like an idiot.

Rationality intruded like a bucket of ice-cold water. He was out of control.

Again.

Shame swept through him as he pushed away from the wall and brushed off his hands.

"Whatever." His voice shook, but instead of anger, it was with disgust. "Keep your goddamn secrets."

Stefan pushed out the door, and went straight down the hall to his locker. It took thirty seconds to change and hit the stationary bike. Stairs would have been better, but he didn't want to risk running into Brit.

It was an unfounded worry because she kept her distance. But it was only after the game that evening—a game he'd fucking dominated—that he realized everyone else had kept their distance too.

For once, that didn't feel like a bad thing.

Numbness had inundated him.

And honestly? It was a relief to finally not feel *anything*.

TWENTY-FIVE

Brit

BRIT HAD SERIOUSLY SCREWED UP.

She should have just invented an excuse. But when Stefan had gone all caveman, demanding answers and getting in her space, she couldn't help it. She'd dug her feet in and pushed back.

Still, that wasn't what had stopped her from telling him the truth, threats from management aside.

No. There was another reason. A deeper one.

Shame.

The elevator opened with a *ding,* and Brit sighed as she stepped into the subdued quiet of the hall. The blue paisley print of the carpet was familiar now, a little slice of home until she established her own.

Which she really needed to get on. Especially if she was going to do this relationship-thing with Stefan. They would need some place more private than a hotel surrounded by paparazzi.

The sharp, all-encompassing shame reared its ugly head again, threatened to burn a hole her throat.

It would have been so easy to confide in him, to come up with a plan. Except, Stefan wasn't the type of man to take something like that lying down . . . not like she had.

How could Brit look him in the eye and acknowledge that she hadn't possessed the strength to act differently?

Ostensibly, she'd made a stand for Bernard.

But Bernard's sick wife hadn't been the only reason she'd capitulated.

Brit wanted to play in the NHL. It was what she'd dreamed of even as a five-year-old strapping on the pads for the first time.

Apparently, she would sell her morals to do so.

"Jesus," she muttered. "Stop bitching and suck it up, Plantain."

"Talking to yourself again?"

The voice made her jump, and her fear was a palpable force, freezing her veins, raising goosebumps on her arms.

It wasn't in Brit's nature to shriek, and she didn't this time. But it was a close thing. At least until her ears and brain took a moment and actually processed the voice.

"Dan!"

She closed the distance between them in a leap, launched herself into her brother's arms.

"Missed you," he murmured, holding her tight.

"Me too."

So, *so* much.

Dan released her, and she bent to retrieve her bag from where it had fallen to the floor.

"Nice digs." He nodded to the wood-paneled walls and lush carpeting that filled the hotel. "A little nicer than where I've been staying."

"Well, it isn't a motel, that's for sure."

He grinned, trailed her to her door. "That would be a step up."

"Afghanistan again?"

Dan shook his head. "You know I can't tell you that."

And *that* was what worry for someone other than herself felt like. She was dealing with a fake relationship because she wanted to play hockey, and her brother was protecting the country.

Nothing like putting things in perspective.

"You okay?" he asked as she tapped the plastic key card against the reader.

His hand on her shoulder made her stiffen for a moment before she made herself relax. "Just peachy."

It was just her brother, for God's sake.

The familiar scent of Dan's cologne—spicy and masculine and . . . *home*—wafted up over her shoulder. "How'd you find out where I'm staying?"

"I'm your older brother," he said and she felt rather than saw him roll his eyes. "It's pretty much my job to know your business." A pause. "Plus, I tracked your phone."

Brit snorted. "Illegal *much*? What would your boss say?"

"She'd probably tell me to keep a closer eye on you." He laughed. "You know Allison worries."

"True." Allison was Blane's mom and also happened to be a bigwig at the FBI. Dan was one of her agents.

But it was true. For some reason, she worried about Brit.

It still boggled Brit's mind that Allison and Sean—Blane's dad—had been willing to take her in, to make such a big commitment so that a girl they barely knew could play on their son's team.

Of course, Brit's *own* parents hadn't hesitated to agree when she had approached them about moving a state away.

But Allison and Sean hadn't hesitated either. They'd

welcomed Brit into their home, committed to getting her to practices and games, feeding and clothing her, making sure she did her schoolwork.

Not to mention that bringing a teenaged girl into a household filled with four boys between the ages of nine and seventeen couldn't have been easy. But they'd done it. And more.

For the three years she'd lived with them, they'd made sure Brit never lost touch with Dan, allowing him to stay when he managed to come up for a game. They'd encouraged, cheered her on, even when she'd spent half a season warming the bench.

More than that, Allison had become a surrogate mother, had stitched together the gaping wound within Brit that had been the result of her parents' indifference.

It would probably never permanently heal, but Allison had helped stop the pain from shading every happy memory with sadness.

A hand waved in front of her face before a saliva-wet finger poked at her ear. "Earth to Brit."

"Ugh. Seriously!"

She shoved Dan's chest hard, had the satisfaction of making him fall back a step. All the drama with management was making her maudlin.

No. *She* was making it that way, with her moping around and growling at everyone. With that thought, Brit shook herself and made a mental note to give Allison and Sean a call. Talking with them always made her feel better.

She had tap the key again before turning the handle and pushing the door open to her room. Dan followed her in. "You this charming with your dates?"

He grinned. "Always."

"Yeah, sure. 'Cuz stalking is sexy."

"Hey"—he turned and threw the deadbolt—"it's sexy when *I* do it."

"Sure." She snorted before going serious. "How's work treating you? Have you been safe?"

"You know me," Dan said. "I'm always safe."

"Except when you're not."

Dan had been shot last year, and any comfort or casualness Brit might have felt for his job had disappeared.

"Hey, come on now," he said. "I was never in any real danger." He took a couple of steps, closed the distance between them, and wrapped her in his arms.

"Yeah, except for the fact that if the bullet had been six inches to the right, you would have been dead."

His face pulled into a masculine grimace, but he didn't deny her statement. "You can't worry about me. I'm always prepared, always careful."

"But—"

He waved her off. "We've had this conversation before, sis."

Brit had a choice. Get into another argument with Dan over something she was particularly sensitive to because of their past—one that wouldn't change a damn thing, no matter how much she nagged—or she could enjoy the fact that her brother was in town for the next little while and shut her mouth.

Which was so. Freaking. Hard.

Dan raised a brow, probably at the screwed-up expression she could feel dragging her lips into a pout.

Dammit. All right. She gave. The breath she blew out was a long hiss. "Okay."

His eyes sparkled. "Just okay?"

"That's all you're getting, so shut it." Her glare should have eviscerated him. Instead, he laughed.

Brothers. For real.

She walked across the room and turned on the bedside lamp then pulled the curtains closed.

Dan sank back on one of the two queen beds, not bothering to take off his shoes. "You wound me."

"Shut up." Bending, she scooped up the room service binder and tossed it on his chest. "I'm too tired to go out. Call and order us some food."

"Bossy."

"You know it."

TWENTY-SIX

BY THE TIME room service knocked on the door, Dan had Pay-per-viewed some terrible action flick, and she'd glanced over the contract for Bernard.

It looked right, but until her lawyer gave her the okay, Brit wasn't going any further with Stefan.

She flipped the contract closed and stuffed it into the manila envelope when Dan didn't move from the bed. "Don't get up or anything."

Her brother just grabbed the remote and turned up the television, until the sound of machine gunfire and shattering glass filled the room.

"I'm so eating your burger," she muttered.

It would totally be worth ruining her in-season diet of rice, greens, and chicken, just to see his face.

"I can take you, squirt," he said. "Any day of the week."

Brit rolled her eyes, but she was laughing as she pulled back the deadbolt and opened the door.

Her lips parted, about to say she could take the tray from the staff member.

Except it wasn't a hotel worker.

Stefan was outside the door. He was in sweats and a t-shirt, more casual than she'd ever seen him.

"Hey," he said softly.

The world went quiet. Still. Everything inside of her froze the moment she saw Stefan's blue eyes, smelled his familiar scent.

"Hey," she returned.

Scintillating conversation from the two of them.

But Brit didn't know what to say or why he was there.

All she knew was that he affected her.

Safe and risky at the same time.

Stefan was a man who wouldn't hurt her physically, wouldn't cage her or throw her naked into a shower. But he was also a man who threatened to unfreeze her heart, to implant a bunch of barbed strands in the organ then grip tight the fibers.

The cool distance, her normal eminent focus was impossible to hold on to when he was nearby.

And if the contract currently sitting on her desk checked out, that pull wasn't going to get any easier to deny.

Ding.

They turned as one at the sound of the elevator arriving, its doors sliding open with a *whoosh.*

Room service.

The worker was a young Hispanic man who'd delivered to Brit before. Mario wore his standard, a black polo and khakis, but this time his typically wide smile disappeared, and he stuttered to a stop in front of them. "I-is everything okay?"

Brit didn't blame him for faltering. Stefan's presence alone filled the entire space with tense expectation.

The tray rattled, and Stefan reached out to snag it. "Here. I've got it."

Mario glanced at Brit, curiosity in his gaze. "It's fine," she said and put out her hand for the receipt to sign.

She scrawled her name then placed her usual cash tip into Mario's outstretched hand. "Thanks."

They watched in silence as Mario stepped back onto the elevator. When Stefan turned to face her, his hands held the tray rock steady, and the penetrating gaze he gave her threatened to turn her knees to jelly.

She wanted to close the distance between them, to feel the stubble adorning his cheeks on her palm, her temple, her inner thigh—

No.

Brit locked her knees. He was hot, no doubt. Even a little sweet. But she was tough. She was the first woman to play in a professional NHL preseason game, could out-squat half her teammates . . . and that was saying something.

So no, she couldn't allow her legs to turn to jelly. She couldn't soften toward Stefan, especially not with the truth of what she had to do.

Their interactions needed to be fake, distant, a facsimile of reality.

Because, otherwise, her heart was going to be shattered.

"What?" It was a defensive question. "I live in a hotel," she said. "It's not like I can get my Betty Crocker on."

He laughed. "We need to get you out more."

"Good luck with that." The voice wasn't hers.

Dan had come up behind her without her noticing. She jumped when he whispered in her ear, "Everything okay?"

She nodded.

"Dan," her brother said, reaching past her to offer Stefan his hand.

Stefan glanced at the tray and back at her. His eyes had turned into flecks of ice, the dark black of his pupils standing out in sharp relief against the pale blue of his irises.

She would have chalked it up to jealousy, except Stefan

didn't seem like the type to get jealous. Plus, no man had ever bothered to exhibit such an emotion over her before.

It just didn't compute.

So this must be coming from a captain-like place, protecting a teammate, looking after the team's resources. It was the only thing that made sense. Except Stefan was glaring at Dan, and if looks could kill—

Pushing aside that thought, Brit reached out and snagged the tray.

"Dan, this is Stefan, captain of the Gold," she said into the silence that had grown taut in less than a minute. "Stefan. Meet Dan, *my brother*."

Holding the tray steady, she slipped back into the room. Enough of the worry and angst. Enough stressing about circumstances that couldn't be changed.

She was going through with the fake relationship.

But . . . it wasn't going to happen until tomorrow.

Until then, she was going to focus on the things that were easy to solve.

Fatigue. Boredom. Hunger.

The bed was cozy, the movie stupid but entertaining, and the food would be filling and tasty enough.

She ignored the voice in her head that said the hunger for the man outside her door wasn't quite so easy a problem to solve.

TWENTY-SEVEN

Stefan

HER BROTHER.

A ball of tension relaxed in Stefan's gut. It was irrational, but he found he didn't care.

Dan fixed him with a look that screamed he knew what Stefan's visceral reaction had been at seeing another man in Brit's room.

Rage. Liquid-hot rage that had demanded he sink his fist into the bastard's face.

He'd resisted, barely. Mainly because he had no rights to Brit whatsoever.

At least that's what he kept telling himself.

But it was getting increasingly more difficult to ignore the piece of him that wanted to claim her as his.

Damn the team. Damn anything that stood in their way.

His body was so in-tune with Brit's that he heard the rustle of cloth as she moved through the room, the soft *rattle* of the tray, the *click* of an interior door closing.

The sound of running water filled the air.

"You like burgers?" Dan asked. He seemed as though he were studying every minute nuance of Stefan's expression.

"What?" He blinked.

Dan rolled his eyes. "Do. You. Like. Burgers?"

Okaaay . . .

"Yeah." Stefan shrugged. "Sure."

"Good. There's hope for you yet." He turned and walked into the room, hitching his thumb at Stefan to follow him.

Brit's brother grabbed the plastic key card sitting on the desk next to the television, turned, and fixed Stefan with a glare that could have peeled muscle from bone. "I'll be back in an hour. You eat. You talk and take care of the pain in her eyes. But you *don't* fucking touch. Got it?"

Stefan nodded. The water still ran in the bathroom as Dan left.

Brit's room was pretty standard-issue for the Gold. Two queens, a wall-mounted air conditioner, a desk that doubled as a TV stand, and a small armchair shoved into one corner.

He sank onto the edge of the bed but immediately stood again.

"The bed? *Really*, Barie?" he muttered.

The toilet flushed, the water turned off, and anxiety gripped his gut. He hadn't felt this nervous since sneaking into Tracey Rickman's bedroom his senior year of high school.

Tracey's dad had been very demonstrative during his whole boy-dating-his-daughter spiel. He'd even included props—a pair of scissors and a shotgun—and had been happy to describe what he'd do to Stefan if he ever hurt his *"darling little girl."*

Just the memory had him shuddering.

The door to the bathroom opened, and Brit walked out.

"Ready to eat?" she asked. "I'm starv—"

Her words cut off as she spotted him standing in the space between the desk and the bed, his arms akimbo.

"What are you doing in here?" The question wasn't snapped out as he'd expected. Brit had proven over and over how tough she was. But in this, she just seemed curious.

Cautious but curious.

"Your brother invited me in."

Her brows pulled down into a frown, and he found that his fingers itched with the urge to smooth it away.

God, she was pretty.

Stefan liked women—all shapes, sizes, and ethnicities. He'd dated across the spectrum, but he had a particular weakness for the girl-next-door look.

Brit was that personified.

A light dusting of freckles across the bridge of her nose. No makeup, slightly flushed cheeks, and delicately pouty lips that he wanted to taste.

Of course, she'd probably sock him if he tried.

His mouth twitched. Brit scowled. "Is there something funny?"

"No." And because he loved the way she looked when she was a little discombobulated, he said, "I actually came to apologize."

His mom had torn into him when he'd returned home after the game . . .

"The fire in your eyes wasn't the good kind, Stefan," she'd said. *"It's not healthy for you or the team."*

"It's fine, Mom," Stefan had replied. *"And it worked. We won."*

Her scoff had come in the form of a loud snort. *"Your team won because they were lucky and the opposing goalie let in two soft goals."* Then she'd hugged him, as if to soften the blow, and whispered in his ear, *"You play better with a clear head. You know that. Bernard knows that. Fight fire with clarity, honey. With a blast of freezing-cold water that snuffs out the other team.*

Not with a blaze that will flame out quickly and ratchet up everyone's tension."

Of course, she'd been right.

Definitely about the way he'd played. His mom had a knack for seeing the game in a way that made it impossible for Stefan to ever discount her opinion completely.

What she didn't know, however, was that her advice could also be applied to how he'd handled the situation with Brit.

"Apologize?" Brit asked, that frown back, his fingers burning with the need to stroke it away.

No. He'd promised Dan he wouldn't touch, and he hadn't come here for that anyway, would never take advantage of Brit in that way.

But—and it was a really fucking-big but—Stefan *wanted* to touch her.

"I shouldn't have pushed you," he said and forced himself to meet her eyes. "You don't have to tell me anything you don't want." His throat got a little tight, and he cleared it. "I didn't have the right to demand anything from you. I'm sorry."

The pause as Brit processed his apology was long and uncomfortable. But just as he was about to say something else—to grovel further—she spoke.

"What if I'd said the secret was something you should really know?"

The question was quiet. Hesitant.

"How could it be?" he asked bluntly. "We hardly know each other. You've been with the team less than a month. What kinds of secrets could you possibly have that involve me?"

Her eyes dropped, and she murmured something he couldn't make out.

Two steps brought him within touching distance, but he resisted the urge. Instead, he bent a little, crouched so that he could meet those brown eyes, and asked again gently, "What secrets?"

Time stretched. The frown disappeared, her expression softened, and he thought for sure she'd tell him.

Then her lids fluttered closed, a breath passed through those kissable lips, and when she looked at him again, all of the softness was gone.

In its place was something different entirely.

Heat. And determination.

He retreated a step.

She closed the distance, walking forward until her breasts were pressed firmly against his chest, until he could smell the delicate floral scent of her.

That fragrance was at odds with her career, with her intensity on the ice, but Stefan was beginning to think it might fit perfectly with the woman underneath.

She went up on tiptoe. Pressed her mouth to his.

And suddenly, thinking was the last damned thing on his mind.

TWENTY-EIGHT

HER LIPS WERE SOFT, her mouth slightly tart. She tasted of desire and just . . . sweet.

So damned sweet.

Heat arrowed straight toward Stefan's groin, sensation exploding across his nerves. Liquid heat flooded his veins.

And Brit . . .

Her name was the sole recurring thought that cycled through his brain—*Brit. Brit. Brit*—until even that thought ceased.

He yanked her close, plastering her to his chest, and pressed them so tightly together that even a knife would have a hard time separating them.

Brit was tall, and he didn't have to bend much to keep kissing her. He stroked his tongue across the opening of her lips, swept inside to taste her more fully.

Her hands tugged at the hair on his nape, hard enough that his mind cleared slightly.

Oh shit. He froze. Had she not wanted this? Was he going too fast? Overwhelming her?

Stefan yanked his head back, dropped his arms.

"Brit. God. I'm so— Oof!"

She'd shoved him. It was so unexpected that he stumbled back and went down . . . onto the bed. Not a second later, she was on top of him, straddling his hips and bending to kiss him again.

His body said, *"Hell yeah."* But there was something in *her* body that began to make warning bells go off in his mind.

A stiffness, maybe. As though she were distancing herself from the moment.

Her hand reached between them and gripped the hard length of his erection.

His eyes rolled into the back of his head. *Holy shit.*

Maybe he was reading too much into this. Because Brit's fingers on him, the rough strokes through the thin cotton of his sweats were heaven. He needed—

Stefan scrambled to hold on to his sanity.

But her fingers stroking him, wrapping around him and pumping . . . it was too damned good.

At least until he got a glimpse of her expression.

His arousal disappeared like so much smoke.

Because Brit's eyes were wet.

No tears had actually escaped—the moisture was contained by her thick blond lashes—but the sentiment was there.

She was hurting.

And he had a fucking hard on.

Had. He'd *had* a hard on.

Stefan gripped Brit's shoulders with gentle hands and set her away from him before sitting up on the bed.

Their breathing was rapid, loud puffs almost in unison.

"Why"—he began, but she went rod stiff, her eyes dropping to the garish red, blue, and gold patterned bedspread, and that quickly, Stefan banked the question. He stood—"don't we eat before the food gets cold?"

She was frozen for a long moment, staring at him with wide eyes until he took the cover off one plate of food—the hamburger—and sat down to eat. "I'm assuming the chicken and rice is yours, but I'm happy to trade."

"My brother—"

"Is giving us time to talk."

Her lips pressed down into a firm line. "I don't want to talk," she said, petulance in every syllable.

Stillness invaded him, followed by confusion and frustration and . . . a shit-ton of anger. He had no clue what was going on with her, what strings she was pulling, only knew that he was ridiculously attracted to her, and that she was a damned good hockey player.

Beyond that, he was lost. Which pissed him off.

"And you wanted *that*?" he asked pointedly, tilting his head toward the bed.

Silence.

It stretched, fraught with tension, until finally, finally she whispered, "I did want it."

"Bullshit."

The word was torn from him, almost violent in the delivery. Brit jumped, but he didn't feel guilty.

Not for pressing this. Not for trying to understand. Not for—

"You had tears in your eyes, and your body was stiff as a board," he said. "You may think me a fool you can manipulate, but I damn-sure know when a woman wants to fuck me. And *that*"—he waved a hand—"wasn't it."

"It's not— I—" Her voice was pained. "My past—"

All at once, he wondered why he'd come at all, why he'd bothered to think she needed an apology.

His behavior might have been atrocious, but hers was worse.

They'd been building something—camaraderie, a friendship . . . the potential for more.

Her secrets had shit on that.

"You know what," he said, plunking the cover back onto the plate. "I'm not hungry after all."

He stood and left.

TWENTY-NINE

Brit

TEARS.

The salty, stinging fuckers had been conspicuously absent from Brit's life for a really, *really* long time.

Yet in the last few hours she'd shed too many of them to count.

About fifteen minutes after Stefan had left—the door closing with a firm finality that made her heart ache like hell—Dan had come back.

He'd taken one look at her face before shoving her over on the bed she'd still been sitting on and pulling her into his arms. They'd watched that stupid action movie from start to finish, her pretending not to cry and him pretending not to notice.

Now it was a quarter past four, and Dan was snoring in the bed next to hers. Their food from the previous evening sat untouched on the desk, and Brit was both not tired and beyond ravenous.

Quietly, she slid from the bed, snagged some clothes, and walked into the bathroom.

She felt vulnerable and fragile and completely deserving of Stefan's frustration. He'd heard her talking to Bernard, knew she was keeping secrets that involved him.

After slipping on her sweats and tank top, she quietly left the room. Maybe she couldn't run to the arena because of the media coverage of the team, but she damn-sure could tear up a treadmill.

Except the hallway wasn't empty.

"What are you doing here?" she hissed, torn between going right back inside the room and sprinting passed the man sitting on the floor.

Stefan's head jerked from where it had been resting, chin on his chest.

Long fingers thrust through his hair, mussing the dirty blond locks. "Waiting for you," he said.

"Waiting—? You can't *wait* in the hall. Why didn't you just knock?" Her voice was slightly shrill, and she made herself modulate the volume. She might not be sleeping, but the rest of the hotel was. "If the media caught wind of you sitting outside my room, they would . . ."

She trailed off, realized she was about to crap on the pink elephant in the room.

"Is that what this is about, then? The bullshit in the press?"

All she could do was shrug. He had no freaking idea. When she carried through with what management wanted her to do, the local reporters who were following them would turn into many, many more.

"I heard you crying."

Quiet words that threatened to melt her.

Brit couldn't let it happened. She'd committed to do this, to help Bernard, to not give up her own career.

Her sigh was both silent and accompanied by an internal bitch slap.

She'd really made a mess of things.

Yet when had that ever stopped her from doing anything?

She was the first female goalie for an NHL team. She could be friends—*more* —with a hunky defensemen.

And, if nothing else, she could endure.

Of course, the problem wasn't exactly enduring. Stefan made her feel too much. Which—

So what?

He made her feel.

Big effing deal.

It was time to woman up, lock down her heart, and just do it.

Stefan was a playboy anyway. He'd get tired of spending time with her in a month or two—hell, maybe a couple of weeks —and they could go their separate ways.

She ignored the little voice inside her mind that was shouting to consider Stefan's feelings.

What happened if *he* felt too much? What if she broke *his* heart?

Hysterical laughter welled up. Like that would ever happen.

Stefan's heart didn't get involved. Ever. She'd seen the pictures, the parade of women through the media, knew his reputation.

There was no way *she* could hurt *him*.

Holding that thought tight, she blew off his concern, tried to minimize his statement about her crying. "I *am* a girl, you know."

His pause was brief.

A beat later, his eyes locked with hers, and the corners of his lips turned up. Just that easily, the tension between them faded.

"That—the girl thing—I think, is most of our problem."

Brit snorted, extended her hand, and helped him to his feet. "Come on."

He followed her onto the elevator and she pushed the button for the gym. "Hope you're ready to run."

Stefan chuckled. "Is this where I say I'm always ready?"

"Wouldn't have it any other way."

He grinned at her, and she smiled back. The strange fluttering in her chest had nothing to do with him. It was heartburn. Or gas.

Definitely gas.

The doors slid open on a *ding,* and Brit started to step off, eager to escape, to gain that perfect distance between them again, but Stefan stopped her with a hand on her arm.

"Hey," he murmured, and when she glanced up into his eyes, she saw they were serious, the easy affability of the moment before completely dissipated. "I'm sorry I made you cry."

"Yeah," she said. "Me too."

Distance.

Ha. That was a joke.

THIRTY

"I KNOW you're keeping secrets from me," Stefan said all of ten minutes later. He'd popped up in front of her treadmill like a freaking whack-a-mole.

Brit froze and immediately almost ate shit. Jumping with a move that showed her impressive reaction time—thank you very much—she landed with her feet on the plastic sides and glared at Stefan.

"Don't do that," she snapped.

"Don't tell the truth?"

Here they went again. He wasn't going to let this go, and she didn't know how to move forward without giving him *something*.

"Look," she said. "I already told you. There are things about me I can't share. Secrets that aren't mine to tell—" She broke off, jabbed at the stop button, the *whir* of the motor as the belt slowed the only noise in the quiet gym. "I—"

Her eyes flicked up, and her frustration faded.

He looked so earnest standing there, like a little boy trying to coax his puppy into rolling over.

And, *damn her*, she wanted to oblige him. Except she

couldn't give in for a stale-as-hell biscuit of affection, for the mere potential of what-ifs and maybes. Not if she wanted to come out of this unscathed.

So she went on the offensive. "Why does it matter to you?" she snapped.

Stefan frowned, stepped back and, sensing victory, Brit pushed just a little more, enough to place a barrier between them that would protect her but, hopefully, not alienate him.

It was her job as a goalie, always looking ahead, always planning the next three steps before the players on the ice had even grasped step one.

"Look," she said again. "Everyone has secrets. I'm no exception."

"I'm not asking you to spill every dirty entry from your diary, for God's sake. I just want to know the secret that involves me."

Part of her wanted to tell him. Part of her thought he *deserved* to know, and it would be so much easier to not carry the guilt and shame and worry. But if she told Stefan, and he went to management, Brit had no doubt that Susan would carry out her threat to void both contracts—hers and Bernard's.

She couldn't let that happen.

But she also didn't think Stefan would let it go unless she gave him *something*.

"Okay fine." She released a loud sigh, called on every one of the skills she'd honed in her many interviews, and lied. "Bernard wanted to bench you for the stunt you pulled against the Ducks."

Stefan's eyes narrowed, but there went the corners of his mouth again, twitching upward and looking all-too-kissable as they did so. "*That's* your secret?"

Of course not, but she was already all in.

"Yup. I told him we'd talked and you had promised not to do

it again. Don't make me regret standing up for you." And then she released the big guns. "So tell me what it was like to date Kelsey Lake"—the famous movie star he'd dated and dumped—"Is she as pretty in person as in her movies?"

"Oh." He glared. "You're mean."

"I've been told that a time or two." Brit tilted her head. Her heart was pounding, but amusement had crept onto the edges of her emotions, and it steadied her. There was something about Stefan that just made it so damned fun talking with him. "So are we going to be friends?"

He stared at her and several tense moments passed, each ratcheting the turmoil in her gut, because no matter her previous confidence, Brit thought Stefan still might say *"Screw it"* and be done with the whole damn thing.

Finally, he blew out a sigh. "You're asking a lot," he said. "I don't trust easily—"

God, did she know how that went.

"—but I'm going to trust you in this, and hope your other secrets won't come back to bite me in the ass."

"No ass-biting, promise." He smirked and she grinned. "So can we braid each other's hair now?"

"Only if you paint my nails first."

She stepped up onto the treadmill, turned it on. "Fatal flaw, Barie. You paint your nails *after* you do your hair. Don't want to mess up your mani."

He took the machine next to hers. "I can't believe we're having this conversation."

Her heart lightened. "I'm a wealth of information."

Stefan turned up the speed so it matched hers. "I'm impressed."

"Yup," she said and hit her button so the treadmill went just a little faster than his. She might be pursing this relationship for a whole host of complicated reasons, but Brit still liked to win, couldn't step away from a challenge.

And there was definitely challenge in Stefan's eyes.

He sped up, two clicks more than her speed.

Yeah no. That wouldn't do. Three *beeps* on her own machine.

"I can also do a mean smoky eye," she announced.

He glanced at her, jaw agape. "A *smoky* what— Shit!" He slapped at the stop button and jumped clear of the belt when he almost fell.

Brit started laughing so hard she had to hit her own button and step clear.

"You did that on purpose," he said, glaring at her while she tried to catch her breath.

"I regret nothing."

He huffed out a sigh and sat on the end of the machine. She did the same on her own treadmill, enjoying the sensation of just being next to him, of smelling the spicy scent of him, mixed with the salty tang of sweat.

It was probably a sign of insanity that she thought the scent of his sweat was sexy—because, really, what was she going to do next? Sniff his dirty shirts? But Brit found she didn't give a damn.

"You can't really do a smoky eye, can you?" he asked.

Hell no, she couldn't. Even putting her hair into anything more complicated than a ponytail was impossible. "I'm a woman of many talents."

There was a brief silence before they both started laughing again, even harder than before.

Stefan was a good man. Funny, charming, athletic—a trifecta of temptation wrapped into a muscled package of sex appeal. But the draw was more than that.

She liked being with him. Which was the most dangerous

part of the entire situation. Standing, she wiped her hands on her sweats, and climbed back on the treadmill. "Let's finish this workout and get to the arena."

An hour after they'd arrived at the rink, her lawyer called to tell her the contract was sound, and she walked it over to Bernard's office so he could sign.

It took her almost that long to convince him to scrawl his chicken-scratch-of-a-signature on the paper, but the relief in his eyes when she finally convinced him it was okay made the whole situation worth it.

She delivered the contract to Devon and watched as he signed his name beneath Bernard's before making two copies.

By the time she'd delivered Bernard his printout and stashed her own in her backpack, she was feeling very much like a law intern.

But it was done.

She was doing this. There was no option of going back.

Especially not after pictures of her and Stefan sitting on the ends of the treadmills, laughing their heads off and smiling at each other exploded all over the Internet before she'd suited up for the mid-morning skate.

Susan approved apparently, if the indiscreet thumbs-up the older woman had given her in the hall was any indication.

Blane—who was walking next to her—frowned. "What was that?"

Brit shrugged. "That's Susan. One of the board members."

They stepped into the locker room. "I know *that*. What's with the thumbs-up?"

"No clue."

"Brit."

She glanced up.

Blane's expression was worried. "You know I'm here for

you, right? If you're ever in over your head? This thing with Stefan—"

Her heart swelled, and she couldn't resist giving him a hug.

Blane froze for a heartbeat before hugging her back.

She wasn't surprised. She'd never been a touchy-feely kid, and after the incident, things had gotten worse.

Brit couldn't remember the last time she'd initiated a hug with someone other than her brother.

"Thanks," she said before covering Blane's hesitation with a laugh. "Things with Stefan are complicated. He's a good guy, but the press"—*and management*—"is insane."

"Hey, at least they won't ask if you're gay anymore."

She rolled her eyes heavenward. "That's a positive, I guess. But only a small one, because now they just want to know every detail of my relationship with Stefan." The press were still pushy, relentless, and unfortunately, a necessary evil.

"And do you?" Blane asked.

Brit pulled back and gave him a blank stare even as her heart jumped. What did he know? "What are you asking?" Her tone was controlled, careful.

"Do you have a relationship with Barie?"

"I—" She sighed, the truth and lies all tangled up. "Maybe." Hell, she didn't know where they stood at that moment.

"You like him."

No point in denying it. "Yup."

Blane was quiet for a beat before his lips tugged up. "Barie and Brit, sitting in a tree. K-I-S-S—"

"I can't believe you!" But she was laughing. He made a kissy noise, and she smacked him. "You know you may be my brother in everything but blood"—she glared —"but don't forget I caught you checking out my ass the last time we were together."

"Yeah, no," he said. "You're *definitely* not my sister." He met her gaze full on. "As you well know."

Idiot. Why had she brought that up? She laughed again, this time awkwardly with a dash of old guilt thrown in. Because she *did* know that. Problem was, her mind might see Blane as a strong, attractive male, but her body said, *"Meh."* That hadn't made things easy on their friendship, and she generally wasn't so callous with Blane's feelings, didn't joke about what couldn't be.

Or at least she hoped so.

She sighed. Social skills. Seriously, she needed to improve hers.

"Hey. It's okay." Blane touched her hand. "I know you don't feel the same. We covered that enough times over my teenage years for me to write you off as a total lost cause."

Her smile was small and tinged with misery. She was a lousy friend and an even worse surrogate sister.

"Brit." He squeezed her hand. "I'm fine. It was a joke. Let it go."

"You mean like how I *punched* your crush out of you?"

"Exactly. So abusive." He gave her sad puppy-dog eyes, but at least they held no genuine hurt. "My nose has never been the same."

She gave a mock shudder. "Let's hope your kissing ability has improved, okay? Because that much tongue—"

"You wound me." His hand went over his heart, as though to protect the precious organ, before his tone took on a serious note. "My kissing ability aside, I count you as my friend and I will kill anyone who hurts you. Okay?"

There her heart went again, expanding like a balloon.

"Okay." She bumped her shoulder with his. "Thanks."

"I'm still going to ogle your ass."

Her laughter was loud, accompanied by a shake of her head. "Wouldn't have it any other way."

THIRTY-ONE

Stefan

STEFAN WATCHED Brit walk into the locker room, Blane at her side. It took everything in him to curb the vicious jealousy tearing at his insides.

He wondered if she'd seen the pictures before quickly dismissing the notion. No, she couldn't have. She looked too happy and relaxed for that.

After the first news story, she'd been violently angry, the cloud of her anger perceptible.

Now he wondered how pissed she was going to be when she *did* see them.

Or if she discovered he actually liked the pictures.

The images of the two of them laughing as though they'd just shared the world's funniest joke had filled him with such a sense of rightness that it had been almost painful.

He'd had to breathe through the longing, the desire to claim her as his own.

Brit had set boundaries, and he'd obey them.

Except, after the scene in her hotel room, he didn't really know what those boundaries were.

Was that a red herring? Some sort of self-destructive tendency to self-harm? She certainly had other hang-ups with personal space.

Though—he watched her hug Blane—apparently not with her former teammate.

Maybe it was more. Perhaps she was simply as attracted to him as he was to her.

Did the reasons really matter? They'd be stupid to act on it anyway.

Blane leaned close to her, his expression serious and a twin of Brit's. It made Stefan's gut clench. He wanted to be the one she turned to.

Where in the hell had that come from?

They could be friends—and maybe they were already tentative ones—but he didn't need to be her lover, her partner—

His lace snapped.

Forcing a breath, he pulled off his skate and yanked out the broken lace. Before he could go in search of a new one, Rich, the equipment manager, had brought a replacement.

"One-twenty and waxed, right?" Rich said, confirming the length and texture preference before setting a new lace in Stefan's hand.

"Yup. Thanks, Richie."

Two minutes later, Stefan's skates were on, and he was pulling on his practice jersey. He was on the black team today, which meant, for some God-awful reason, Bernard had decided to pair him with Stewart.

Clearly, he'd pissed someone off in his last life.

But he was captain, and that meant he needed to get along and work with every person on the ice.

Practice was a lesson in perseverance.

Mainly because Stewart was a pain in the ass.

Only when the coaches weren't directly next to them, of course, only when screwing up the play made someone else look bad. Mainly Stefan.

When one of the coaches was watching, Stewart was a lesson in proper play, but when they rotated to another group . . . Mike pulled shenanigans.

He made Stefan skate to pucks he should have taken, threw passes without looking . . . was uncooperative, lazy, and generally uninspired.

Which mostly made Stefan want to punch him in the face.

He didn't, of course. But the fantasy of his fist colliding with Stewart's nose and blood gushing everywhere was what got Stefan through that interminable practice.

Still, Bernard wasn't an idiot, and whatever had kept the coach off ice the previous week hadn't done so during the last few practices.

He saw more than Stefan gave him credit for.

"That's it for today. Hit the showers," Bernard told the team as they gathered at center ice. "Take the morning off tomorrow, but be here for a pre-game meeting at two."

The guys disbanded, headed for the locker room. "Stewart, Barie, wait."

He and Mike both stopped, Stewart with a teenage-sized sigh, and Stefan with a quiet sort of resignation.

Dread tied his intestines in knots. What—

"Ladders. Twenty. Each side. Go."

Stefan's relief was strong. The skating drill sucked, but it was better than being benched, than losing his captaincy. He skated toward the far side of the ice, ready to get it over with.

"Why?" Mike asked.

Stefan gave an inward groan halfway to the goal line. For

fuck's sake, that man could not keep his goddamned mouth closed.

A sharp trill of Bernard's whistle. "Thirty."

"But—"

"Forty."

Finally, Mike shut the hell up and skated over to where Stefan waited.

"Together," Bernard said as he stood over the Gold's logo at center ice. "Go." He blew his whistle.

Stewart burst forward from the goal line in a show of speed that was both unnecessary and excessive. They'd need all of their strength to finish, especially post-practice.

The drill was deceptively simple, just skating and stopping at every line from one side of the ice to the other. But there were a lot of lines.

Blue line. Stop. Red line at center ice. Stop. Far blue line. Stop. Far goal line. Stop.

And they only had to do it forty times . . . per side.

Not to mention, Mike had basically set them up to fail with the pace he'd started.

Still, Stefan wasn't the type to back down from a challenge. It had taken everything in him earlier to cease his pushing Brit for her confidence, and then he'd only succeeded because he figured he'd win her over eventually.

But he wasn't going to yield to Stewart. Not when he trained harder and longer than every other damn person on the team. Not when he could still draw breath and move his legs.

No fucking way.

Sprint. Stop. Sprint. Stop. Rinse. Repeat.

By ten, Stewart was sucking wind.

By twenty, Mike's pace had slowed to a snail's pace.

By thirty, even Stefan's legs were burning. But Mike was in

worse shape. He was green, looked ready to blow chunks, and they still had ten more to go.

It was on the second half of thirty-three that Stewart stumbled and fell. He scrambled to get up, only to fall again.

Stefan didn't think, just reacted. Closing the ten feet of distance between him and Stewart, he shoved his shoulder under Stewart's arm and pulled him to his feet.

"Keep moving," he gritted.

"Fuck off," Stewart growled.

"I want to get the hell off this ice. So shut the fuck up and skate."

The last seven were torture—with him all but carrying Stewart—but finally they finished.

Bernard had been passively standing at center ice as they struggled. Now he blew his whistle. "Cool down then hit the showers. I expect you both to be on time tomorrow."

He skated off the ice without a backward glance.

The silence was deafening.

Or it was until Stewart unloaded. "Do you want a fucking medal or something? Always got to be the hero?" he screamed, shoving at Stefan's chest. A feather would have had more impact at Stewart's level of fatigue, but that didn't stop him from unleashing a few more choice words.

Stefan had enough. "Dude," he said and shoved Mike back, not bothering to help the other man up when he hit the ice for the second time. "I couldn't give two shits about you as a person. You're lazy, just barely talented enough, and a first-class asshole. I do what I do for the good of the team. Not you. *Not ever.*"

"Who do you think—"

Stefan cut him off. "Let me guess. You're going to give me some version of 'Who do I think I am?' or 'Do I know who you are?'" He rolled his eyes. "I know *exactly* who you are. You're a self-entitled bastard who has no sense of team. Do what you want. Just stay out of my way."

He turned and skated off the ice.

Brit was standing in the hallway leading back toward the locker room, still in her gear, her face serious.

"Hey," she said when he stopped in front of her.

His hands were clenched inside his gloves, and his blood pressure must have been off the charts, but his voice was calm enough. "Hey."

Brilliant conversationalists, they were.

And great, now he sounded like Yoda.

"Are you all right?" she asked.

He nodded.

"Good." She bent and picked up her helmet from where it sat on a chair then turned to walk down the hall.

Stefan followed her in silence. Until he couldn't.

"Why'd you stay?" he asked.

"Why did you help Stewart?" she countered.

He paused, both mentally and physically. They were next to the wall of pictures, game shots of each of the former captains. Just four of them, since the Gold were a new team.

They'd had a similar wall in Calgary when he'd played with the Flames. But as an older team, the Flames had history, rows and rows of history.

His shot was on *this* wall, a picture of him skating in full black and gold.

It was weird seeing himself there, imagining that his photograph would in the beginning of a long line of captains, that he would be part of the history of the team—

If the Gold didn't fold.

The possibility sat like a rock in his gut.

"I helped him because I had to," he said, not looking away from the pictures.

"Exactly," Brit said. "Which is why you're the best person on this team to be captain and"—her voice faded as she slung her helmet on her head—"why I hope we'll manage to stay friends when this is all over."

Her first statement made his mind spin, her confidence in him intoxicating.

She was already pushing into the locker room before the second half of her sentence hit home.

" . . .stay friends when this is all over?"

Letting Brit keep her secrets had just gotten a lot harder.

THIRTY-TWO

STEFAN WALKED into the house to the scent of lasagna and . . . the sound of his mom being sick.

He'd dropped his messenger bag on the floor and was hauling ass before the front door slammed shut behind him.

His mom was in the small bathroom, kneeling on the ground, retching into the toilet.

"Mom—" he began.

She waved him off, shoved the door closed in his face.

Her cough was violent, and he tried the knob. Locked. "Mom—"

"Don't make me send you out of the house for another night. *I'm fine—*" She retched again.

Stefan stood for a minute outside the door, listening to her suffer and wishing for the millionth time since he'd found out about her illness that he could shoulder the burden for her.

Anger, violent and intoxicating, rushed through him. He wanted to destroy something, punch the wall, bust through like a tornado—

Which would help absolutely nothing.

Of course, he might feel a hell of a lot better if the object he was busting through was Mike Stewart's face.

With a muttered curse, he turned, walked to the fridge, and pulled out a bottle of water. The freezer held some damp, cold cloths, so he grabbed one for his mom.

By the time he'd set both on the counter, the toilet flushed, and Diane staggered out, her face blanched and her brow sweaty.

"Sit down," Stefan murmured and grabbed her arm to help her do just that. He pressed the cloth to her forehead and put the bottle of water in front of her just as the timer went off.

"The lasagna—"

"I'll get it," he said.

But as he pulled the pan out of the oven, his mom slapped a hand over her mouth and bolted for the bathroom again.

It was barely a decision. He took the pan and was out the back door before the thought had processed.

Pan and all went into the garbage before he went back inside and opened every window in the vicinity. Next, he cranked the vent over the cooktop to high.

Stefan allowed himself one moment to let the anger rage. Then he tucked it away, saved it for motivation for later.

Cancer was a Class-A asshole.

But that wasn't a new fact, and his mom needed him more.

By the time Diane came out from the bathroom a second time, Stefan had opened a can of chicken noodle soup and was heating it up on the stove.

He moved to help her, wanting to make sure she didn't fall, but she glared at him and shook her head, pulling out the chair, before sitting down in the careful movements of someone who felt like shit.

God, she is ridiculously pale.

It took every bit of discipline at his disposal to stay at the stovetop and stir the fucking soup. When it was warm, he poured it into a mug—his mom preferred to sip it rather than use a spoon—and got some saltines out of the pantry.

"So," he said as he brought both over to her, "well done on the whole christening the porcelain-goddess thing."

His mom almost dropped the mug she'd brought to her lips. "Stefan, that so isn't funny."

He'd been intending to force a smile, to push the joke forward, to inject some fucking levity into the situation. But his mom's reaction was so typical, so *mom-like* that he didn't have to force anything.

Lips twitching, he said, "It's pretty funny."

"Stefan Benjamin Barie. Me puking my guts out is *not* funny." But her lips were curving too. Blue eyes so similar to his own narrowed even as amusement clouded their depths.

She sighed, crossed her arms. The smile grew.

"Okay. Fine. It's a little funny. *But* . . . know that next time you're sick or throwing up because you're hungover, I'm laughing in your face."

He laughed. "I thought you were the parent. Aren't you supposed to be all saint-like?"

Her snort was loud. "If you think that about me, then I've failed as a mother."

Happiness filled him, buoyed his mood. His mother had always had enough personality for three people. She was spicy, high-spirited . . . and every other damn adjective he could think of for firecracker.

Cancer had drained that away. To see her like this—even for a moment—gave him hope that things might actually be okay.

"Ha," he said. "As if you could believe that with a son like me."

"A son with an ego the size of a planet?"

"A son who is—" He faltered for a moment. Normally he

would have said something about being a successful captain for an NHL team or the leading defensemen. But after that practice he wasn't feeling all that successful at anything hockey-related. *Shit.* Now she was looking at him, and he blurted the first thing he could think of. "—going to sit down with you and watch *Dancing with the Stars.*"

The strangled gasp of air that followed came from his mouth, not his mother's. Had he really just locked himself into watching a crappy show? Into several hours of hell interspersed with interrogations during the commercial breaks?

On the smooth meter, it was about a minus five.

His mom gave a little laugh before picking up her soup. "That expression. Since when have I ever pushed you to talk?" When Stefan snorted, she shook her head. "Okay, when in the *last couple of years* have I pushed you?"

He snorted again. Really, sometimes she was delusional.

"Oh my God. Seriously, kid. You're pissing me off." She fixed him with a glare "I. *Don't.* Push. Now eat some lasagna. I'll give you couple of hours before I start pestering."

He sighed, and any dredges of hope that throwing her favorite show at her would knock her off the scent disappeared.

His mother was nothing if not a lesson in perseverance.

He wouldn't have it any other way.

"I love you, Mom."

"I love you too. But don't think that's going to get you out of *Dancing with the Stars.*"

For fuck's sake.

And he still had to tell her—

"About the lasagna . . ."

STEFAN'S MOM had snapped at him about wasting the cooking

she'd slaved over, made even worse because he'd thrown away her favorite pan.

Then as abruptly as she'd yelled, she'd stopped, pressed a kiss to his cheek, and murmured, "You're a good boy, Stefan. The best a mother could ask for."

Such a small thing, those words, the affection. His mom was hard to predict sometimes, tough and strong as nails. But he'd never once doubted that she loved him.

Always, she'd been free with her affection, unwavering in her support.

It was because of *her* he'd gotten so far.

Even when things hadn't worked out with his father, when she'd been abandoned and newly pregnant, when his dad copped out on child support, his mom had been there.

Early morning practices. Long drives to tournaments. Skimping money for new equipment—

"I like you with Brit."

"What? How—" He broke off because, really, those pictures had been *everywhere*, and his mother was all over any news story involving him.

He should pay her instead of his publicist.

"She seems like a nice girl."

"She is."

His mom gave him a penetrating look. "Baggage?"

Stefan shrugged, but because his mom would understand, he told her what had happened.

"She's skittish around men. Freaked when I came up behind her. That's why we . . . in the pictures . . ."

Why they had ended up in Classic Bedroom Position #1.

"Do you think she's been sexually harassed?" his mom asked then added, after a pause that said way more than the words, "Or maybe more?"

He started to say no.

How could Brit have possibly been hurt? She was tough, strong, and vibrant. Could kick ass with the best of them.

That couldn't be ignored.

But it also couldn't be ignored that she was still smaller than every member of the team, that if she was taken by surprise—from behind—or outnumbered . . .

Something could have happened.

He could imagine how *easily* it might have happened.

"I—"

Good God. A memory swept over him. He'd cornered her in the locker room, pushed into her space, trapped her against the wall.

It was scary to think how easy it would have been for him —*for anyone*—to take advantage.

But there hadn't been fear in Brit's eyes. Not that time. When he'd pressed his body to hers, her russet irises had been on fire, had scorched him with fury and desire.

She wasn't scared of him. That much he was sure.

Still, she'd all but admitted to having a multitude of secrets and if his mom's inkling about the nature of Brit's secret was correct, if she'd been hurt or violated, she would need to the chance to tell him on her own terms.

It wasn't something she should be ashamed of—not that feelings often followed logic and reason.

Shit. He didn't like this—

"Okay, seriously, how is he still here?" his mom said, pulling Stefan from his thoughts and pointing to the celebrity chef that was fumbling his way through a terrible rendition of a tango. "He's the worst."

"He *is* pretty bad," Stefan agreed. And the costume—glittery and with more fake feathers than a peacock—was horrendous.

"Ba-ad?" Her question was punctuated by a yawn. "He's absolutely terrible."

"Here." Stefan tucked a blanket around her shoulders then winced as he stretched his aching legs in front of him. All he wanted to do was lie down. "How long is this show anyway?"

He'd spent a full hour cooling down after the practice from hell. Thirty minutes on the stationary bike, followed by stretching, and then hitting the PT suite for some targeted massage. Not that any of that had helped.

His quads were on fire, and the burn would only be worse in the morning.

"Two"—his mom yawned again—"hours."

There was no way he'd make it. After staying up the previous night with Brit and now the sleep-inducing, so-called entertainment of the show . . . well, he'd be lucky to make it through another dance.

Turned out he didn't have to.

His mom was snoring even before the chef got his scores.

He waited a few minutes, made sure the DVR was recording, then gently lifted her in his arms and carried her to her bedroom.

As Stefan tucked his mom in, he couldn't help but remember all of the times he'd woken up in his bed after falling asleep on the couch, couldn't help but wonder how many times she must have done the same thing when he'd been little enough to carry.

It made his heart ache.

Because the fragility in her expression, her innocence as she slept, raised a wave of fierce protectiveness in him, stronger than he ever thought possible.

He would do *anything* to protect her.

Even fish her favorite pan out of the trashcan.

THIRTY-THREE

Brit

GAME DAY.

Two words that incited excitement and anxiety in most hockey players. There was always the odd athlete who managed to stay calm, or worse, who was good enough to play professionally but hated the sport itself.

That wasn't Brit.

Even if she wasn't starting in tonight's game, she would be on the bench with the rest of the team, ready to step in at a moment's notice.

There was absolutely nothing like being in an arena filled with screaming fans, listening to chants encouraging the team, chased soundly by the slightly tipsy segment of the crowd yelling that opposing players sucked.

It was familiar. It was an epi pen to her heart without the assistance of drugs.

"Ready?" Frankie stood next Richie, who had opened the door of the car for her. They appeared to just have arrived at the arena, their coats still on and bags slung over one shoulder.

"Heck yeah." She thanked Josh for driving her and stepped out. "Is the extra security necessary?" She pointed to the fenced lot, the gate now patrolled by a half-dozen guards. And that wasn't counting Richie and two others closer to the entrance. "There are hardly any journalists out today."

Despite Stefan's night at the hotel and the resultant pictures of them on their respective treadmills, most of the media had moved on to far more exciting things—a scandal in the governor's office and a celebrity having her baby.

Susan would be disappointed, not that Brit cared.

She was doing this her way, one that wouldn't sacrifice herself or Stefan or the team.

And regardless of the idiotic attempt in the hotel room, she wasn't ready to go further with Stefan. If things happened between them, it wouldn't be driven by the fake relationship.

It needed to be pushed by real feelings.

The assault hadn't broken her, exactly. Brit had even had sex since then.

Okay, not much. But enough that she knew she wasn't going to turn back into a virgin.

But it was different with Stefan. The other times had been filled with distance, and that was okay. That was what she'd needed. Release without emotion.

They'd felt good. She'd had orgasms, had gone home with a sense of satisfaction.

Yet, she'd frozen in that bed because Stefan *was* different. She couldn't keep a part of herself back, couldn't frost over the threads of emotion—of respect, caring, *affection*.

Stefan had felt it, had demanded more.

And she'd wanted to give it.

Her body didn't want distance, not when he was melting every last one of her defenses.

" . . .journalists," Frankie said, and Brit blinked, trying to remember what she'd asked before her mind had gone straight down its favorite daydream.

Stefan.

And his glorious mouth. And hands. And abs.

And—*shit*—arms and . . .

"Management seemed to think they would be back in force," Richie said and hurried to open the door to the arena. "More security isn't bad. The reporters were ravenous just a few days ago. They want everyone to be safe."

The equipment manager smiled at her, and her heart melted a little bit. He was so sweet.

"Thank you, Richie," she told him, sincerity in her tone. "Thanks for keeping us safe."

His cheeks creased even as they went a little pink. "It's nothing," he said. "Just my job, after all."

"Still." She squeezed his hand as she passed through the door. "Thank you."

So management thought that the press might return. Because of the game? It was against one of their biggest rivals, the Sharks. But that wasn't unusual. They would play the other local team eight times that season. It—

Her heart sank.

Management wasn't guessing the press would be back because of a tough game.

Nope. It was a message.

They wanted something to happen. Something that would guarantee press coverage.

And the envelope in her locker—filled with only a single paper that read, *MORE*—confirmed her instincts.

Funny how the truth of what she was doing hadn't really hit home till then.

Funny how she felt more violated by those four letters, by

something that was really only her own fault—for agreeing in the first place—than she'd felt at any point in her life.

The crinkle of paper was only vaguely satisfying as she balled the note and chucked it in the trash.

This crap could wait.

She had to push her feelings aside and focus on getting ready for the game.

Her team needed her.

TURNED OUT, that wasn't exactly true.

Julian had the net, and the team won easily. Brit cheered them on, wincing whenever the guys took a bad hit—because seriously, even though they were big, tough hockey players, getting checked still hurt—and shouting encouragements as they battled it out on the boards.

She'd lost her head for a second when Blane and Stefan collaborated for a gorgeous 2-on-1 goal, screaming like a banshee when it went in.

By the time the final buzzer sounded, her throat was slightly sore, and she was hopped-up on adrenaline.

Such was the life of the backup goalie. So often the bridesmaid and rarely the bride.

Though with Beausoleil in potentially his last season, more ice time should be coming her way soon.

She hoped.

Because seeing her team out there and not playing was almost unbearable.

Patience, Brit reminded herself. *Keep working hard, and it will come.*

She followed the team back into the locker room, waited

through the post-game interviews, gave a couple of sound bites when the media asked her opinion.

By the time she'd finished, most of the guys were gone or were in the shower. Frankie caught her eye from across the room, and she nodded. Far as she was concerned, their post-game ritual should continue.

When they played on home ice, whether she was in net or not, they worked through a couple of buckets of pucks.

She needed to improve her blocker side, and Frankie had a knack for placing shots.

He crossed over to her. "Same thing?"

Brit nodded. "It's not good enough yet."

Frankie grinned. "It's getting pretty damn close, though."

"Then we'll have to make it harder."

He clapped her on the shoulder. "Like the attitude, Brit."

She did too. It was easy with Frankie. He had an inbred optimism and positivity that made her want to work harder than she'd ever done before.

It wasn't like she'd been a slacker on her previous teams, but having Franklin Todd at her back gave her confidence.

Plus, it was nice to not have a coach yell after every play, to actually hear some positive—*gasp*!—things, instead of everything she did wrong.

"Let's do this," she said and led the way back to the ice. It was freshly cut, all the maintenance done, a pristine sheet of white and red and blue. "Sure Ken doesn't mind if we mess up his ice?"

"Not at all. He always does a cut"—referring to the Zamboni clearing off the excess snow and laying down a thin layer of water to fill in the divots and scratches in the ice—"first thing in the morning."

Brit skated to the goal that had been set up for her, scuffing up the crease in her usual manner, as Frankie pulled on his skates and grabbed the bright orange bucket.

He poured the pucks onto the ice—at least fifty of them—and used his stick to spread them haphazardly around.

"Ready?" he asked once he was done and took up a position just inside the blue line.

She tapped the ice with her stick, gave a nod.

Crack! came the first shot. It was low and to the outside, and it was a scramble to cover the angle, especially when she'd expected a high-glove side. But at this point, it was almost cheating if she knew where the shot was going.

She wouldn't know in a game, after all.

No one was going to tell her where they shot, and though she could study up on a shooter's preferences, there were simply too many players, and they were too good at shooting *anywhere* for her to keep track.

She dropped to her knees, pushed hard, and slid to the far side of the net. The puck hit her pads, rebounded wide.

Brit didn't worry about exactly where. Instead, she was scrambling to her skates.

Because Frankie had moved and was already lining up the next shot.

It continued like that for a long while, Frankie occasionally calling out a pointer or adjustment before peppering her with more shots.

By the time he finished shooting—she'd lost count after sixty-two—her legs were shaking, and her hip flexors were on fire.

At least the bruise on her shoulder finally felt better, its only reminder an occasional twinge.

She'd just stretched her arm out, testing the joint when she caught a flash of movement.

They weren't alone.

The slight blast of fear was as normal as it was annoying. A breath slid out from between her clenched teeth, and she forced herself to calm.

Calm.

She wasn't alone. Frankie was there. And no one was coming up behind her.

Plus, even if they were, Brit needed to get the hell over that particular trigger. Three years was long enough.

Only once her heart had settled from a sprint into a jog did she allow her gaze to swivel.

Bernard, Blane, and Stefan were sitting on their bench. Apparently deep in conversation, though their eyes were on Frankie and Brit.

"You're there," Frankie said, skating over. As she stretched, he went over a few more points. They were small tweaks, but she knew they'd make a huge difference.

"Thanks for staying," she said. "I know it makes for a late night."

"Not at all, Brit. Anytime."

"I'll help you with the pucks—"

"I've got it."

Bernard's voice surprised Brit. She hadn't realized he'd put on skates. They looked ridiculous with his slacks, button-down, and tie. He'd shed his suit jacket, at least, but the beat-up boots with shiny silver blades were still incongruous with his professional attire.

"I can—"

"I've got a few things to talk with Frankie about," Bernard said before a twinkle entered his eyes, "and I'm fully capable of picking up some pucks." A twitch of his lips. "I may have done it a time or two."

"But—"

He gave her an even look, one that was determined and

intense and very . . . well, coach-like. At least the amusement in his eyes hadn't faded. He made a shooing motion. "Go."

It was an order, and Brit had too many seasons of coaching under her belt to not obey.

"All right." She hesitated. "Thanks."

"Go on," Frankie said. "It looks like the boys are waiting for you."

Brit glanced over, saw he was right.

"But don't forget to stretch properly. You don't want to tighten up."

She nodded then skated over to the bench and stepped up to Blane and Stefan. They had been in a pretty intense discussion, one that stopped when she approached.

Blane had that look, the big brother, protective stare, but Brit couldn't find it in her to be annoyed.

Yes, she already had a brother, but it was nice for another person to have her back.

"Did Dan make it in okay?" she asked Blane as their awkward trio walked down the hall to the locker room. Her brother had attended the game, but Brit wasn't sure he'd be able to find his way to the family waiting area, even though she'd given him the proper clearance. The tunnels were decidedly maze-like, even for an FBI agent.

She probably shouldn't have kept him waiting by practicing with Frankie, but Dan had never given her crap for following her dreams and wouldn't hold it against her now.

He nodded. "Yup. He's waiting in the PT suite."

Brit frowned. That was weird. But then she remembered Mandy and knew the petite brunette was very much Dan's type.

That's to say . . . she's a woman. Who's single.

"Seriously?"

Blane nodded. "I'll see if I can peel Dan out of there and meet you in the locker room."

"Thanks." She turned to Stefan. "We're going to dinner. Want to come along?"

It was an invitation she would have made to anyone. Brit was inclusive by nature, knew what it was like to be on the outside, and didn't like feeling as though she'd left anyone out.

But with the tangle of emotions in her mind, with the task management had given her—the job she'd *agreed* to—knotting with the things she *wanted* to do . . . well, it felt wrong.

Stop whining. Stop seeing an ulterior motive in everything.

Except, she *did* have an ulterior motive.

Brit sighed inwardly. This was the way things were. She either followed through—

Or she didn't.

But she couldn't keep beating herself up for it.

Maybe she could get her and Stefan out of this unscathed. If she played things carefully, maybe they could remain friends.

Because she felt too much to casually dismiss Stefan.

How could she risk hurting him?

THIRTY-FOUR

HIS HAND on her cheek startled her.

Brit glanced up, saw Stefan was very close, blue eyes staring down at her full of concern, his suit-clad body only inches from hers. The rich spice of his aftershave filled the air, and they were near enough that Brit could see the scars on his face—a thin slash above his brow, a small, jagged dash across his chin.

"What is it?" he asked, brushing his fingers down her cheek again. *God,* how she wanted to lean into the touch, to lose herself in the feel of the slightly calloused roughness against her skin.

The truth.

It would be so damned easy to tell him the truth. To lay it out there and let the chips fall where they may.

"Have you ever been in the middle of doing something that you're already regretting but you can't stop?" she blurted.

He stiffened and leaned back slightly. The distance wasn't much, given the narrow hallway they were in, but it still hurt. Especially when those blue eyes went a little cold. Stefan stared at her, studying her as though he could see right through every protective layer she'd ever erected.

She looked away. "So dinner? Yes?"

There was a long moment of quiet, then Stefan tugged her ponytail. Cautiously, she flicked her gaze back to his and saw the chill in his expression had been replaced by something Brit really hoped was understanding.

"Yes," he said. "And also"—quieter now—"yes, I have."

She smiled broadly, and the happiness she felt at the small acceptance in his eyes made her tongue loose. "Good. I like spending time with you." She mentally groaned but couldn't stop more words from coming. "You're funny and sweet and a good hockey player—"

Shut. Up.

Good God, her social skills needed an overhaul. As in a little more smooth and a little less verbal diarrhea.

Girls didn't just tell guys they *liked* them. Not so explicitly, anyway.

For fuck's sake, she was terrible at this. At life in general.

"I like spending time with you too," he murmured.

Oh.

Funny how one sentence from Stefan, and things were all right.

"Are we going to do this, Brit?" He took a step toward her. There was less than a foot between them, and good Lord, how she wanted there to be none.

"D-do what?" For a second she thought he knew about her plan with management and the media. Then she got a good glance at his eyes.

They were molten, burning as he watched her.

Her breath caught. Because—*holy shit*—never, *ever* had a man looked at her in such a way.

Not when she'd been fully dolled up. And especially not when she was sweaty and wearing hockey gear, the slight funk of wet equipment permeating the space between them.

"Explore this thing between us." He leaned in, pressed a kiss to the corner of her mouth.

"Th-thing?"

Lips on her jaw. Her throat.

"This attraction. The chemistry threatening to ignite the room." Teeth on her neck, a sharp bite soothed by a smooth flick of his tongue.

Her sucked-in breath was loud . . . and shaky.

"I don't think we should." The words were out before she'd had time to calculate how it would affect her plan, the feel of his lips—soft and hot and wet—against her skin better than a truth serum.

Stefan pulled back slightly, one side of his mouth quirked in humor. "No?"

This was her chance to tell him everything.

She shook her head. To herself. To him. Not yet. She couldn't tell him yet.

After he knew the truth he might not look at her in the same way, full of laughter and heat and temptation.

"No." Brit couldn't. She needed more time, had to shore up more barriers against Stefan's charm. The allure was too much. It led to too much vulnerability and too damn much of her heart being involved.

He smiled fully then, a flash of bright, white teeth against pale pink lips. "Why not?"

"What about the honor clause in our contracts?" she asked, mind scrambling even as she felt her head tilting on its own volition, as if merely exposing the skin of her neck would draw his mouth back to the spot.

It worked. He kissed just beneath her jaw before stretching to whisper in her ear, "That only extends to dating Gold employees. Not players."

"One could make the case that we *are* employees," she said, humor crawling into her, sweeping aside the anxiety. He was just so . . . Stefan.

He unlocked something inside of her, made it so damned easy to be with him. Comfortable. Warm. Okay—blazing hot and filled with so much desire that she was almost desperate for his mouth on hers.

"One would be wrong," he murmured.

God, she wanted him.

He kissed her then, his fingers sliding into her sweaty ponytail, lacing through the locks without revulsion or hesitation. A little sweat didn't bother Stefan, and it made Brit like him even more.

No other man she'd dated had wanted to be near her postgame. She'd had to shower first, slap on something girlie to hide the scent of her exertion before they'd go out.

It wasn't like she wanted to walk around smelling gross and stinky. She considered herself a decent human being, and with that came well-rounded hygiene skills.

But Brit had always wished the man she was with would want—no, *need*—every part of her, whether or not it was pretty or polished or smelled like freaking petunias.

Stefan being that kind of man wasn't surprising.

He was good, sweet and charming, and—

All thoughts fled as he deepened the kiss.

His fingers trailed down her back, moved forward to brush the sides of her breasts, and a firm stroke of his tongue across her lips had her opening her mouth, completely forgetting they were in a public place where anyone might see.

She couldn't think, couldn't do more than process the electrifying sensations that Stefan invoked.

"I don't know why— Ugh! *Come on!*" Dan's voice was disgusted and loud enough to snap her out of the haze of desire.

Her eyes flew open on a gasp. She started to pull back, but

Stefan caught her head and pressed one more soft kiss to her lips.

"I think that went better than our last kiss," he said with a wink before dropping his hand and turning to face her brother.

Blane stood behind Dan, arms crossed, eyes narrowed at Stefan.

"Go shower, if you want," Stefan murmured. "I'll take care of Dumb and Dumber."

Her brothers—because, really, Blane was as good as one—glared fiercely, but she'd seen Stefan on the ice, knew he could take care of himself.

"Thanks." In her skates and with Stefan in shoes, she didn't have to stretch to kiss his cheek.

Leaving the men to tend to themselves, Brit pushed into the locker room and found it crowded with equipment staff and a few players. There were enough people to make her feel comfortable, so she hit the showers and dressed.

For the first time since management had thrown down the gauntlet, Brit felt confident in scooping it up.

She could do this.

Perhaps even make something real of this thing between her and Stefan.

THIRTY-FIVE

Stefan

"I DON'T REMEMBER GIVING you permission to touch her," Dan said the moment his sister was out of earshot.

Stefan resisted the urge to roll his eyes even as he did his best to hold on to the post-kiss glow. Brit was fucking incredible and her mouth—

"It's not yours to give," he told Dan, shifting discretely to hide any evidence of how much he'd enjoyed the kiss.

"I'm her brother."

"And Brit is her own woman," he countered.

Blane stepped forward then, going shoulder to shoulder with Brit's brother and forming a barrier of angry men between him and the exit.

"What are you doing?" Blane asked. "Don't you think that she's going to have a hard enough time without fucking a member of the team? How do you think that will make her look in the media?" He thrust a hand through his short brown hair. "It's already bad enough with the pictures."

"It's not like that," Stefan began.

"Then what *is* it like?" Sharp words from Dan this time. "From what I've seen, you don't stick around. After our parents, *our dad*—" He shook his head. "Brit doesn't need another flakey asshole in her life."

The implication that he was taking advantage of Brit stung, mostly because it was a thought he'd had more than a few times. But he couldn't seem to stay away from her.

He didn't *want* to.

"You don't know anything about me. This thing with Brit, it's more. It's—" God. How could he even begin to categorize what was happening between them? Yes, it was new and intense and he really liked her.

But it was also way more than just a desire to get in her pants.

And still . . . they had hardly even begun.

Stefan blew out a breath. "I don't want to hurt her."

"You've hurt her already," Dan said. "She spent half the night crying after you left her room."

Fuck. He'd known that, of course, had heard how upset she'd been through the hotel room door and guilt sat heavily on his heart.

"You're a fucking asshole," Blane spat.

Yes. Yes, he was. But it was also—

"All we did was talk." Or close enough because he definitely wasn't going to tell Blane and Dan about the kiss or the way Brit had sprawled on top of him, pressing every sweet curve and lithe muscle against him.

Stefan shook his head, shoved the image to the side.

"I needed to know—" He broke off, not wanting to divulge what little he knew of Brit's secrets. "She was upset about something else, and tap dancing around the draw between us was only making things worse," he said, ignoring the glowering expressions on the men's faces. "I can't guarantee Brit and I are going to end up with a white picket fence and two-point-four kids, but I do know she's the first woman to ever make me want that."

Blane snorted. "It'd be better if you just left her alone."

"Be real. I've seen the way you stare at her," Stefan snapped. "If Brit had chosen *you*"—he glared at Blane, the idea of Brit in the other man's arms, of kissing the tall, good-looking forward made Stefan angry on a bone-deep level—"you wouldn't turn her away. You'd grasp the chance and hold on until your fucking fingers fell off. Don't piss on me because I feel the same damn way."

"I—"

Dan put his hand on Blane's shoulder and squeezed, cutting off the other man's words.

They stared at each other, a standoff in which none of them were willing to budge.

Stefan had decided to go for it with Brit, regardless of the secrets and complications, and he just didn't have it in him to kowtow to anyone. Brother or old friend aside.

Brit was different. He wanted her, would do whatever it took to keep her.

"It goes without saying," Dan began before pausing and shaking his head. "Fuck it, I'm going to say it anyway."

He stepped into Stefan's space, crowding him, not stopping until they were nose to nose. "You've hurt her once already, so there goes your free pass. Know that if you do *anything* to hurt her again—or to hurt her chances of playing in this league—I will break every bone in your body and then dump your ass in a military prison so secret you will never, *ever* see the light of day again."

Stefan felt the blood drain out of his face but didn't look away.

He was sincere in his intentions, didn't want to cause Brit

pain. He liked her—probably way too much, given the circumstances.

"Noted. I won't hurt her. And"—he hesitated, wanting to choose his words carefully—"if there is any sign that my presence would do something to jeopardize what she's worked for, I will walk away, immediately and without a fight."

Stefan would. He knew that in the very fiber of his being. It would be hard as hell, considering how strongly he felt for her in just the short time they'd been dancing around each other. If and when he felt more, it would be agonizing.

But it would be a hell of a lot worse if *he* were the reason she didn't achieve her goals.

That was completely unacceptable.

Dan stuck out his hand, and they shook. The cool approval in the other man's eyes made Stefan relax slightly, until he turned to Blane, whose expression could have sliced clear down to the bone.

Well, tough. He was just going to have to deal.

Stefan stuck his hand out. "We cool?"

Blane was silent for so long that Stefan didn't know if he was thinking of punching him in the face or considering putting the tension between them aside.

Probably punching.

"We're cool," Blane finally said and took Stefan's hand, "as long as you stick to your word."

Stefan fixed the other man with a look. "When have I ever not stuck to my word?"

A grudging nod. "Fine."

Brit breezed out of the locker room just then, her hair wet and slicked back into a ponytail. She wore a fitted blazer and slacks with a white button-down, her messenger bag over one shoulder.

He crossed over to her, took the bag, and slung it over his own shoulder. "You stretch?"

"Yup." She nodded. "I'll do some more after dinner. But for now, I'm too hungry to do anything else. Let's get some food."

He glanced at Dan, who was watching them with silent, assessing eyes, waiting for him to step out of line, probably, then Blane, whose expression had softened when Brit came out. When he saw Stefan looking, it turned to granite.

This was going to be a blast.

"Come on," Stefan told them. "I know just the place."

THIRTY-SIX

AFTER STEFAN STEPPED out to make a quick call to check on his mom, he joined the others, and they took Blane's SUV to the restaurant. It was south of San Francisco, a small hole-in-the-wall burger joint in the town of Belmont.

The decorations were the weirdest, campiest around. Blood-red velvet curtains ran floor to ceiling, and the light ranged from dim to sketchy.

Headshots of celebrities, politicians, athletes, and gangsters flitted across the flat screen mounted on one wall in an odd slideshow of young and old, popular and infamous.

Thirty people at most could fit inside, but this was closing time and the chef had never failed to make room for him.

Tonight was no exception.

They crammed themselves into a booth in the corner, three athletes, plus Brit's brother, imitating sardines in a can.

Maybe the booth would have been fine for normal people, but he, Blane, Brit, and Dan weren't normal.

Well, Dan was, he supposed. But Brit's brother was still huge, an inch taller than even Blane and broader across the shoulders and chest. And at six-four and two-hundred-twenty pounds, Blane was no slouch himself.

Stefan was slightly more *petite*, as the boys liked to tease him—only six-one and two-hundred-and-five pounds.

Brit was—

Hell. He didn't know. A couple inches shorter than he was. Maybe about the size of Blue Robertson, the Gold's rookie this season. So probably, five-ten or eleven and a hundred-seventy-five, maybe even a hundred-eighty pounds. She was toned and well-muscled, but goalies got away without the bulk a skater needed to make a presence on the ice.

As they squeezed in together—he and Brit on one side, Blane and Dan on the other—Stefan was thankful that Brit was next to him, not just because her thigh pressed against his felt really fucking good or because the delicate floral scent of her shampoo was teasing his nose . . . but also because Blane and Dan looked like two adults sitting at the kids' table.

He had to bite back a grin when Dan shoved Blane over. "My ass is halfway in the aisle."

Brit snorted. "Dramatic much?"

Blane joined Dan in glaring at them. "Why did we let you pick this place again?" he asked Stefan.

"Because this place has the best bacon-and-bleu-cheese burger on the planet," he said. "And because milkshakes. 'Kay? Enough said?"

"We shouldn't be drinking milkshakes," Blane grumbled.

"Seriously," Brit said. "We've got two days off. I, for one, am having a burger and a milkshake. Mint chocolate-chip. Or maybe cookie dough. Or maybe—"

Laughter swept through Stefan. "Like ice cream, do you?"

She shifted in the booth, turned to smile at him. "Maybe just a little."

"Are you kidding?" Dan asked. "Ice cream is your crack."

"For real," Blane said. "Once she stole my skates and wouldn't tell anyone where they were for a week because I ate her Cherry Garcia." A martyred expression crossed his face. "I had to wear *rental* skates."

"It was Chubby Hubby," Brit said with a chuckle. "And that was the third time you'd eaten the entire pint. After *I'd* bought it."

"We lived as a family. We shared everything."

Stefan's brows pulled down. He'd known Brit and Blane were close, that they'd played on the same team in juniors. But living together? *That* he hadn't known, and as much as he tried to ignore the pang of jealousy in his gut, it was still there, caustic and burning.

"Now children," Dan began, "I know you had your differences—"

"Oh geez, Blane," Brit cut in. "We lived together for three years, and you ate more of my food than Dan did during my entire childhood."

"I was a growing boy."

Brit threw her head back and laughed. Hard.

The sound was electric, and Stefan felt every nerve in his body stand up and take notice. He wasn't the only one.

Though the restaurant was almost cleared out, there were a few patrons still nursing beers . . . or the occasional milkshake. At Brit's laugh, their eyes turned her way. The dim lights made her hair shine like spun gold and her skin look like a bowl of peaches and cream he wanted to lick up.

Or maybe that was just him.

Because the sound of Brit's joy unknotted something within Stefan, made him hope.

Made him want.

God, how he wanted.

The server came over then and took their order. It was nearly impossible to take his eyes off Brit, to focus on the words.

Thankfully, he only had to nod when asked if he would be ordering his usual.

"I love you, you know that, right?"

For a second, Stefan thought that Brit was talking to him. Then he realized that she was looking at Blane.

Christ.

The feeling that swept through him wasn't jealousy.

It wasn't.

Nor was it liquid rage as he studied Blane's face and saw the intense longing there.

Because he *should* be feeling relief—relief it wasn't him that Brit was in love with, relief she was referring to the brotherly, platonic love she felt for Blane.

It made no sense for him to want to hear those same words. They'd barely stumbled into the start of something, and there damn-well shouldn't be any desire on his part to plant his flag—rhetorically speaking—and claim Brit as his.

Good God. It hadn't even been a month since he'd first seen her in the arena's parking lot, struggling to pull her bag from the trunk of her crappy car.

There would be no flag planting, at least not in the whole put-a-ring-on-it, cave-man-style claiming.

Things were tentative, new. Light and easy.

For now.

Blane blinked, and the longing was gone, replaced with a mock-frown. "I still won't ever forgive you for the rental skates."

"Good Lord," Brit said, exasperated, but her lips were twitching. "A woman does one thing—"

"It was a *huge* thing."

"Not Ben-and-Jerry's huge."

Dan caught Stefan's gaze and rolled his eyes, throwing a

sigh of frustration in for good measure. "Children, can we forget about something that happened almost ten years ago?"

Brit put up her hands. "I can. Don't know about Hulk over there, though."

Blane's lips twitched. "I seem to remember buying you a fresh carton of ice cream."

"Oh! That's right." She released a little breath and smiled broadly at Blane. "You did! That was really sweet." Her eyes narrowed. "Still not going to apologize."

Stefan snorted. He couldn't help it. This side of Brit was new. Relaxed and . . . just really, really cute.

"What?" She turned, brushing against him in the tight confines of the booth.

Not that he minded.

Nope. In fact, he wanted her closer and, figuring she wouldn't make a big deal about it since they were in a public place, he stretched out an arm across the back of the booth and closed the few inches between their upper bodies.

She fit perfectly. Having her against him was right.

Utterly right.

"What?" she asked again.

"Nothing," he replied. "I just didn't know you were so . . ."

"Weird? Is that what you were going to say?" She frowned, tried to put some distance between them. Stefan didn't let her. Instead, he wove his fingers through the ends of her ponytail and tugged the slightly damp tresses gently.

"No." He glanced across the table, saw that Blane and Dan had moved on and were talking about something else, then bent so he could whisper in her ear. "So damned cute. So sweet I want to lick you up and see if you taste as good as you sound."

"I'm not—" Her cheeks heated. "That doesn't even make sense."

He shrugged. "Doesn't make it any less true."

"Oh—"

The server returned with their drinks then. An Oreo milkshake for Brit and beer for him, Blane, and Dan.

Brit took a sip of hers, and a look of such pleasure suffused her face that Stefan's cock twitched.

Shit. Between the flag planting, the talk of licking, and now the soft moan of pleasure as Brit took another sip . . . he'd be lucky if his brain had any blood left in it.

Fortunately for him, he didn't need to speak. Blane, Brit, and Dan dominated the conversation.

Stefan was happy to listen as they teased each other about things that had happened during their respective childhoods.

It was nice to know they'd had so many good times together, that laughter and memories had come easily.

His own childhood had been good, of course.

But it had also been a little lonely.

Without a father, without siblings and his mother working so damned hard, the house had been quiet far too often.

The guys on the team had been his family. But it was a fluid one.

Rosters shifted continuously as players aged out, moved, or were cut from the team.

There hadn't been too many constants.

Funny how he'd never recognized that before.

Their food arrived, and the four of them dug in, polishing off the half-pounders with ease. It was always amazing to him how much food hockey players could put away.

Even Brit finished her burger, though she took off all the produce before she ate it.

"No veggies?"

She grimaced. "Not by choice. I eat the damn things because Rebecca requires it, but on a cheat day? Hell no, I'm not choking down some lettuce."

"I can throw some quinoa on there for you."

Rebecca was the team's dietician, and she was notorious for her nutritious, but not-very-tasty food plans. Not that the diet didn't work.

Stefan had never been more in shape, never felt so strong on the ice, and that wasn't just the extra workouts. It was Rebecca's food and Mandy's physical therapy.

And Brit.

He felt his lips curve. A trifecta of women making his life better. He'd better not let that thought slip out.

Brit would give him no end of crap just for having had it.

Still, as he sat next to her, reveling in her scent, in the way her body had relaxed and gradually softened against his, Stefan thought he might get a kick out of telling her.

Just to see those brown eyes spark at him.

"Thanks for inviting me," he murmured into her ear as Blane related a funny story about a Gold defensemen *losing*—with the help of the team—his jock, not wearing it to practice, and then unsurprisingly—and with an *accidentally* misdirected shot by his D partner—getting hit right in the unprotected area.

He'd only heard it about a hundred times since it had happened.

Sometimes hockey players were more like children than well . . . children.

"It's nice to get out."

Brit turned her face up to his, a slight frown pulling her brows together. "Why would you have a problem getting out?" She cocked her head, and her tone was light, but her eyes held a note of seriousness that he couldn't ignore. "Do you have a secret love child? A wife?"

Brit didn't know it, but the explanation was simple. He didn't go out because his mom was sick, and he was on the road enough that he didn't like leaving her when he was in town.

"Just a dozen or so," he joked, instead of telling her what was really going on. "You don't know it, but I'm making a run to star on the show *Sister Wives*."

She snorted. "You're an idiot, just so you know. And also, how do you even know about that show?"

"My mom," he said. "She's all I've got, and we spend a lot of time together." He hesitated before telling her part of the truth. "Actually, she's living with me for a while. It's nice."

Brit stared at him, and he waited for it. For her to make fun of him because his mom was living with him, to make a comment about him being a mama's boy or the like.

She didn't.

Instead, she just smiled and said, "That's really nice for you both." Then she settled back against him and joined the conversation again, adding her side to a childhood story Dan was sharing about some mishap while skiing.

Easy acceptance. How strange.

How wonderful.

They stayed at the restaurant way past closing, the four of them each having such a good time that apparently no one wanted to leave.

There was a lot of teasing and laughter, and when Stefan finally peeled himself out of Blane's SUV and got into his own car, he realized he couldn't remember a time when he'd had more fun.

Sharing it with Brit, with her dash of cuteness and gentle smiles, made it simply the best night of his life.

THIRTY-SEVEN

Brit

FOR ONCE, Brit didn't pull herself out of bed before the sun was up. Her brother had left for the airport a couple of hours before, bussing a kiss on her cheek before telling her he'd see her soon.

There would be no early morning run, no stairs. The Gold had a player's meeting and light practice the following day before they left on their extended road-trip. But, for now, she was going to be lazy in bed.

So the knock at the door was completely unwelcomed.

With a groan, she slid out from between the sheets and walked over to peer through the peephole.

Then wanted to bang her head on the door.

She'd forgotten to put on the *Do Not Disturb* sign. The knock came again, along with the sound of a keycard being pushed into the lock. Brit glanced down, made sure she was decent, and threw back the deadbolt.

"Hi," she told the surprised maid. "Sorry. I don't need cleaning service today."

"Oh! I'm sorry, Ms. Plantain. I didn't realize you were in today."

"It's my fault," she told the woman. "I should have put the sign on."

"Do you need fresh towels?"

What she needed was to crawl her butt back into bed and turn on some crappy morning television show, to veg like a mofo, so that by the time she emerged, all of this guilt she was feeling over deceiving Stefan would have disappeared.

Instead of saying any of that, Brit shook her head. "No, thanks." She reached down and hung the sign on the outer doorknob.

Thirty seconds later, she was in bed and watching a celebrity answer interview questions about his latest film release.

Part of her admired the suave way with which he deflected the less-than-flattering inquiries about an anger scandal in the not-so-distant-past, but the rest of her was disheartened.

This was what it would be like with Stefan, a relationship that was all veneer and a smooth finish, but zero substance underneath.

Truth hit her like a slap shot to the gut.

The reason she was so torn up about this fake relationship was because it was the first time in her life she'd spent time with a man who *could* be more.

So much more.

The door to the next room slammed shut, echoing through the walls of Brit's suite, and she sighed.

Gold management had offered her a new contract a few days before.

And she'd signed it.

But whether they'd presented it because of her game play or solely because of the stuff with Stefan, she didn't know. The contract itself didn't have the biggest payday or the longest terms—just two years—but her agent had managed to eliminate the two-way part of her clause, so she'd be staying in the NHL for at least that long.

Which was more than Brit could have expected, and though she wasn't stupid enough to believe the agreement with Stefan didn't factor in, she was relieved to be in one place for a while.

Unless, of course, management traded her.

And that was a lovely thought for so early in the morning.

Signing the revised contract also meant the Gold were no longer paying her for her lodgings. She'd been planning on keeping the room at the hotel until the team got back from their nine-game road-trip, but with the morning free, maybe she should begin looking for an apartment.

The vacuum turned on next-door, making the decision for her.

Le sigh.

She shoved out of bed and took a shower where she spent a fair amount of time shaving her legs and underarms before washing and conditioning her hair.

Just because she was a professional athlete didn't mean she couldn't feel like a woman.

After de-Wookie-fying herself, she toweled off and dressed. Then instead of slapping her hair into its normal ponytail, Brit dried it carefully. She even put on mascara and blush.

Being in an ice rink for most of the year wasn't exactly conducive for a nice summer glow.

Her fingers hesitated over the lip-gloss before setting the tube aside. She couldn't abide the sticky slimy stuff. No matter that it made her lips look *"lush enough to kiss"*—which was an exact quote from the sales person who'd convinced her to buy it.

Brit had worn the damn stuff once—and it had worked as

promised—but the tacky residue it left on cups, not to mention her teeth, hadn't been sexy.

Her blond hair framed her face in even layers. It shined, even in the fluorescent lighting and was the single physical thing where she took the most pride.

Obviously she was in shape, but her shoulders were broad, her thighs muscular, her breasts barely existed.

Whoever said that more than a handful was wasted hadn't met her.

Stefan would be lucky to get a finger-full.

Brit caught that thought and shoved it away then scowled at her reflection.

"Seriously," she muttered. "No more thinking yourself in circles."

But it was hard.

She had never felt this way before. Even as a teenager she'd been more focused on hockey than boys, and the few crushes she'd had later hadn't gone anywhere . . . even more so after the assault.

At this point, she wasn't exactly over what had happened, but she *had* come to terms with the fact that it didn't define her.

She wasn't delusional, didn't think she was magically better, especially because having someone at her back still made her uncomfortable as hell.

But she'd push past it.

Just like she pushed past everything else that had stood in her way.

She was living her dream. Everything she had hoped for was finally within her grasp.

So maybe—just maybe—she could grab on to some dreams in the other parts of her life as well.

And maybe Stefan could be part of that dream.

She walked out of the bathroom, picked up her phone, and

called the real estate agent Stefan had recommended to set up an appointment in an hour.

Then Brit sucked in a breath, bolstered her courage, and called him to come with her.

As she spoke to him, his sleep-drenched voice like roughened velvet against her skin, she wasn't thinking about the fake relationship. Wasn't calculating the next move that would get them media attention, wasn't worried about management.

This moment was about her.

For one damned moment, it could be about her. About what she wanted.

Which was Stefan.

For however long she could have him.

THIRTY-EIGHT

"TOO SMALL," Stefan said as he glanced around the unit's single bedroom. A queen bed took up almost all of the available space, but there was a small walk-in closet that was plenty big enough to store her collection of jeans, t-shirts, workout gear, and odd pair of game day slacks and button-downs.

Brit was wearing one of her a *nice* t-shirts today, meaning it was new and lacking in stains and holes. Between that and the makeup and her blown-out hair, she'd surprised Stefan.

His eyes had gone wide when they'd met up in the hotel's lobby, and his hand had come up, as though he wanted to touch the strands.

Brit had wanted that too, had wanted his fingers tangled there, pressed against her scalp as he took her mouth in a searing kiss—

It had not really been the time.

But with the bed right there in front of her and the real estate agent having stepped out to take a call, Brit was once again reminded of how tempting Stefan was.

Really, really tempting.

"You okay?" he asked, walking out of the closet and stopping in front of her. He was close enough that she could feel the heat from his body, see the slight scruff of his stubble.

Hear the grumble of his stomach.

Her lips twitched. "I'm sorry," she told him. "I monopolized your morning. I'll buy you lunch."

He gave her a mournful look. "I'm withering away. I'll be skin and bones soon."

"Ha." She snorted, but couldn't—didn't *want* to resist reaching out and stroking the firm muscles of his chest.

They were granite beneath her palms. If granite was scorching hot . . . and lickable.

She brought her other hand up, squeezed his pecs.

What had she been thinking about handfuls earlier? Because this was a really nice one.

Stefan sucked in a breath and stepped closer. Her teeth found her lip, bit firmly, attempted to find control, when all she really wanted to do was ask him to take off his shirt or, better yet, to slip her hands under the soft cotton and take matters into her own hands.

She'd slid them down the rock-hard planes of his abdomen to do just that when he spoke.

"Brit?" The question was soft, husky, and laced with enough desire that her thighs trembled.

"I like spending time with you, remember?" she said, staring up at him as her fingers trailed along the hot, *hot* skin just under the hem of his shirt.

One corner of his mouth turned up. "I know. Me too." But he took her hands in his and carefully pulled them from his skin.

She stuck out a lip. "I thought we were going to explore this thing between us."

His smile grew. "We are."

"Then—" She tried to free herself.

He held firm.

"—why won't you let me—"

The door to the apartment opened and the agent, Lisa, called to them. "What do you think?"

"Because we're not alone," he murmured, the light blue of his eyes darkened with what she hoped was desire and not annoyance. Her eyes darted down, saw the erection straining against the front of his jeans.

Oh yeah, desire. For damn sure.

Not that she was in any better shape.

If he'd touched her, stroked those fingers down and between her thighs, he'd have found her soaked—

"Just give us a moment to finish our discussion," Stefan called.

"Sure thing!" Lisa called back.

They listened to the agent's heels *clack* across the floor, until the noise stopped in what Brit thought was the kitchen.

"You," Stefan said, squeezing her fingers, "are dangerous as hell."

She smiled.

"That wasn't a compliment."

Humor tempered the desire eating at her. Slightly. "I'll still take it as one."

Sex goddess wasn't a role she typically undertook. Hell, normally she was a little shy in the bedroom. But Stefan brought out another side of her . . . and she liked it.

In fact, the attraction between them was so crazy, so *huge*, it might have been frightening had he not been right there with her. She knew she wasn't alone.

She laughed.

Who would have thought?

Stefan's brows pulled together. "Now you're playing with

me? Teasing?" A flash of temper, which sent a little shiver down her spine, crossed Stefan's face.

"Isn't that kind of the point of foreplay?" she asked.

His mouth dropped open in shock and his breath hitched.

A little bubble of hope expanded in her chest, competing with the tangle of desire and guilt, pushing them both to the side until all she felt was happiness because she was in this man's presence. Stretching up on her toes, she pressed her mouth to his.

The kiss was short and hot. But just as Stefan put his arms around her to pull her even closer, she stepped back.

"You're sexy," she told him.

"Brit—"

For some reason, spending time with Stefan gave her confidence in her own skin, made her feel gorgeous, wanted. Competent.

She had no clue why.

Or if it was him at all.

Maybe he'd unlocked something. Or maybe she was finally growing into her own.

Whatever it was, Brit decided she liked it. She headed for the door only to stop a couple of inches from the threshold and glance back at him over her shoulder.

"I want you," she said.

In bed and out of it . . . and then right back in it.

Stefan muttered a curse that made even her ears—and she'd long thought herself beyond the effect of swear words—turn pink.

He prowled toward her, and Brit found that somehow her feet had become glued to the ground. Still watching him over her shoulder, she couldn't move.

Or maybe it was that she didn't *want* to move.

"Turnabout is fair play," he said. "You know that, right?"

His hand came up to her nape and squeezed. His chest pressed against her back, hard and unforgiving.

A slight pang of nervousness unfurled in her abdomen, but before she'd even had a chance to register the sensation, Stefan whipped her around and slammed his lips down onto hers.

Anxiety withered. Desire roared.

A heartbeat later, he was gone, pushing through the door, a whispered "Oh, there will be foreplay" trailing in his wake.

Brit stood there, her fingers pressed against her swollen lips, heat raging in her skin, her nerves zinging like the needy bitches they were, and tried to figure out how Stefan had turned the tables on her so easily.

Then she decided she didn't really care.

Because if he kissed her like that . . . as if the world would end without one more stroke of her tongue, as though her mouth was the sweetest temptation he'd ever experienced then he could turn the tables any damn time he wanted.

Lisa's voice chimed in from the kitchen and jump-started her into motion.

Brit smoothed her hair from where Stefan's fingers had mussed it, sucked in a breath, and stepped from the bedroom.

As she walked, she forced herself to focus on the apartment. Built-ins lined one wall, and the kitchen was tiny but held stainless appliances, white countertops, and cabinets. Gauzy shades covered the wall of windows.

It *was* small.

But it was perfect. Airy and cozy and just a couple of blocks from the Gold's arena.

The single bathroom wasn't luxurious, but it would do, especially paired with the decent-size living space, and cute kitchen. She loved it.

Of course she had to consider that it would be tight when Dan came to stay. But he was used to sleeping in all sorts of crazy places. He could sleep on the floor or a blow-up mattress.

Or she'd get a sleeper sofa. There was room enough.

"What do you think, Brit?" Lisa asked.

"I'll take it."

THIRTY-NINE

Stefan

HE HATED FLYING.

Seriously hated it.

So much so that if there were a boat, a bus—hell, a covered wagon to get him to the away games, he would have signed up in a heartbeat.

But, of course, he hadn't.

Not only did the team's insurance require them to travel only on approved vehicles, he was the *captain*.

His place was with the team.

Brit laughed a couple rows up from where he was seated, liquid warmth and lightning wrapped in one. It fired his nerves, made every cell perk up in rigid attention.

Blane said something that made her laugh again, and a sharp slice of jealousy cut him deep. *He* wanted to be the one who made Brit happy, wanted to sit next to her, absorb her smiles, her sweetness.

But it wasn't Stefan's place to monopolize her time, and if she didn't want to sit with him, didn't want to give unspoken confirmation that the rumors circling in the media, being whispered in the locker room were true . . .

He wasn't going to stand in her way.

They might be pursuing the chemistry that threatened to flay him to the core, but he hadn't laid claim to her.

Which sounded positively barbaric, stupidly alpha male.

Brit would certainly kick his ass for even having had the thought. And yet, he almost didn't care, would take the verbal chewing with enthusiasm . . . if it meant she could be his.

But—

What?

It was complicated? Hell, yes it was. It was a risk? Definitely. He felt more with Brit since—well—ever.

It was new.

That was the notion that gave Stefan the most pause.

And the reason he was sitting five rows behind her, admiring the golden tint of her hair, the slender slope of her neck, the confidence in her hands as she gestured wildly.

She'd been strong when she'd first come to the Gold—it would have been impossible to get there any other way—but in the almost six weeks since she'd first walked into the Gold's arena, he'd witnessed her strength grow, mature into granite laced with . . . caring, maybe?

But instead of weakening the stone, the undertone of affection for her teammates tempered its core, made it even more solid.

She didn't just care for *him*, though he was egotistical enough to think that was part of her transformation.

It was more than that.

Brit was committed to the team with her whole heart. Even her staunchest critic could see that, and they were only five games into the regular season.

A season in which she'd played maybe ten minutes total, but

a season during which she'd been to every practice—optional or otherwise—had been engaged and cheering for their team even while on the bench.

Hence, the so-painful-his-spine-itched distance between them.

But because the draw between them was so new, he wouldn't do anything to risk her career.

Not even when his heart ached to be beside her.

"That bad?" Max asked from his seat next to him. His D-partner always took the window seat, leaving Stefan and his nervous energy free to get up and move around.

Or Max had every time after their first flight together, after Stefan had crawled over him a half-dozen times to pace the aisle.

Further that, Stefan didn't pretend to misunderstand what Max was saying. They'd known each other far too long to play those kinds of games.

And last year's horrible season had created bonds too deep to sever.

"Bad," he agreed. "Really fucking bad. I've never felt like this before."

Max sighed, leaned back in his seat, and took out his ear buds. "It's a really bad time . . ." He hesitated then said, " . . .for both of you."

"I know."

"Might be better if you let her go."

Fury made his fists tighten. He banged one on his thigh. "It's not that easy."

"Why?"

Only three letters, but enough to give Stefan pause.

"I don't know," he said. "I've tried to ignore this thing—whatever it is—between us, but I can't. She's in every thought, every fucking heartbeat."

He bit off the rest of the words before they came. Part of it was because he wanted to save them for Brit. The other part was that *if* he said it—gave voice to the feelings that threatened to unnerve him—he would be even more vulnerable.

"So then what? You continue with this relationship? What has management said?" Max fixed him with a look. "You know, after Gordaine and Rhonda," he said, referring to the rape scandal and resulting investigation that had ended up with the Gold's former captain being banned from the NHL altogether, "management enacted strict rules against fraternizing with staff."

"Brit's not staff."

"She's close enough, and sooner or later someone is going to mention something. Hell, I'm surprised the media hasn't pounced on it already."

That was true enough. The media *hadn't* zoned in on the similarities between him and Brit and Gordaine and Rhonda, and for the first time he wondered why that was.

"My name's cleaner than Gordaine's ever was."

"It's not pristine, though."

"No one's ever accused me of rape."

"No one's ever accused you of getting close enough to try."

"It hasn't been *that* long. My playboy past is still out there."

Max rolled his eyes. "Playboy? Dude. You've hardly even gone out. In the last two seasons we've played together, I can count on one hand the number of times you've been out past midnight, and two of those times have been with Brit in the last month."

"You and I go out," he said, trying not to focus on the fact that he sounded like a defensive teenager. "We've *gone* out."

His friend snorted. "Yeah. For one beer, and then you're safely abed by eleven."

"It's not that simple." Part of it had been his fatigue with the party scene.

The rest of it . . . he sighed. It was hard to be in a partying mood when someone he cared about was sick. And his mom hadn't been well for a long time—two bouts with cancer in four years would do that to someone.

To that end, it was just as easy to settle the ragged edges with a beer or two at his own house.

No media. No women. Just quiet solitude and distance to keep his emotions safely boxed away.

Until Brit had broken the seal, and all sorts of feels had inundated him.

Feels?

Yup. He was losing it, and most of him didn't even give a damn.

"Yeah," Max said. "That's what I figured."

His friend was quiet for a moment, as though waiting for Stefan to spill his guts. But the thing was, Stefan just didn't have it in him.

After a minute, Max sighed. "Okay then."

Stefan nodded. "Okay."

"What are you going to do about Brit?"

"I'm going to win the girl." He shot Max a solemn look. "Just carefully. Very, very carefully."

Max grinned. "That's my boy. Smart wins over—"

"Stupid every day of the week," Stefan finished.

They bumped fists. "Hope it works out for you, buddy."

Brit laughed again, and they both looked forward.

"Me too. Me too."

FORTY

THEY PLAYED in Vancouver the next night and the game went horribly.

It wasn't anyone's fault in particular, just that everyone seemed flat, and nothing was clicking on the ice. In a rare show of temper, Bernard chewed their asses in the locker room between the second and third periods—a misguided but fairly common attempt at motivating professional players to do better.

Stefan never understood that.

Yelling didn't make him play better. It made him worse. Suddenly his hands were a little shaky, and he was jumpy with the puck.

Calm and relaxed was when he played the best.

Some guys played well angry. That just wasn't him, for any sustained length anyway, and it wasn't most of the guys on the team.

Thankfully, Bernard didn't lose his shit too often. Further that, it was hard to argue his sentiments of lazy play and uninspired offense.

Especially after they let in a fourth goal all of twenty-three seconds into the third—making Stefan a minus three for the night.

Two seconds later, Bernard pulled Julian, and Brit took over. It wasn't even that Julian was playing poorly. The move was typical for NHL teams, a way to stall their opponent's momentum and shake their own team into action.

The swap worked.

Not only did Brit play magnificently, practically standing on her head as she was peppered with shots from her first seconds in the game, but her presence actually changed the tenor of the game.

So much so that the Gold finally started playing.

Unfortunately, not soon enough.

The forwards managed to sneak three goals in on the Canucks' goalie but couldn't quite snag the tie.

The locker room was silent after they'd filed in to get undressed. Nineteen men and one woman, sitting on wooden benches as they peeled off their sweaty gear.

Bernard hadn't let the media in yet, and he wasn't in the room proper.

Stefan knew it was a sign for him to step up, to say something.

Trouble was, he didn't know what.

Brit did, though, and her simple words a few minutes into the silence made him fall for her even more.

"We can do better."

That was it. One sentence that was both truth and motivation.

It was also enough to loosen Stefan's tongue.

He tossed his jersey into the dirty pile in the center of the room. "No more," he said. "No more flat performances. Brit played her ass off—"

"Julian too," Brit interrupted, with a serious expression. "Jules gave it everything he had."

At her words, most of the guys glanced up, and many nodded in agreement. They knew the game was on them, knew they had to do better.

"Yes, Jules played well too," Stefan said, making sure he met Julian's eyes, that the goaltender understood he meant the words. "But we can't rely on our goalies to save us. We need to do more."

"Barie's right," Blane chimed in. "I know we're better than this."

"Agreed," said Max.

A lot of the guys gave their support, some with words, some without. But everyone was positive.

Except Stewart.

"Everyone has an off night," he said.

Excuses. The man was full-to-the-brim of lame-ass excuses.

"We're professional athletes," Stefan told him. "We don't have the luxury of an *off* night. We get our shit together, or we won't be around for another season."

Stefan let the room absorb that for a moment. Those that were on the team last year understood how precarious their position was. Half of the team had been cut, most of them—the son of a bitch Gordaine, notwithstanding—without real reason.

It was easy to blame losses on poor coaching, on a lack of support from management, or a young roster.

That wasn't this year.

Management had given them every perk imaginable. They had a good coach who rarely—mid-game verbal assault aside—made mistakes. Their team was beyond talented.

They had plenty of ice time, a decent schedule, state-of-the-art training equipment.

So this sad attempt at hockey wasn't on the higher ups, wasn't on Bernard.

Nope.

It was all on them.

"Stefan's right," Brit eventually said, breaking the terse silence. "There are so many waiting in the wings, ready to pounce on every opportunity. I know. Blue knows."

She nodded at the rookie, who softly replied, "Yeah."

"If they want it more, we're already screwed." The emotion in her tone was fierce, then her lips quirked, and it was pushed aside by the amusement dancing across her blue eyes. "Now this may be my second X chromosome talking, but I'm happy to be here with you guys. I believe we have the talent to do well this season. I believe in us." A beat of quiet. "So do you think you all can get your shit together?"

The guys laughed and continued undressing.

"That your idea of a motivational speech?" Henry, one of the fourth-line wingers called.

"What, Henry? You want me to get my pom-poms out?" Brit called back, before blowing on her fingernails and rubbing them on the strap of her plain black sports bra, in a job-well-done sort of way. Her chest protector and jersey had already been discarded, and she knelt to begin taking off her pads. "I just call 'em as I see 'em."

Henry wolf-whistled in response, and Brit laughed, that wonderful, full-bodied mirth that lightened a room of testosterone-laden jocks.

"You can put it in your spank bank," she said, "but I don't want to hear about it."

"Burn, Plantain," one of the guys called.

The team laughed and began exchanging a series of increasingly bad jokes and innuendos . . . which grew even louder when Henry blushed.

They ribbed the forward then each other until Bernard came in and announced, "Players meeting, eight-thirty tomorrow morning. Plane leaves at ten, and afternoon practice right after we land."

Normally this would have made the team groan—an extra meeting and practice on a game day, interspersed with the team's scheduled flight to Chicago.

But not one person, not even Stewart—who appeared unusually subdued—made a face.

In that moment, Stefan felt like he finally understood his role as captain.

It wasn't that he needed to be the best on the ice or come up with the most original motivational speech, a la Herb Brooks in *Miracle on Ice*.

He just needed to support those who were the best at the moment, who could capture the essence of the room with a well-timed insight.

Sometimes, he thought it might be the best player both on and off the ice, as Brit had been today with her impressive goal-tending and no-fluff words.

Sometimes, it might be those that could loosen a room full of stressed-out players, like Henry had done.

Sometimes, it would have to be him.

But that was okay.

Just knowing he could sometimes share the burden made the task that much less daunting.

FORTY-ONE

Brit

STEFAN'S EYES MET HERS. "Thank you," he said and took off for the showers.

Brit shook her head.

Sometimes the man really didn't get it. A thank you wasn't necessary.

In fact, when someone thanked her for doing something she should be doing anyway, Brit almost felt *less* responsible for her actions.

Especially when she got gratitude for something that *really* should be expected. Some things were optional, and those deserved a thanks. Some—like pushing her teammates and herself to do their honest best—did not.

Maybe it was totally screwed up, but that was the way her mind worked.

If the expectation was there that the team would support each other, would encourage, would deliver a much-needed kick to the ass when necessary, then the road to the playoffs was already half-paved.

"His heart is in the right place," a masculine voice to her right said.

She glanced over at Julian, something inside her settling at the even tone.

There was always a moment of awkward when she relieved a starting goalie. Yes, of course, she wanted to eventually be in Jules' position, but having to actually see him when she'd basically taken the position—even for a limited time—from him was uncomfortable.

He sighed when she looked back down at her pads and continued undoing the straps. "You're not going to make this weird, are you?"

She wanted to say *"Who me?"* but she'd already made things strange enough with her awkward staring. Instead, she shrugged.

"Hey," he said and waited until she looked up. Another sigh. "Yup. You're going to make things weird."

"I'm—" Brit blew out a breath. "Fine. Okay. I *am* making it weird. It's just . . . I've always been a backup, and now to have this chance to maybe work my way into starting. And with an NHL team . . ."

Jules was quiet for a moment, his hair only slightly damp from the early crack he'd got at the showers, but when he spoke, the words surprised her. "I was a backup too."

"You were?"

"Yup. Never thought I'd be more." He shrugged. "Then the starting goalie got injured two weeks after the trade deadline, and it was on me."

She set her pads to one side then turned to face him fully. "What happened?"

"That year we won the whole damn thing."

The mix of pride and reverence in his voice made her ache.

She wanted *that*, so badly. Wanted her name immortalized on that silver cup.

"What did it feel like?"

"Everything and nothing." That made her jaw drop open, and he grinned. "Don't look so shocked. It's like any big event. Tons of buildup, so much pressure and working, working, working. Then you've done it, and . . . it's just over." Jules gestured at her equipment, stacked next to the bench. "You get undressed. You celebrate. You move onto the next season. Only it seems even further from reach, because you've already tasted it and know how hard it is to grasp."

Brit was still digesting that long after Julian had gone, and when Mandy came over to pull her into the modified therapy room, she was more than ready for a distraction.

"Shoulder?" Mandy asked, all but shoving her onto the padded table.

"It's fine."

Mandy glared. "You said it was fine when the damn thing was swollen and you had reduced range of motion." She narrowed her eyes. "Tell me the truth."

"It's a little sore. But in a tired way, not injured way."

"You'll tell me if that changes." Her gaze bored into Brit, fierce and intense as hell.

Brit raised her hands in surrender. "Promise."

In a blink, the sternness in Mandy's expression faded away, and the other woman smiled brightly. "Good." A nod toward Brit's raised arms. "And good range of motion. Keep up those exercises."

She nudged Brit to lie face down on the table and began massaging the tight muscles in her shoulders. "So tell me about Stefan," she said. "He is, without a doubt, the hottest guy on the team. That chest . . . those arms . . ." Mandy sighed. "Damn, girl.

I'm jealous. Half the time, I want to pull him in for treatment he doesn't need, just so I can touch him."

A wave of cold fear had swept over Brit at Mandy's initial words—the fear of discovery, fear of someone finding out the truth about her and Stefan—but all that quickly, the fear was replaced with jealousy, surging hot and unhindered.

She turned her head and glanced back over her shoulder at Mandy. Okay, glared. Because, dammit, she'd been pressed against those muscles of Stefan's and didn't want anyone else touching . . . or fantasizing about touching.

Mandy grinned. "Guess that look says it all." She dug her fingers into a sore spot, and Brit grunted in discomfort. "Come on, just dish already. A little girl talk makes the world go round. Plus, who else am I supposed to talk to. Rebecca? You know she's about as fun as watching paint dry."

With a snort, Brit plunked her head down on the pads. Rebecca *was* pretty serious and not a whole lot of fun.

"Point made," she said. "But I'm not really good at the whole girl-talk thing."

Especially with non-hockey-playing girls. At least she could connect with the guys on the team about the sport, but chatting with Mandy about hair or men made her downright uncomfortable.

"We'll practice."

Which sounded about as fun as talking with Rebecca, but Brit sighed and didn't protest as she endured the alternating pain, pleasure, and icy cold that was the storm of Mandy's fingers mixed with the therapist's patented muscle cream.

Good God, the woman had strong hands. If she weren't all of five-feet-and-change, Brit would have told her to get her ass in gear and start playing. "You're not funny," she muttered.

"If it makes you feel any better, I'd admire Stefan all day, but when it gets down to it, I like my men a little burlier."

"You're so little, they'd smother you— Fuck!" The therapist had dug firmly into a particularly sore spot.

"Sorry." Mandy chuckled. "Okay. No, I'm not. You've got a smart mouth on you." She popped Brit on the shoulder then dropped down onto the table next to her. "We can't all be tall and willowy like you, Brittany Plantain. Some of us girls have a little meat on us . . . and like our men with the same."

"Meat?" Brit stopped and glanced over at Mandy, lips twitching. Sometimes her mind went really dirty, she couldn't help it. Okay, she *could* help it, but being around guys and their plethora of sexual innuendos and bad jokes has turned her into a twelve-year-old boy. "Really?"

Twin spots of pink appeared on Mandy's cheeks, clashing with her pale skin and red-hued hair. "I didn't mean—"

"Uh-huh. I think there's a dirty mind in there. Hiding under two tons of cuteness."

"Two tons?" A grin. "Jeez, girl, I just told you I was insecure about my size, and you bring up my weight."

Panic seized Brit for one long moment. Until she saw the humor in Mandy's eyes. The other woman was devious.

Biting back a smile, she said, "Okay. Maybe three."

"Bitch."

They looked at each other and cracked up.

When they'd finally gotten themselves back under control, Mandy bumped her shoulder against Brit's. "Did we just become friends?"

Brit nodded solemnly. "I think so." For once, she might have actually met another woman she could be herself with, another woman where things weren't her trademark awkward.

"Good. I'm tired of hanging out with cavemen all the time," Mandy said.

"Other women besides Rebecca work for the Gold."

"Yeah." Mandy shrugged. "There are a group of us, but I'm the only one that travels with the team."

"Well then, we'll need to stick together."

The other woman snorted. "Heck no. Any spare time you've got will be spent with Stefan."

"It's not like that," Brit protested, even as she wondered why she bothered. Management wanted it to be more. She and Stefan wanted it to be more. So why put the qualifier on it now?

"Then what's it like?" Mandy asked. "Because the pictures of you two are smoldering."

"It's attraction."

And possibility. The delicate hope for more.

But it was also a fragile future that could be easily torn apart if Stefan found out the real reason for her initial interest, for her moving forward into something she wouldn't have normally touched with a ten-foot pole, chemistry or not. Probably, the same was true for him. They both understood that any relationship between them would be complicated.

Inter-office dating on steroids.

With an inner sigh at the mess that was her life, Brit rose from the table and tested her shoulder. No matter what they said about Mandy, the woman knew what she was doing when it came to muscles.

Just hopefully not Stefan's.

"If that's attraction, then sign me up," Mandy said.

Brit chuckled, but it wasn't filled with humor. Or at least not entirely. "Attraction complicates things."

Mandy stopped cleaning the table with a disinfecting wipe and raised a brow.

Way to go. Draw even more attention to the convoluted mess between her and Stefan.

"I'd say be careful," the other woman murmured, "but it seems like you already know that."

"Yeah."

Mandy tossed the wipe then walked over. "Okay, then I'll say this. Stefan might seem like an open book, calm and with his shit together, but he feels as much as the rest of us. He's just really good at keeping it bottled up, making it seem as though everything is superficial and doesn't matter."

"How do—?" Brit bit back the question then shook her head at herself. She *wanted* to know—despite feeling jealous that Mandy might understand Stefan better than she did—and asked anyway. "Did you and he—?"

"*God no.* I don't shit where I eat, no matter how much fun it is to look. Plus, remember? Burly men." She shrugged, her expression going a little serious and a whole lot wicked. "But I work closely with you all on a daily basis. It's hard not to get to know each of your nuances." She raised one brow, chasing it with a penetrating look. "All of them."

"So what you're saying—"

Mandy's lips tipped up into a smirk. "Is that I know all."

Now damn, that was a frightening thought.

FORTY-TWO

"COME OUT WITH ME?"

Brit jumped at the sound of Stefan's voice ambushing her the moment she stepped outside the room.

"Jeez, ninja. Don't sneak up on me." Her hand pressed against her chest, tried to soothe the racing tattoo of her heart within. "And it's late. I want to shower and sleep."

"I can help with that."

She snorted. "It's a simple matter of you wash my back . . ."

"Exactly."

Walking into the locker room, Brit noticed that the pile of jerseys and undergarments in the center of the room had disappeared. Her gear was stacked and waiting for the equipment manager to store for their next plane ride.

Never let it be said the Gold staff weren't efficient.

The guys had already finished with their showers, and the room was hushed. Which meant she was showering back in the hotel room.

Maybe it was crazy to feel like a crowd would save her if any of the guys tried to grab her again. A group hadn't stopped the men in the past, but she'd also been the only one showering when it happened.

And so somehow, the notion had become hard for her to shake.

She felt safe when she wasn't showering by herself. She felt exposed when she was.

In the twisted logic of her mind, it made sense.

Maybe someday, she'd get past it.

Today wasn't that day.

Because seriously, she had enough crap on her plate.

"I'm exceedingly skilled with a loofa."

Her mouth dropped open at the soft words, their cheese factor nearly infinity. She was just about to give Stefan a boatload of crap about it when she turned and saw the expression on his face.

It appeared superficial. It seemed light.

Until she looked closer and realized the offer was much more significant than that. He was trying to make her laugh, to relieve some of her stress . . . because Stefan knew there was something about the empty locker room that made her nervous.

That was when Brit knew.

She *had* to tell him. Needed to be honest in this way, since she couldn't in so many others.

"I was . . . well, I want to say attacked, because that's what it felt like." She cleared her throat, pushed past the lump in it. "But it wasn't so much that as some sort of sick ritual the guys had for new players."

His nostrils flared, and his eyes darkened, the light blue going almost navy. "What do you mean?"

She shrugged. "A few years ago . . . the team I was playing on . . . well, they have a tradition." She swallowed hard. "I wasn't immune."

"What. Do. You. Mean?" he asked, somehow managing to

inject intensity into the question without actually raising the volume of his voice.

"I mean"—she sucked in a breath and told him the truth —"they waited until I was alone in the shower then came up behind me, held me down, touched me . . . then doused me with icy cold water. They tried to say it was their way at making me feel like part of the team because every single player endured it. I-I just thought it was going a different way."

"You thought they were going to rape you."

The air in her lungs shuddered out on a long, shaky exhale. The floor became blurry through the lens of her tears, but her voice was rock steady. "The way"—her eyes closed—"Their hands. I—" Finally, she breathed out and lifted her chin. "Yes."

And that was the truth. The piece that had shaken her to her very core. Those men had taken something from her—stolen her safety net, ripped away a place where she'd felt protected.

Hockey had been her happy place. Until then.

It had taken her years to find her way back.

Stefan's voice shook with fury. "That's assault. It's wrong."

"Yes."

"But why—"

Brit knew what was coming. It was the inevitable course of questioning. Why had she let it happen? Why—

"Didn't I do something?" She laughed without mirth, the words coming fast now, almost frenzied in their effort to escape. "Except I did. I reported the incident to the head coach. I thought it was a matter of misunderstanding, that they needed to know it was wrong to do it to anyone, male or female. And they . . ." Brit blew out a breath. " . . .they said all the right things, even made a show of pulling the guys into meetings. But at the end of the day, *I* was the one they let go. It was *me* who scrambled to find another team, another contract, and position. That's why this thing with Bernard—"

Shut up!

The thought burst through to the forefront of her mind, silencing the flow of words.

Stefan watched her for a long moment. When he finally spoke, it wasn't to question her further, to pounce on the slip. No, his words, when they came, were supportive.

"You did the right thing."

She shook her head. "I'm not so sure."

"You did."

"My career suffered." It had been rough trying to find another team, and even though she'd eventually managed to secure another contract, Brit had thought her dream finished.

"Maybe," Stefan said. "But you're here now."

He took a step toward her, raised a cautious hand. That tentative action undid her, and she closed the distance between them, nestled into the expanse of his chest. His arms wrapping tight around her were better than making a tough-as-hell save.

Those arms soothed, managed to make the past feel like it was very much in the past.

"Did you ever think about going to the media?" His question was gentle in a way that might have pissed her off, if it were anyone else, but coming from Stefan, it was okay.

Brit didn't allow herself to think about why that might be.

"Yes," she told him. "But there were pictures, and I thought if it all came out, the pictures would too. My career couldn't recover from that."

The old saying that pictures were forever was true. They shaded a person's image, always crept back in when someone was in the news. And a story about a hot button issue?

That would have been regurgitated time and again.

Every time a similar story surfaced, the media would have said, *"Remember that time when the professional hockey team got caught assaulting Brit Plantain?"*

She could have never just been a goalie striving to make it like other players.

She would never have been just the first female goalie on an NHL team.

No.

She would have been a victim.

And Brit couldn't abide that.

"Come on," Stefan said a few minutes later. He dropped his arms, and the sensation of their loss was intense. She wanted to stay curled against him forever, to stay safe and warm. Protected.

Then his fingers laced with hers, and the warmth returned, melting the frosty numbness making popsicles of her insides.

"We'll go to the hotel," he said. "You'll shower. I'll order room service, and we can eat."

Her eyes flashed to his, suspicious. "Are you trying to finagle an invitation to my room?"

"Who me?" he asked, anything but innocent.

She felt her lips twitch. Stefan was charming for all his deviousness, and delight replaced the hooked tendrils of the past.

"And what will *you* be doing while I'm showering?" she teased.

"Watching TV."

Uh-huh. "So this is all about using my TV?" she asked.

"Yup." Stefan shook his head. "I've heard your room is nice than mine."

Brit rolled her eyes, but just as she was about to call him on that bit of BS, he leaned close and whispered in her ear, "I'll also be imagining you naked and wet. My mouth on those perfect breasts, my hands on your ass. Picturing pulling you close as I dropped to my knees and . . ."

The rest of the image he painted in her mind was hot and dirty and . . . sexy as hell.

She wanted—

But he didn't let her catch her breath, just continued painting the scene, his husky voice sweeping over her like calloused fingers drifting down her spine. "I'll be imagining all of that, planning, knowing that when we actually get to be in a shower together—one that's not filled with a bunch of our teammates"—he added with a rough chuckle—"it'll be even hotter than I can imagine."

Holy hell.

Her thighs trembled, the ache between them intense.

And that was only with words.

Still, Brit had never been one to let someone else win, not in sports and not in life.

It wasn't in her nature.

So she found her voice, rose on tiptoe, and whispered in his ear, "But what if I wanted there to be a bunch of other dudes?"

He shivered, his fingers clenching on hers. But then her words must have penetrated because he reared back in comical outrage and glared at her.

She smirked. That would do.

"Come on, Romeo," she told him. For once, she was in the moment, and the tenterhooks of the past were very far away. "I like your plan."

FORTY-THREE

Stefan

STEFAN HADN'T BEEN KIDDING when he'd told Brit he would be imagining her naked and wet, droplets of water skating down her skin . . . all that creamy skin exposed for his mouth, his fingers, his co—

He cursed, grabbed the room-service menu off the desk in her hotel room, and tried to push the images from his mind.

It wasn't that he didn't want Brit—the raging boner tenting his pants was more than enough evidence to the contrary—but it was too soon.

She was vulnerable . . . and they were on date three.

Of course, his dick would like to remind him that the countless hours they'd spent together in the company of their teammates and the dinners with Blane and Max and Dan added to that.

They did.

But it was still too soon.

Stefan had slept with enough women in his lifetime to understand that sex was just sex.

And he wanted more than sex with Brit.

But that wasn't the only reason for his hesitation. Although she'd opened up to him, he couldn't help but feel there were more secrets she was hiding, more he needed to know before they took that final step.

Not to mention they had practice and a game tomorrow. If they were going to sleep together, he wanted to take his time, to keep her up for hours into the night.

This wasn't the right moment.

Which he was going to remember, even if ninety percent of his blood was currently in the southern half of his body.

The shower turned off.

"Christ," he muttered and quickly phoned in the order before sinking down onto the edge of the bed. He turned on the TV and cranked the volume, not wanting to engage his imagination further by listening for any faint clue of movement as Brit dressed.

His phone buzzed, but he ignored it because the door to the bathroom opened, and he nearly swallowed his tongue.

He'd seen Brit naked, but this was somehow even sexier.

Her face was washed clean, her blond hair pulled back into a scattered ponytail—which was all he registered before his eyes were drawn back down to her body.

A pale pink silk tank top encased those breasts he'd been fantasizing about, her nipples beaded beneath the thin material, clearly illustrating the fact she wasn't wearing a bra.

He bit back a curse, struggled for a semblance of control. She was the personification of temptation.

Her legs were bare except for the smallest pair of flannel shorts he'd ever seen, miles and miles of bare skin flushed slightly pink from the heat of the shower.

Stefan's fingers actually ached with the need to touch.

Brit tugged her ponytail, a nervous gesture that made her

appear all of fifteen-years-old for a moment, but when she smiled and gave a rueful shrug, any thoughts of youth disappeared.

She was all woman.

He wanted her.

"I don't really do the matching lingerie thing," she said.

"Wh-what?"

With a sigh and an eye roll, she walked over to him. "I'm not super girlie."

"Like fuck you're not." He was practically sitting on his hands, so he didn't grab her.

Her lips curved up, and she stopped less than six inches from him. Close enough that her delicate feminine scent coated the air between them.

"You know, I've never felt so powerfully sexy before," she said, stroking a single finger down his shirt, pressing the column of buttons lightly into his skin and setting him on fire, "but hearing your voice go all growly . . . Damn, I kind of like the way you make me feel, Barie."

Sweet baby Jesus, she was a menace.

"Me too," he agreed, even though Brit was making his balls turn permanently blue.

And apparently, she had no plans to stop because she plunked herself down in his lap, leaned close, and pressed her mouth to his.

No preamble. Just hunger, plain and simple.

She wrapped her arms tight around his neck, mouth opening, their tongues tangled in intimate embrace.

Stefan's control snapped.

He grabbed her hips, pulled her flush against him, and twisted one hand into her ponytail, angling her head so he could plunder it even more deeply.

Brit moaned. The sound was sexy as fuck.

He needed more. More skin. Her pinned beneath him. He needed to be inside her.

His fingers found the hem of her tank top and swept it up and over her head.

"I need to get my mouth on these," he said, placing one hand at the base of her spine to coax her closer as he bent to take one pink bud in his mouth.

"What—*Oh!*"

She arched and her soft moan of pleasure echoed through him, ratcheting his arousal to even higher levels. *God.* The woman was hot. Twisting, he tossed her to the mattress and followed her down. She spread her legs, effectively positioning himself in the place he most wanted to be.

Of course, it would be a lot better minus his pants, but he'd promised himself—

Her thighs wrapped tight around his hips, and she moved, undulating against him in a rhythm that literally made Stefan see stars.

He gripped the comforter fiercely, trying desperately to not blow his load in his pants. "Stop," he ground out.

"I can't," she said, panting. "I need—" She rubbed against him again, and he couldn't stop his hips from pressing forward, the layers of fabric between them creating both delicious friction and intense frustration.

He wanted—

"Stefan," Brit panted, "please."

It was in that moment he realized he'd never be able to deny her anything.

Good intentions gone, he reached between them and slipped his fingers beneath the waistband of her shorts, pressing firmly against her clit. She was wet and hot, the dampness of her arousal soaking through the fabric and onto his slacks.

"Please," she said, as he stroked her. "Please. Please. *Please.*"

He circled the bud, stroked until she was writhing beneath him. White intruded on the edges of his vision, blurring all reason, shrinking this moment until he didn't think, until his sole reason for existing was to bring Brit pleasure.

"Oh fuck!" she cried, and her thighs clenched hard around his hips, trapping his hand between them, grinding against his erection. She bucked wildly as her orgasm made her break apart.

That was it for him.

Pleasure exploded in his brain, tore down his spine, and into his groin.

He came in a rush and collapsed on top of her.

Holy shit. "Holy fucking shit," he said aloud when he could breathe again.

Brit looked up at him, wide-eyed and flushed. She brought her fingers to her lips and he noticed that her hand was shaking. "What the hell was that?"

Stefan hadn't come in his pants since he was a teenager. Five minutes with Brit, and he'd regressed fifteen years. But for some reason he was grinning, probably because even though his dick hadn't been where it wanted to be, the orgasm had still been the best of his life.

"That, I think," he said, "was chemistry. A shit ton of it." He flopped to the side and stared up at the ceiling.

They glanced at each other then burst out laughing, so loudly they barely heard the knock at the door.

Stefan reached down, picked up Brit's tank top, and tossed it to her. He gestured at the wet spot on his slacks. "I think you'd better answer the door."

FORTY-FOUR

STEFAN GRIMACED and adjusted his pants as Brit set the tray on the desk. It was a lot more uncomfortable than when he was a teenager.

She turned to face him, pointed at his slacks. "Take 'em off."

And immediately he was hard again.

"Not for that." She yawned. "As sexy as this *chemistry* between us is, it's getting late." Raising her hand up, she twitched her fingers. "Take off your pants, I'll wash 'em in the sink."

"You don't—"

"You're on your own with your underwear, though." Brit was talking a big game, but her cheeks were pink.

He raised a brow. "What makes you think I'm wearing any?"

Her mouth dropped open, and he smirked. How she was such a mix of sweet and sexy, confident, and innocent he would never know. But he loved all of those things about her . . .

Loved.

Holy shit.

That may be the first time Stefan had ever thought the L word with respect to a woman who wasn't his mother.

He went very still, studied the emotions coursing through him.

Somehow the notion of loving Brit didn't actually scare him.

Now wasn't that something?

"Stefan?"

He looked up; saw Brit studying him with concern. "You okay?"

"I'm better than okay." In one smooth movement, he rose from the bed and pulled her close. The kiss he laid on her was sweet and gentle, and it *still* filled him with raging desire . . . even more so when she responded without hesitation.

Kissing her until his control threatened to erode for the second time, Stefan forced himself to drop his arms and step back.

"Start eating," he told her and brushed his thumb across her reddened lips. God, he wanted to kiss her again. "I'll take care of the pants . . . and underwear."

He set his phone and wallet on the desk before going into the bathroom and stripping down. After rinsing both his pants and boxer briefs with soap and water, he hung them up to dry before hopping in and taking a quick and frosty shower.

Brit had used every towel in the bathroom for some reason or another, so he scooped one off the floor before drying and wrapping it around his waist.

When he emerged, it was to find Brit curled up against the headboard, a plate balanced precariously in her lap.

She had the determined look of someone who was finishing a plate of food simply because it was good for them.

Not that he blamed her. The regimented diet Rebecca recommended got really old *really* quick.

"That good, huh?"

Brit grimaced but determinedly shoveled in another bite and swallowed. "It's good for us."

"Yes," he said and picked up his plate. "It is. But that doesn't mean it doesn't get boring."

"True." She chewed and swallowed another bite before glancing up and smiling. "But don't think I didn't see what was hiding under the other cover. How'd you know?"

Stefan sat next to her, tucked a stray blond strand behind her ear. "That you don't like chocolate but love mint chocolate-chip ice cream?" He shrugged. "I have my sources. And that makes no sense by the way."

"It makes total sense. You don't taste the chocolate! And besides, ice cream is in a different realm than other desserts. In ice cream, having some chocolate is totally acceptable."

Stefan grinned even as he heard his phone buzz again. He needed to check that, but he didn't want to leave Brit's side. Not yet.

"Your very random dislike of various types of chocolate aside, I want to know everything about you, Brit." Wanted to know all the little things that made her tick. His heart gave a hard squeeze as he realized he meant those words with every piece of his soul. The depth of feeling he had for this girl . . .

He cleared his throat, concentrated on his plate, feeling both at peace and a whole lot vulnerable. "So anyway, choke down that rice and chicken so you can have some ice cream."

When Brit didn't answer, he looked up.

Her face was sheet white, and her fork was almost vibrating, her hands were trembling so badly.

"Brit? What's the matter?" he asked. Had he revealed too much too soon? He'd thought she was right there with him.

"Stefan," she said. "I need to tell you something. I"—she broke off, shook her head—"I . . ."

"What?" he asked when she stopped again. "What is it?"

"I don't really know where to start."

"It doesn't matter," he told her. "Just start *somewhere*."

"Management—"

His phone began ringing, and normally he would have ignored it.

But it was his mom's ringtone.

"Hang on," he told Brit. "I need to answer that."

"Of course, but I need—"

He wasn't listening closely. His phone was already on his ear. "Hello?"

No response.

"Mom? Are you there?"

"Stefan?" Her voice sounded weak and fragile.

"Mom?" His gut twisted. "What is it? Talk to me."

"Stefan?" She sounded disoriented. "I . . ."

"Mom!" he said sharply. "Focus. What's going on?"

There was some crackling, the sound of heavy breathing. Until, "Fell."

"Where are you?"

"Kitchen. Blood."

He whipped toward Brit. "Call 911."

FORTY-FIVE

Brit

THE PICTURES of Stefan exiting her hotel room clad in only a towel made the media circuit the next day.

Management was thrilled.

Brit didn't give a shit.

Stefan's mom had cancer, and she was manipulating him into a relationship.

Enough was enough. The contract didn't matter. She was going to tell Susan she was done and damn the consequences.

Being on the phone with 911, relaying Stefan's instructions as he frantically tried to keep his mom alert and reach someone who could get over to his house, had been both heart-wrenching and terrifying.

The moment the dispatcher told her that the paramedics were with Stefan's mother, that Diane was alive and responsive, Brit had shoved Stefan out of the room and told him to pack.

"I'll call Bernard," she'd said, "and arrange the flight. You go and pack."

"I don't—"

Brit had put his wallet and phone in his hand, gestured at the towel. "You'll need clean clothes at least," she'd said. "Go. I'll take care of it."

A car was waiting fifteen minutes later, the flight booked, and Stefan had been home before the sun rose in California.

Brit hadn't slept a wink, not until Stefan had texted midmorning after she and the team had landed in Chicago, telling her that his mom was alive and in the ICU.

Bernard hadn't canceled the meeting or the afternoon skate, and she'd been grateful for the distractions. The mood on the ice had been subdued but determined, and the Gold had handily beaten the Blackhawks with Jules in net.

Later, alone in her room, she texted Stefan and asked how his mom was doing.

No response. But fifteen minutes later, her phone rang with an unfamiliar number.

"Hello?" she asked after picking up.

"It's me."

"Stefan. Thank God. How's your mom?" Nervous energy bunched in her legs, and she began pacing the hideous-green-floral carpet.

"She's okay." Brit released a breath as he continued talking. "Out of the ICU now that her blood pressure has stabilized. But she's still dehydrated, and her blood sugar was very low . . . No surprise, that, since she can't keep anything down."

God, Stefan had to be so frustrated, helpless as he was in the situation.

"I'm so sorry," she told him. "Is there anything I can do?"

"No," he replied. "You've been great, Brit. Thank you. But . . ." A beat of quiet. " . . .did you see the photos?"

Had she ever. "I did. I'm sorry," she said. "I didn't think—"

"Not your fault." His voice dropped. "Any pushback from management?"

"None."

His breath rattled across the speaker of her phone. "Good. I thought maybe Bernard—"

"He didn't say anything." In that moment, she wanted to tell Stefan everything, to lay it out there and take the brunt of his anger.

She didn't.

Because Brit didn't want to heap one more thing on him, not then, not when he was already dealing with so much.

"Hey," he said, "the game went well, huh? I saw the score. Hang on—" But Stefan broke off, and she heard murmured words in the background. He came back on the line. "I've got to go. My mom's awake."

"Okay, let me know if I can help in any way."

"You've already done enough, Brit." He said goodbye and hung up.

She *had* already done enough. Just not in the way he thought.

Because Brit knew that, whatever the consequences to her or Bernard, she couldn't do *this*—the lies and deceit and regret—anymore.

She threw on a jacket, packed her bag, and went down to Bernard's room. He deserved a warning, time to get things in line, because she didn't doubt for a moment Susan would make good on her threats.

The door flew open before she could knock, and her coach seemed to know what she was going to say before she spoke.

"It's all right, Brit," he said, when she stumbled through the words. "Don't worry about me. These months have let me get things in order. Even if management cancels the contract, we'll be okay."

Brit found she had to take him at his word, because if she

didn't, if this course led to someone else—Bernard's wife—getting hurt . . .

She already had way too much guilt on her plate.

Swallowing that down, she said, "I've got to go back to San Francisco. Help Stefan."

Bernard nodded. "Take a cab to the airport. I'll arrange a flight. It'll have to be commercial, though. The team is flying out in a couple of hours, and the plane wouldn't make it back in time."

It was better that way, better she didn't use team resources for personal use. Better that she didn't give Susan any more ammunition.

Once Brit was in the cab, she pulled out her phone and sent a text. Her show of spine, of damn-the-consequences-and-move-forward was long overdue.

But at least it was there.

No more, Susan. I'm done.

Brit made it into SFO on the last flight of the day. It was just after midnight, but her body had been in so many times zones over the last few days it didn't know which way was up.

All she knew was that her place was by Stefan's side.

When things were calmer, when his mom was in the clear, she'd confess everything and deal with the consequences. Even if it meant losing him.

But for now, she was going to be there for him, reciprocate the support he'd shown her.

She shouldered her duffle and walked through the airport. It was deserted enough that her presence only garnered the occasional second look.

There were a few cabs parked outside the terminal, so Brit hopped in one at random and directed the driver to the hospital. It was only when she was a few minutes out that she realized Stefan hadn't told her what room number his mom was in, or even the floor.

Surely, he would have hired security with all of the press. Devon, the Gold's GM, had released a general statement saying that Stefan would miss a few games because of a family emergency, so it wasn't common knowledge his mom was in the hospital.

But that didn't mean the media wouldn't find out, or that Stefan wouldn't take precautions.

And he didn't know she was coming.

Brit could picture it, a hulking security guard standing outside his mother's door, turning her away and, at just the sight of her slightest hesitation, hauling her out the front door of the hospital.

That would give the press something, wouldn't it?

"Not well planned," she muttered to herself and wondered if she should just go back to the hotel. Her apartment wouldn't be ready for another week. Maybe she should just try to catch up with Stefan in the morning.

She started to tell the cabbie, "Can I—"

"Here you are," he told her as they turned into the hospital drive, and, just at the same moment, his radio clicked with a call for another pickup. His impatience was a tangible thing when she hesitated, and he barely waited a heartbeat after she closed the door before speeding away.

Maybe she should call another cab.

It was a silly thought. Ridiculous.

Except now that she was at the hospital, Brit was second-guessing herself.

She'd done a crazy thing, leaving the team. Bernard would pull in a goalie from their minor league team, so at least Jules would have backup, but her leaving was risking her position and any momentum she'd made in the games she'd played.

Bernard understood why she'd left. Still, this was professional hockey. If she wouldn't step in, someone else would be happy to take her spot, and she really didn't like the feeling that she'd put her career in jeopardy.

She'd acted on pure instinct that morning.

The team had been in Chicago and the Gold's AHL team was located in nearby Evanston. It had been an easy fix in her mind. The team would be fine, and Stefan needed her support more.

Except, did he?

He and his mom had been on their own for a long time, Brit knew that.

And he hasn't asked her for help.

Yet she couldn't shake the feeling that he didn't ask for help because no one had ever been there for him, because he and his mom had always needed to do it on their own.

So she shouldered her bag and walked inside. She was staring at the directory, trying to form a brilliant plan of attack when the elevator dinged, and Stefan walked out. His reaction was almost comical—feet skittering to a stop and eyes widening, his mouth opening and closing his mouth a few times.

She didn't hesitate, didn't think, just strode across the distance between them and threw her arms around his neck.

"What are you doing here?" he asked. "What about the team?"

"I needed to be here more," she said and had never felt a stronger truth.

He straightened with a jolt. "Brit," he began, "that's incredible, but you can't—"

She *tsked* and dropped her arms, even though the same thoughts had crossed her own mind only a few minutes before. She'd just realized something incredible.

Stefan was important. More important than so many other things.

Maybe even more important than hockey.

"I talked with Bernard," she said, tucking away that thought to ponder later. "It's fine."

"I—"

"Where were you going?" she said, interrupting what was probably going to be an argument for her to get on the next damn plane and get back to the team. "I'll go so you can stay with your mom."

Stefan was quiet for a beat. Then he smiled, and the impact of it was a nuke to her senses.

Damn, she liked him. Hell, that was a lie.

She loved him. Good God. She *loved* him.

Which was a notion that pretty much rocked her to the core and rendered her deaf, dumb, and stupid.

Thankfully, Stefan was still talking and she had a minute to get her crap together.

"My mom kicked me out," he said. "I was going home to sleep for the night."

Oh. Well, that made her cross-country flight seem awfully pointless.

"Come with me."

Her eyes shot up. "Wh-what?"

"Come home with me," he said. "Let me hold you, to know that, without a doubt, one of the two most important women in my life is safe and whole."

Every bit of air in Brit's lungs *whooshed* out of her on a rapid exhale. "I'm important?"

He touched her cheek, eyes shining brightly. "Yes, sweetheart, you are."

Her heart clenched because some part of her had understood that, but to hear him say the words, especially with the guilt tearing her up inside . . .

It made her want to grasp every damn second she could possibly spend with him and hang on as tight as she could.

To savor. To remember. Because when she told him the truth—

"So? Will you come?"

She didn't even hesitate. "Yes."

Stefan didn't reply with words, but something in his expression released. Relaxed and opened. He nodded, scooped up her bag, and led her to his car.

She followed without reluctance.

He was an incredible man, and Brit was determined to do something good, something *right* by him.

So that if this thing between them went down in flames and carved out a chunk of her heart, crushed it into oblivion, it could at least be said that she'd tried to do something solely for Stefan and his well-being.

In the meantime, she was going to wring out and hold tight to every happy moment she could.

Especially if that meant another moment in Stefan's arms.

FORTY-SIX

THE DRIVE to Stefan's house was short and mostly silent. It wasn't uncomfortable, exactly, but Brit had experienced more relaxed car rides.

They talked about his mom for the first few minutes. She was staying one more night in the hospital as a precaution but would probably be released by the following afternoon.

"I called the home-care agency we've been using, and a nurse is going to stay with her twenty-four hours a day for a while." He slanted a glance toward her as the car slid to a halt at a red light. "Mom's not thrilled, but she's also decided not to argue."

Brit figured it would be hard having help around all the time, especially for someone who appreciated her independence, but it was clear Diane couldn't be left alone.

"Maybe you can eventually arrange it so they just stay when the team is on a road trip?" she asked.

Blue eyes warmed before they returned to the road.

The sensation enveloped her, comforted way more than they should have as an independent woman herself.

But she was hopeless when it came to him, grasping up every crumb of approval, of desire, and caring.

What was it about Stefan that made her crawl? She wasn't broken any longer, wasn't a desperate person. But with him—

Perhaps it was because he'd do the same for me.

They were experiencing this crazy rollercoaster of a desire together and Brit thought that if it had been *her* mother who'd taken ill, Stefan wouldn't have hesitated to drop everything too.

It was at the very center of this draw between them. A deep-seated . . . *trust.*

Fuck. Except nothing was based on trust. Her heart stuttered before she shoved the sensation away. Regardless of management forcing her hand with Stefan, they hadn't poisoned every piece of what was between them.

They couldn't force her to feel, dammit.

And she felt so, *so* much.

So much it threatened to well up and swallow her whole, threatened to make her run the other direction and distance herself from the potential of future hurts. The potential they might not be able to overcome an obstacle Stefan didn't even know existed.

But an inner voice reminded her he was in this too, that he seemed to feel as deeply as her, and that was enough for her anxiety to lessen, for her emotions to settle back down.

It was easier to be vulnerable when she wasn't alone.

Stefan's fingers found hers in that moment, lacing their hands together and giving hers a gentle squeeze.

"That's a good idea," he said, about the in-home nurse. "My mom would probably agree to that."

There were lines of strain around his mouth and eyes—fatigue, stress—and Brit's emotions revved again. But this time they weren't centered on her. They were focused on Stefan and how she so desperately wanted to take away his pain and worry.

"Probably?" she asked, keeping her tone light. "You seem to have a knack for hanging out with women who give you a hard time."

His gaze didn't leave the road, but the side of his mouth she could see turned up. "Pushovers are no fun."

Her laughter filled the car. "So, I'm seeing the man cave. I expect posters of swimsuit models and a boatload of black leather."

He snorted. "Then you're going to be surprised."

"*Naked* posters?" she asked, affecting a scandalized expression. "No, you probably keep the naughty stuff where your mom can't find it. Oh! I just realized!"

"What?" His question was amused.

"I'm dating a man who lives at home with his mother." She shook her head in mock-reproof. "I really need to make better life choices."

Stefan's eyes shot to hers, his smile soft, his expression warm.

"You're both ridiculously cute and completely transparent. But I appreciate the moment of lightness. And"—his smile transformed, went a little wicked—"don't think I didn't see those magazines with shirtless male celebrities in your hotel room."

"*That* is a completely different situation."

"Oh? How so?"

Well, shit. "It's . . ."

"I'll save you," he said, turning into the driveway of a neatly kept bungalow.

It was a bit modern for her taste, with a flat roof and wide windows, but there was no doubt it was well cared for.

"Naked men and naked women are not all that different and also . . . we're here."

They got out of the car—Stefan snagging her duffle from her

before she could toss it over her shoulder—and walked up the driveway.

"You don't park in the garage?"

He had what she thought of as the typical athlete's car, a sleek Mercedes with a big engine, butter-soft leather seats, and enough gadgets to make her dizzy.

It put her crappy, little Toyota to shame.

"My mom parks in the garage."

If she hadn't already fallen for him, that matter-of-fact statement would have done it.

"Come on," he said, and she trailed him up the two steps to the small porch. Someone had left on an exterior light, and Brit could just make out a set of chairs and a small table on one side of the structure.

What would it be like to sit outside on a lazy Sunday morning and drink coffee, do the Sudoku?

The Sudoku?

It was strange it hadn't hit her before that moment, maybe not exactly surprising, considering everything else that had led to her and Stefan's relationship and the whirlwind of emotions since.

But Brit had been so wrapped up in the guilt and then in her reaction to him—the flaming desire—that she hadn't really digested the fact that she liked Stefan.

No. That she'd fallen *in love* with him.

So deeply that her daydreams had shifted. Instead of fantasizing about playing in front of a crowded arena, of hoisting a silver cup, she was thinking about lazy mornings in Domestica.

Part of her said those feelings were okay, a normal course of human nature and that she could afford to focus on *something* besides hockey.

The bigger piece was panicked.

She couldn't afford to let off the gas now, couldn't risk losing her dream. Not now. Not so close to completion.

Plenty of people had relationships as professional athletes. It was a job, after all.

But this wasn't just a relationship. This was a tangled mess of deceit and intense sexual attraction.

And somewhere along the way her heart had gotten involved.

Shit.

Shit!

She should leave, fly back to the team, and—

Slightly roughened hands cupped her cheeks.

Brit started to pull away, needing the distance. But Stefan didn't let her.

Those fingers slid into her hair, threaded through the blond locks, and pulled her against his chest.

"Thank you," he murmured after a moment, "for being here."

The panic began to ebb, the racing beat of her heart slowing, matching the steady pace of his.

A moment later, he'd shut the front door to the house and snagged her hand. "You need to get back to the team."

Brit let him tug her down the porch steps and back toward the car before his words processed. That was what she wanted.

Right?

Except what was she going to do now? Fly back across the country, back up for a game when she would be too exhausted to perform well. Knock down the kid called up for a chance at an NHL game.

She'd been that kid too many times, didn't want to take that opportunity away. Not even if she had to pay dearly for it later.

"No," she said. "I'm here—"

"I promised myself . . ." Stefan said, towing her forward. " . .

.that I wouldn't do this. Wouldn't do anything to screw up your dreams. It's amazing you came . . . *so damned amazing* . . . but I can't let you take the chance."

His words—his actions—calmed her.

She reached up to slide her arms around his neck and kissed him.

She poured all she had into that kiss. Every fear, every feeling, every bit of the blazing heat that boiled just beneath the surface anytime she was near him.

No more panic attacks. What she had with Stefan was important, valuable, and she was going to grab onto it.

Maybe it would be her happy ending. Maybe it would bring nothing more than a broken heart.

But at least she would know.

Looking back, she would know that she had explored the potential of what might be.

Only when her brain screamed for oxygen did she drop her arms. Grasping his hand, she picked up her duffle from where he'd dropped it to the ground then walked back to the front door.

"It's enough," she said, "that you were willing—" She broke off, shook her head. "The promise is enough. Later, we can argue, but for now, let's eat and recover."

FORTY-SEVEN

Stefan

VULNERABLE.

Stefan was feeling remarkably vulnerable with Brit in his home, which made him a total baby. But if there was ever a day for a free pass . . .

Even now, the fear still gripped him, still made his insides feel like shards of ice.

The flight home had been interminable, the longest of his life. Every worry, every shoulda-woulda-coulda cycling in his mind like Sisyphus and his perpetual boulder pushing.

Finally making it to the hospital and finding his mother exhausted but coherent had made his eyes burn in relief.

He'd stayed with her until she'd kicked him out for some *real* rest, not wanting to go even then, but knowing that arguing with her not only didn't do any good, but also only tired her further.

Stefan glanced over at the sound of Brit coming into the kitchen. They'd slapped together some PB&Js and scarfed them down before she'd gone off to change for bed.

"Everything okay?" he asked.

She nodded, and he couldn't get over how young she looked with her hair pulled back, her skin slightly pink and makeup free. The first word that came to mind was *angelic*.

The second was *his*.

A woman who would soon be in *his* bed.

Except . . . that wasn't what this was about. Brit had come back to help him, to show support, and, fact was, they weren't ready for that step yet.

No matter the wood he was sporting at just the thought of her in his bed, naked between his sheets. He bit back a curse—

"I'll sleep on the couch." His house had only three bedrooms: his, his mother's, and a third that had been converted into his office.

Brit frowned, walked across the room, and glared up at him. "Do you *want* to sleep on the couch?"

Fuck no. He didn't. "It's fine."

"Uh. No," she said, "it's not fine. It's stupid."

"I don't want to take advant—"

"Oh for Christ's sake, stop playing the staid and moral hero of the romance novel that is our lives. If I didn't want to be in your arms tonight, I would have let you put me on a plane back to the team." She hesitated and a hint of indecision slid across her face. "But if you'd rather have your space . . ."

This woman was seriously going to be the death of him.

She'd always drawn him in. He'd always thought her beautiful. But it was so much more than just attraction. It was fire. Kindness. A good heart and a spine of steel. A dash of innocent.

So, *hell yes,* he wanted to have her in his arms. Stefan wanted that and so much more.

He wanted to kiss every inch of her skin, to lick and suck and bite, to taste her . . . everywhere.

"No," he said. "I don't want space."

With a single step, he pulled her against his chest and slanted his mouth across hers, suckling her bottom lip before sweeping his tongue into her mouth and plundering it with a kiss that expressed how he felt very much the opposite.

Space? No.

He wanted nothing between them. Not now. *Not ever.*

After releasing her mouth and pressing a line of kisses across her jaw, down her throat, he tucked an arm around her waist and led Brit to his bed.

Where they stared at each other awkwardly.

Her gaze flicked to the bed, and she bit her lip. Paired with her cloud-patterned fleece pajamas, she looked sweet enough to lick.

"What side do you—"

In a swift move, he closed the space between them and swept her into his arms.

She squealed, a shockingly feminine sound that made him smile, and began to protest. Except he'd already pulled back the bedspread and tossed her atop the sheets.

His shoes were off a moment later, followed by his pants and socks. Barely a heartbeat passed before she was back in his arms.

"Wait," she murmured before squirming from his embrace and sliding off her pajama bottoms. "These are too hot to sleep in."

His brain short-circuited.

If before he'd merely been turned on, now he was starving for her. Seeing her ass barely contained by pale pink silk, witnessing a peekaboo of flesh as her tank top rose an inch, feeling the soft skin of her thighs against his shredded Stefan's control to the finest filament.

She'd accused him of being a hero earlier, but with her in his arms, lithe muscles and delicate curves pressed against him, he was feeling decidedly wicked.

As if she heard every thought in his mind—or probably more likely felt the raging boner tenting his boxers—Brit rotated to face him and stroked a hand gently across his jaw.

"Tomorrow, hotshot," she said. "Tomorrow you can prove to me that you know how to use that . . . rifle?" Her mouth turned up before she yawned. "I'm looking for a suitably dirty euphemism, but I'm just too tired."

Her head snuggled against his chest, blond hair that smelled of roses and apples catching on the stubble of his jaw.

If he had been the only one tired, Stefan probably would have pressed on.

But Brit had called upon his every protective instinct from the very beginning. She was tired, and even if he hadn't been bone-wearingly exhausted, he would have still done the same thing . . .

Wrap her in his arms, tug her close, and hold her as she slept.

He dreamt of a blond angel who made him feel so, so much.

IT WAS AMAZING, he thought, when he woke hours later, that there was never any question of where he was, of who was in his bed.

Brit was in his arms where she belonged, and everything was right in the world.

He savored the moment, for just a few heartbeats, before carefully reaching one arm over to his nightstand.

Somehow he'd ended up on his back, Brit sprawled across him blanket-style, one of his hands cupping his favorite ass in the entire world.

Yeah. Definitely not a hardship.

Resisting the urge to massage, he snagged his phone and checked his messages.

It was just after seven, which meant they'd barely slept five hours, but he needed to make sure all was fine with his mom.

He scrolled through his notifications, saw a text sent not fifteen minutes before.

Discharging this afternoon. I don't want to see you before noon.

The order made him smile.

I'll come in whenever I want, Mom. I'm an adult and therefore order-proof.

The " . . ." signifying her typing a response popped up on his screen.

You'll always be my baby.

A pause before another message came through.

Therefore I'm forever allowed to give you orders.

. . .

He snorted then replied.

Love you. See you at noon.

"Your mom seems great," the sleep-rumpled voice came from just below his chin.

"Did I wake you?"

Brit shook her head then tilted it back so she could meet his gaze. "I was just dozing. I didn't mean to . . . eavesdrop, if that's even possible with text messages." She nodded at his phone. "Sorry. I should have let you know I was awake."

His lips twitched, along with his fingers . . . and not the ones on his phone. "You mean, take away my fun of holding onto *this*?"

Her breath hitched. "You make a good point."

"I know," he said and bent to kiss her.

"Wait!" She threw up a hand and thrust it between their mouths.

"What?"

Her eyes darted to his and away. "Don't you need to go to the hospital?"

"You didn't see that part?"

"No." She shook her head. "I mean, yes I did. But—"

"But my mom is a force," he told her. "I've learned to pick my battles, and this isn't one I want to fight. I'm not waiting until noon, but we don't need to rush over."

"Oh."

He set his phone down on the nightstand and used his free hand to grip her thigh where it was slung across his hips.

Her skin was like velvet, and the heat of her teased him, even through the layers of their underwear.

"Any other questions?"

"No."

"Good," he said, pulling her fully on top of him. "So come here."

She didn't hesitate, and it felt almost as good as the sensation of her body against his. Soft against hard, and so goddamned gorgeous she took his breath away.

Her hands grasped the top of his shoulders, her pelvis covered his—

That was pretty much when he stopped thinking, when his reservations of the night before disappeared.

There was only taste and sensation, desire and heat.

"Stefan," Brit moaned as he swept his hand under her tank top to cup one perfect, apple-sized breast. Her thighs clenched his hips, and she ground against him in the same heart-stopping, perfect rhythm that had made him come like a schoolboy two nights before.

Using his other hand, he gripped her waist, stilled her motion in a futile effort to gain control.

He was ready. She was ready. But he *needed* to make this good for her.

"Please," Brit said, squirming against his hold.

"Hold on, baby." He flipped them, pinned her to the bed. In a flash her tank top was shoved up and his mouth was on her breast.

Her fingers slid into his hair and she gripped the locks hard, almost painfully tight. But Stefan didn't care. The feeling grounded him, made him want her even more, until the burn of desire was coursing through his blood like a swollen river rushing down and escaping its shores.

He switched breasts, reveled in her moan of pleasure.

The buzzing began at the furthest reaches of his mind, a barely perceptible annoyance . . .

. . .that got louder.

And louder.

Until the fact that his phone was ringing finally penetrated his consciousness.

Brit seemed to come down to earth at the same time. "Your mom?" she gasped.

Stefan was already moving. He pushed up and picked up his phone without looking at the caller ID.

The masculine voice hit him right in the gut.

"Heard about your mother," his father said. "How much money do you need?"

FORTY-EIGHT

"WE DON'T NEED anything from you," Stefan spat into the receiver. He started to hang up, but his father's next words gave him pause.

"It's not your place—"

The man had the gall to try and reprimand him.

His absentee father, the sperm donor who hadn't made a single goddamn appearance for the first half of Stefan's life wanted to tell him what was *right*?

Stefan laughed harshly. "You gave up your place to talk to me like that about thirty years ago, *dad*," he said. "What gives you the right to interfere now?"

Silence met his eardrums. Maybe the bastard had hang up.

A soft hand touched his arm, startling him, and he stared down into Brit's concerned eyes. His anger, if not faded, then at least banked.

He cupped her cheek for a second, shook his head when she pointed at the door, a brow raised in question. "Stay," he murmured. As painful as this was—ripping open one of his oldest childhood wounds—he still wanted her next to him.

His father finally found his tongue. "You don't understand—"

"Look," Stefan said. Brit's presence enabled him to calm his tone, to be an adult when his father never had. "This isn't up for discussion. You left. You decided you had better things to do than be a father. There's no place for you in my life or Diane's." He sucked in a breath. "Just move on. You're good at that."

"I can't—"

"I *can't* have this conversation. Stay away, *Dad*," he said and hung up.

Tossing the phone onto the nightstand, Stefan struggled for calm. He wanted to punch a dozen holes in the wall, wanted to scream and yell like a child.

But it had always been like that, hadn't it?

His father could gut him faster than any other person on the planet.

Arms wrapped around his waist, and Brit pressed her cheek to his back. It was amazing how such a small thing could bring comfort.

A hug. Only a hug, and yet the torrent inside him calmed.

He waited for her to ask him questions, to push for an explanation.

She didn't.

Which was what gave him enough strength to open up.

No judgments. No matter what, he'd receive no judgments from Brit.

"My dad left my mom before I was born. He couldn't handle being a father. They married young, barely out of high school. I came along a few years later." He swallowed. "I get it was tough to have that much responsibility, but still."

Brit's breath hitched, a soft puff of heat across the bare skin of his back. "Still," she agreed then hesitated before saying, "I'm sorry."

"I'm not," he said and gently removed her arms, turning so he could look her in the eyes. "My mom was everything. She"—he got a little choked up, had to breathe, to push down the emotion—"gave me so damned much."

Delicate feminine fingers traced the light plaid pattern of his bedspread. Stefan longed to lace his hand with hers then realized she had already given him that right.

So he did.

Instantly, the jagged tears in his heart weren't quite so painful.

"When did your dad come back?" His head jerked in surprise and she gave him a soft smile. "Seemed the likely consequence, given that phone call."

"I was thirteen. He showed up at a game." The memory was imprinted on his consciousness, the day his father had tried to shred the family he and his mother had struggled so hard to create. "I looked up in the stands, saw my mom, her face pale, talking to a man."

Fear had swept through him at seeing his mother so diminished. Strong, tough, feisty as hell were the most frequent adjectives used to describe her. But in that moment, she'd been a poor impersonation of herself.

Anger had followed directly after, and he'd started to get up, ready to leave the bench to go help her.

"Luckily my coach had noticed too, and he stepped in." It still made Stefan furious, the sheer arrogance his father consistently displayed. "Turned out there was nothing to get in the middle of. My dad had decided to sue for primary custody, and since the rink was conveniently close to his house, he'd come to deliver the papers."

"Oh my God." Brit's voice shook. "Did he win?"

"No." So many people had testified, written letters and donated money. They'd even shown up in court. "A teammate's dad was a lawyer. He took mom's case for free, and he won. And, luckily, I was old enough that the judge took my desires into account."

A blond head on his shoulder, a firm squeeze of his hand . . . small acts of comfort, but ones that sewed Brit into his heart.

"I'm glad."

"Me too," he said. "My father didn't even ask to see me before he loosed his lawyers on my mom." Stefan gave a brittle laugh. "And the thing is, my mom would have let him visit, because, ultimately, she wanted me to have the chance at a father. But he decided that just because he'd made a couple of million, he'd steamroll her into it."

"What a prick."

That made a slightly more natural laugh burst out of him. "Agreed."

They sat on the bed for a few moments, Brit curled up into him, their hands laced together.

"Thanks," she eventually said.

"For what?"

"For sharing your story with me." She pushed back a stray strand of blond hair. "I know it wasn't easy."

He bent, pressed his lips to hers. "Isn't that what being in a relationship is about?"

Her teeth found her lip, bit down. "Is that what this is?"

"Is that a stupid question? Yes." He smiled when her expression turned affronted. "But I have the feeling you want me to say the words. Brit, you and me, we're together. You're different. You're *special*."

"But—"

He waved a hand. "Let me say this. I don't do connection easy. I spent so long pouring everything into the sport, trying to make up for all the sacrifices my mom made, not wanting any distractions"—he cupped her cheek—"and regardless of the multitude of supposed women the media likes to pretend are parading through my door, I don't date."

Brit leaned into his hand and closed her eyes. "Everyone told me you were a playboy," she murmured.

He snorted, and her eyes flashed open. "Ask Max if you don't believe me. I'm more of a homebody than a partier. But the media did get *something* right. I didn't do relationships . . . until *you,* I never wanted to."

"Oh." Her gaze stayed focused on him, light brown and gentle, but there was also something almost dark lingering beneath the surface. He waited for her to say more, to respond.

"Oh?" Stefan finally asked. "Just *oh*?"

He'd poured his heart out and *that* was her reaction?

"I'm processing," she said after another tense moment. "It's just . . . I've never felt like this with anyone else either. It's"—her voice dropped to a whisper, vulnerability evident in her next words—"it's actually kind of scary."

His heart squeezed tight. God. The things she did to him. "Then we'll be scared together."

"Yeah?" she asked.

"Yeah," he agreed before wrapping her in his arms and pulling her close.

They sat in peaceable silence for a few minutes, Stefan stroking one hand through her hair and just absorbing the moment. Never had it felt so right to just . . . be.

So," she said eventually, shifting so that her legs lay across his lap. His hand slid from her hair as she tilted her head back to look up at him. "Anymore skeletons in your closet?"

"None." His fingers found the bare skin of her thigh and stroked. "Well, none, unless you count the love child."

She sucked in a breath even as she smacked him across the chest. "That isn't funny."

"It's a little funny." He slid his fingers higher and longing slammed him right in the gut. "Come down here." Bend down and kiss him.

"What—"

"Never mind," he said. "I'll come to you."

Tumbling her back onto the mattress, Stefan took her mouth. He plundered, poured every bit of want and need, of affection and love into that kiss.

Brit took it all and gave back more.

She was open to him. Willing. And he was more than ready to take.

FORTY-NINE

Brit

HOLY SHIT, the man could kiss.

Brit was surrounded, her mouth inundated, her body almost on the brink of overstimulation. Stefan was on top of her and the heat of his skin seared her, even as the hard planes of his body pressed against hers.

Frankly, she was always aroused just from being in Stefan's presence. But *this?* In his bed with just two layers of cotton separating them?

Her desire had been launched straight into the atmosphere.

"Now," she said, tearing her mouth from his to gulp in a huge breath. Her heart tap-danced in her chest, her thighs quivered in anticipation. "Hurry."

She literally couldn't wait another second, didn't want to take the chance to be interrupted again. She wanted to seize the moment and . . . well, quite simply, Brit wanted to screw the man's brains out.

"I don't want to rush this," he murmured. "Not now. Not that I've finally got you here in my bed."

"We've been circling this for—*ah!*—months now . . ." She gasped when his lips found a particularly sensitive spot behind her ear, moaned when his tongue followed suit.

"We've barely known each other for *two* months." A kiss to her throat, her collarbone . . . lower . . . to her breast.

"Long enough." Teeth found her nipple through the fabric of her shirt, tugged. "God! Stefan!"

"Not for me." He sat back slightly, smirked down at her, all smooth skin and muscular lines. "I'm the man with the playboy reputation, remember? I'm the one who needs to demonstrate my *skills.*" His expression was pure male—aroused, intoxicating, swelteringly, sexy male.

Her mouth watered for a taste. "Skills . . ." Callous fingers trailed up her abdomen. " . . . I don't give a damn about skills." When she reached for him, he batted her hands away, and she released a frustrated breath. "For God's sake, Barie! Fine, you've got *skills*. Now hurry up and show them off already."

Stefan grinned before his hands found the hem of her tank top and pulled it off. "I fully intend to."

Then those hands were on her breasts, and his mouth joined the party, and Brit decided, really, who was she to stop him?

Especially since he was playing her body as if it was his very own personal instrument.

Mouth trailing south, he kissed her ribcage then her stomach, each hipbone, and finally in between.

His hot breath soaked through the cotton, almost scalding against the damp heat of her. He pressed his palm there, just firm enough that a bolt of pleasure made stars flash behind her eyes.

One tug, and her underwear were off. One shift, and his shoulders pushed her thighs wide.

Good God, the man's mouth should be sainted.

And his tongue. *Definitely* his tongue.

It took her less than a minute to explode around him. She was still gasping when Stefan reached across her, into the nightstand, for a condom.

"Last chance," he murmured when it was on and he was poised above her.

In response, she grabbed his hips, pulled him down. "Now."

He slid into her on a smooth stroke, filled her to completion, and never had she felt more right, more whole.

His groan of pleasure undid her. "God, Brit, you feel . . ."

This wasn't the time for more words. Movement. She *needed* him to move.

"Shh," she ordered, twisting her hips. Her breaths came in short bursts. "More. Now."

Stefan bent to take her mouth in a heated kiss, and then he was pounding into her.

It was hard and rough—and just exactly what she needed.

And when he reached between them to stroke her, to give her the pressure necessary to push her over the edge, she disintegrated emotionally, literally broke into pieces that he deftly caught, one by one, and somehow managed to put back together, making her more instead of less.

A heartbeat later, he shattered, and she returned the favor.

IT FELT like hours before they managed to pull themselves from the bed. After a quick shower—together, because really, what was better than hot water and an even hotter man beside her?—they dressed.

"You don't have to come, you know," Stefan said. "You can stay here, enjoy the free day."

Brit slanted a glare at him, apparently fierce enough that he raised his hands in surrender and drove them to the hospital.

Diane obviously wasn't happy to see her son.

"What are you doing here?" she snapped. "You need more rest— Oh!" Her eyes landed on Brit, hovering cautiously in the doorway.

Despite her resolve to accompany Stefan, Brit was feeling as though she'd made a mistake in coming. Who wanted visitors when they were in their sick bed?

"Come in," Diane said, gesturing Brit forward. "Oh Lord, I'm a mess." She patted her hair. "But never mind that. You're Brit, and you're even prettier in person!"

Brit, not completely comfortable with such compliments, gave an awkward shrug. "Um . . ."

Diane raised her hand, and Brit found herself taking it . . . then being tugged down into a hug. "You're supposed to say thank you when someone pays you a compliment."

"Mom," Stefan warned.

"I'm only stating the truth."

Brit snorted, and Diane glanced at her, gave a wink. "Now go get your woman a coffee. And don't come back for at least twenty minutes. We need to chat."

Stefan shook his head. "I don't think—"

"It's okay," Brit said.

He hesitated.

"Go on," she told him. "But water, not coffee, please." She couldn't stand the disgusting stuff.

Diane patted her hand. "Oh, we're going to get on just fine. I know it."

The glee in Diane's voice made Brit smile. It widened when Stefan gave a groan. "I'm in trouble, aren't I?" he asked.

"Loads." Brit retracted her hand from Diane's surprisingly strong grip, stood, and pecked him on the cheek. Her voice dropped to a whisper. "Now leave me to endure the third degree."

"You don't have—"

"Shh," she said. "I'm kidding." Well, not about the interrogation—there was no way out of it, that much was obvious—but about his mother. Brit had expected a quiet, reserved, middle-aged woman.

Diane was anything but.

Her presence filled the room, though it wasn't overbearing. Instead, she lit up the space, warmed it in that special charismatic way usually reserved for politicians and celebrity royalty.

It both calmed and unnerved. But Brit was determined to get along with Diane, if only for Stefan's sake.

And, considering the affection in her eyes when Diane looked at her son, that wasn't going to be difficult.

They had at least one huge thing in common.

They both loved Stefan.

When the man himself had left, Brit turned to Diane and raised a brow. "You have questions?"

The other woman's reply was solemn. "Only about a million or two."

They were quiet for half a second then burst into laughter.

"You're the first girl Stefan's ever brought . . . well, not *home* exactly," Diane said, once they'd gotten ahold of themselves. She rolled her eyes at the hospital room and its equipment crammed in along the walls. "You're the first woman I've met that he's dated." A pause. "Ever."

"Ever?"

Brit didn't know whether to be freaked the hell out by the statement—the pressure!—or touched.

"Ever," Diane repeated. "I only knew he wasn't a complete recluse because of the pictures on TMZ. But half of that site is utter crap, so really I only knew that he isn't *half* a recluse." She frowned at Brit. "Why do you look so perplexed?"

Brit tugged a chair over and sat down before answering. "I

guess I'm wondering what your point is." She mentally groaned and clapped a hand over her mouth only peeling back her fingers slightly to say, "I'm sorry. I didn't mean it like that—"

"Shh, honey. I know what you mean." Diane smiled, even as she laid her head back onto the pillow. Her face softened, the confident mask slipping slightly to reveal someone who was tired and perhaps a little scared. "My point is my son started living when you came into his life."

The impact of that statement took Brit's breath away.

"He's had a hard time since—" Diane sighed. "Well, he just hasn't had the easiest time, and now with this damn cancer coming back, I could just feel him slipping farther and farther away. Not feeling. Putting all of his energy into hockey and me."

Her eyes whipped up to meet Brit's, slightly glassy in the fluorescent lighting. "I don't want him to live like that, to be a robot who doesn't feel. I want him to be happy, and you seem to be able to break through the ice better than most."

Brit turned Diane's words over in her mind. They confirmed what Mandy had told her before, what she'd already sensed.

"Stefan's dad called this morning," she said. Brit didn't exactly mean it as a test, but it kind of felt like one.

Diane's breath hitched. "Oh?"

"Stefan told me what happened."

The lines of tension eased from Diane's body. Passed. "So you understand."

Brit nodded. "I understand."

She did.

Stefan's life had been rocked as a teenager. He'd almost been torn from his mom, from everything that was familiar in an act of betrayal by someone who was supposed to love him unconditionally.

"And what about your health?" she asked.

Stefan's mom gave a tired smile. "Surprisingly, despite my

current surroundings, they think I'll be fine. I was diagnosed at an earlier stage but, since it's the second time, my treatment is much more aggressive than before." She sighed. "My doctors back in Minnesota weren't bad at all—they saved my life—but they didn't have access to the same type of medical advances as here in the Bay Area. My prognosis is very good."

"I'm glad," Brit said.

"Me too," Diane replied before giving her an arch look. "I want to be around for my grandchildren."

FIFTY

THAT NIGHT, Brit took the red eye to join the Gold in Philadelphia. She went straight from the airport to morning skate, more than happy to be back on the ice.

Julian had the start, but since they were playing back-to-back again, Brit would get to play the next night in Boston.

He sat down next to her in the locker room after the skate. "Barie?"

"His mom will be okay," she said, hoping it was the truth, that Diane's determination to beat the cancer would make that outcome a reality. "Just threw him, I think."

"Yeah. It's a tough one." Sighing, Julian stood and put on his suit jacket. "Gotta go. My kids are here for the game. Let me know if you need anything."

"Will do," she said. "Have fun."

After he left, Brit sat in the emptying locker room for a few more minutes before forcing herself to finish dressing. There had been nothing from Susan or the rest of management since she'd sent the text saying she was done.

Sooner or later, there would be consequences for her defiance.

But maybe because she was still seeing Stefan, they wouldn't care. It was what they wanted, after all.

Somehow that didn't make Brit feel better.

The entire situation could implode in a hundred different ways—so many more than she'd worried about before she'd originally agreed to the mess.

Brit had a contract, but the higher ups could still trade her.

Or . . . they could release the pictures.

That was probably the worst of it, at least from her perspective.

Those photographs represented a part of her she never wanted to face again, and yet they could be all over the world in a matter of minutes.

Unfortunately, Brit knew that Susan wouldn't hesitate to use them to get what she wanted.

For now Brit was still giving her what she wanted. Kind of. Her relationship with Stefan was in the local news, had been picked up by a national market or two, and attendance at Gold games was higher than ever.

But—and here was the piece that nagged at Brit—what would Susan do now that Brit had tried to yank the reins back?

Susan wasn't the type to take a power struggle lying down, and, not for the first time, Brit wondered if she'd made a mistake.

She snorted, bent to zip up her boots. *Of course* she'd made a mistake. A fucking huge one, agreeing to the deception in the first place.

Yet a part of her couldn't ignore the fact that she probably wouldn't have made the leap with Stefan, if not for Susan's interference.

She stood and picked up her bag. The tap on her shoulder made her jump, but though her heart skipped a beat, and her tongue went dry, Brit didn't freak out by the man coming up behind her. If nothing else, if—no—probably *when* this situation blew up in her face, she could at least say that she'd bettered herself in that slight way.

"Brit?"

Mike Stewart's tentative question made her brows rise.

She turned, glanced up at him. His usual smirk wasn't in place.

"What's up, Mike?"

"I—" He'd never looked so unsure, so insecure. "Can we walk?"

"Walk?"

"Yes," he said. "You and me, go for a walk."

Her recalcitrance must have been obvious because Mike blew out a breath.

"Look, I'm trying to apologize here, okay?" he snapped.

"You are?"

"Yes." The words were ground out.

Brit gave him a beatific smile. Okay, it was tinged with a little mischievousness. "For what?"

"Oh my God," Stewart said. "Please, just walk with me for five minutes."

She paused to make him sweat it a little bit. Her shoulder had hurt like a bitch, and though she'd seen improvement in his attitude since he and Stefan had skated together in the ladder-drill-from-hell a few weeks back, it wasn't like he was Little Ms. Sunshine.

"Please," he said again.

She sighed. "Fine."

He held the door open then walked out behind her. "You heading to the hotel?"

She nodded. "Gonna catch some rest before the game."

"Good," he said. Then nothing.

They walked out of the arena and to the hotel, since it was only a few blocks away.

"You're wasting your five minutes," she told him about a block in, the wind gusting around them, the sound of traffic a distinct roar in the background.

Stewart sighed. "I find now that I'm here, it's harder than I thought."

"Apologies are never easy," she agreed.

"I was a dick." Eyes on the concrete, he kicked at a pile of leaves in their path. "A really big one."

"Yup," she said.

But it was easier knowing that Mike felt some remorse, instead of thinking he was some sort of sadistic bastard who liked to prey on woman and start shit on hockey teams.

And for all the silent-male routine he was pulling now, his eyes were alight with contriteness.

"You really were," she added when no more words came.

His lips twitched, and he shoved his hands in his pockets. "Agreed."

"So . . . you gonna tell me why?"

"Why I'm a dick to everyone, or was one to you in particular?"

Brit tilted her head to look up at him. "Both, I guess."

A breeze kicked up, cold enough that she pulled her jacket tighter around her. California had thinned her blood, made her a wimp about the temperature.

"Well, I'm a dick to everyone because that's who I am." He ran a hand over his stubbled cheek. "But I was a particular dick to you because . . ."

"I'm a girl?" she supplied. It wasn't that much of a stretch.

"God!" Mike laughed, a sharp, harsh sound. "That makes me sound even more like a dick."

"If the shoe fits," she muttered.

He glanced down at her. His expression was mostly amused, but there was something underneath—a chink in his supposed armor?—that undermined the tough exterior of his words.

"I'm going to do better," he said, and his voice took on an earnest tone. "When I'd realized what I'd done, how far I'd sunk . . ."

Mike stopped, snagged her hand, and tugged her to a halt next to him. "Hell, I could have really hurt you. Then Barie stepped in and dragged my ass across the fucking ice during that damn ladder drill because I'd been punished like a twelve-year-old boy." He frowned. "He didn't have to do that. He's too . . ."

"Too good?" Brit tried to bite back her smile. Stefan *was* a good captain and an even better man. She'd never seen him do the wrong thing.

He especially didn't do the wrong thing just because it was *easier*.

"Exactly." Stewart dropped her hand and starting walking again. She trailed next to him. "He always used to rub me the wrong way, like he was trying too hard to be everyone's friend, to ingratiate himself. Now, I realize he's just like that."

Brit chuckled as she approached to the hotel door and pulled it open. "He is," she said, stepping through. "I don't think you'll ever meet a more genuine guy."

"I'd say you haven't known him long enough to make that judgment," Stewart grumbled, "but it's the damn truth."

They walked to the elevators then hit the buttons for their rooms. Typically, the team took over a floor or two. This time, they were split onto two, Brit on the sixth and Stewart on the fifth.

As they went up, she said, "So that was your apology? You break a cardinal rule in hockey, and I don't even get an out-and-out *sorry*?"

She had the pleasure of seeing him stammer before deciding to let him off the hook. "We're good," she said.

His head swiveled toward her, and she raised both hands in surrender. "I *swear*. We're fine, but take it easy on Stefan, okay? He's had a rough go of it."

"I will." The door slid open with a *ding*, and Stewart made to step off before hesitating. "His mom?"

"Should be okay."

Stewart nodded, pushed back the elevator doors when they tried to close. "I'm going to be better," he said. "For the first time in my life, I refuse to fuck up a good thing."

Brit smiled at him, feeling another piece settle into its rightful place inside her heart. Stewart was notorious for his poor attitude. He was good, more skilled on the ice than most, but he'd never been a team player.

Maybe that was about to change.

"As cheesy as it sounds, Stewart," she said, "I believe in you."

His eyes warmed, and the smile he returned was surprising —laced with emotion and almost gentle. "Thanks, Brit. See you later."

She nodded, let the doors close, and rode up to her floor. Less than five minutes later, she'd texted Stefan and changed into her jammies.

His response made her heart feel as though it were filled to bursting with helium.

Miss you. Are you all right with how things went?

He wasn't referring to the red eye or the morning skate.

Feeling pretty fantabulous myself. You?

. . .

Not even a question. Can't wait to see you. I find that my life feels so much more complete when you're near.

Aw. Those words ensnared her heart further. The man was lethal. In a good way.

In the best way.

Her phone buzzed again.

Rest up for the game. I'll be watching.

Brit's phone rang early the next morning, and, hardly awake, she picked up.

"Do I need to ask Mr. Barie his intentions?" Allison's voice was chipper, way too much so for Brit, who hadn't gone to bed until after midnight.

She grunted and rolled over, trying to clear the sleep from her brain. "How are you, Allison?"

"Good," Blane's mother replied. "I'm just worried about my favorite daughter is all."

"You don't have any daughters," Brit said, sitting up.

"*Pish.* I've got one very special one—if not in blood then in heart." Allison's tone took on a serious edge. "And one who I'm slightly worried is going to get *her* heart broken."

"Stefan's a good man," Brit said. "The best kind."

"Then I'm happy for you, sweetheart. You deserve it." A beat then, "Okay, enough sappy stuff. For now, give me all of the locker room gossip. All of the dirt I can't get from my sources at the Bureau."

Brit obliged and listened when Allison returned the favor with family gossip. Blane was the only one of the brothers to make it into the NHL. Two of the others had been successful in the AHL, and one was a college professor.

"I'm glad the boys are doing well," she said before they hung up. "I'll try to squeeze in a visit the next time Dan is home."

"You don't worry about us, honey. Concentrate on playing well. We'll catch up once you're not so busy."

Allison had always been just like that, Brit thought later as she readied herself to take the ice. She understood the game and its demands, and not once had she faulted Brit for going after her dreams.

FIFTY-ONE

Stefan

THREE DAYS LATER, Stefan exited his room and headed for the elevator.

Brit was waiting for him.

Well, *that* particular part was a surprise, since she didn't actually know he was back.

He'd only just arrived in New York and dropped his bags in his hotel room. His mom was home from the hospital and settled, a nurse staying with her for the foreseeable future.

Management had been more than lenient with him—letting him miss four games at a critical part of the season, when the team was just starting to gel. But Stefan was the captain and knew he'd needed to get back to the team.

As hard as it had been to leave his mom, he'd gotten on the plane. Their lives needed to get back to normal, for both his mother's and his sanity, which meant he'd had to trust in the care they'd put in place.

So he was back with the team and, since tomorrow was an

off day, he was going to kidnap Brit for the night then try and talk his way into her room.

It was way better sleeping with her wrapped in his arms than sitting in a dark room all alone.

Stefan smiled as he rode the elevator up a floor and thought of what her face would look like when he'd sweet-talk her.

It wasn't even the sex—though God knew that had been fan-fucking-tastic—but because Brit had a huge heart. He'd seen it. His mom had seen it. The entire team knew it.

For the first time in his life, the thought of holding a woman's heart in his hands didn't frighten him. Stefan wanted to protect the delicate organ. To shelter it.

So he would.

The first step of that was taking care of Brit right back.

His stomach growled, reminding him of his hunger and calling an end to the sappiness that seemed to afflict him of late. He wondered what her reaction to the hole-in-the-wall restaurant would be. It wasn't fancy, but it had the best thin-crust pizza around.

He stepped off onto the floor, and a whiff of roses and apples had his body coming to full attention. Brit was just down the hall, he knew, having managed to wrestle the information from the front desk clerk earlier, and that scent—

It was hers alone.

Stefan was just about to knock on Brit's door when he heard voices. One he knew almost better than his own.

He turned from the room and started toward the sound, anticipation in every cell.

Even as he closed the distance between them, he tried not to listen, not sure if the conversation was private.

But who would have a private conversation in the hallway of a hotel?

Still, he tried not to listen. He really did.

Then he heard his name from Brit's lips.

FIFTY-TWO

"I CANNOT ALLOW you to do this," a female voice said in response. The cadence and tone was familiar, but Stefan couldn't place the sound with a face.

"I'm done," Brit said. "It's wrong. I need to tell him."

The woman's scoffed disbelief was loud.

"It's true," Brit said, and it sounded like she was chewing on glass. "I *care* about him. I can't keep doing this to him—"

"As if I give a shit about your feelings. We had a deal. Bernard—"

"I told you before, I *cannot* do this anymore. Bernard is willing to take the chance."

The other woman made a noise of disgust. "Then Bernard suffers. His *wife* suffers."

"Bernard will be fine," Brit replied. "God knows, he didn't want me to do this in the first place."

Stefan took another few steps, inched toward the voices.

"Bernard will gamble this salary like he's done with the previous six," the woman snapped. "His wife won't receive proper care, and that will be on you."

Brit went quiet, but Stefan could sense her tension, even

from the hall. "You're a monster, you know that?" she said, soft enough that he had to strain to hear.

"I may be a monster, but I'm creating a dynasty," the woman said. Her voice was clear as a bell and confident to a fault. "When people think about hockey, the first team they will think of will be the Gold."

"And if this gets out . . ." Brit said. " . . .if this thing between Stefan and me goes bad, it'll be in infamy."

His gut clenched. If *what* went bad?

"Who cares?" the woman said. "Plenty of other sports teams are infamous. We'll never become a powerhouse without blurring a few lines."

"I won't. Not anymore."

Stefan stopped outside the alcove that held a few vending machines and one icemaker. The rumble of the motor was barely enough to disguise his presence and definitely not their words.

Both women were frustrated and getting louder by the second.

"You can't—" the woman said.

"I can, and I will," Brit all but spat. "Fire me if you want. But I can't do this to Stefan." Her words were laced with so much pain that he felt the slice in his own heart. "The Gold has gotten their press. It's enough. He's dealt with *enough*."

"I'll be the one to say when it's enough," the other woman began.

"No." He stepped into the alcove.

Stefan couldn't focus on how this conversation would impact what he and Brit had been building, not at that moment. This was deeper than that, *more* than the betrayal freezing his insides.

Brit was hurting, and, no matter the truth of what was

between them, he cared about her too much to allow that to happen.

He leaned back against a vending machine. "No," he said again. "*I'll* be the one to say when it's enough."

The other woman was Susan Depratt, he realized, once he saw the perfectly coiffed grey hair and hideous pantsuit. Her eyes were furious, her lips pressed into an unflattering line.

Susan was one of the oldest board members, but also the ex-wife of Donald Depratt, the man who'd funded the Gold's journey to San Francisco.

Which meant she was powerful, connected, and not someone he would normally want to fuck with.

A disagreement with Susan usually led to a few games down in the minors or a multiple-game benching. Sometimes even a trade.

"This isn't any of your business, Barie," she said.

Despite the inherit threat in the words, Stefan bristled. It sure as fuck was.

It involved *him*. It involved Brit.

"Does Devon know?" He asked the question of Brit, completely ignoring Susan for the moment.

Her eyes were wide, and perhaps there was the slightest glimmer of tears. But Stefan couldn't focus on that.

Not right now.

He stepped toward her. "Does Devon know?"

A nod.

Dear God. How far up did this go? The GM was involved. A high-ranking board member was involved.

And Brit.

Who'd been new to the team.

Probably threatened. Or at least cajoled into . . . what?

He realized he didn't know yet.

"What exactly did they have you do?"

"It"—she shook her head—"it doesn't matter. It was wrong. I knew that from the beginning. I shouldn't have done it."

"Done *what*?" he asked.

His gut was sinking fast now, a heavy anchor pulling it down, filling the cavity with dread.

"It wasn't *all* about them," Brit said, her words coming rapid and jumbled. "I-I liked you. I didn't— I wanted to spend time—"

"Might as well tell him, girl," Susan said and there was something gleeful about her tone. "Ms. Plantain was to seduce you into a relationship so the team could get more press. But now that you know, you can help with that . . ."

His eyes slid closed on one long, slow blink.

Susan kept talking.

He ignored her, opened, and turned to Brit. "Is it true?"

Her eyes met his, fell away, clear brown pools of despair, and any hope he'd held onto until that moment disappeared like so much smoke.

But he had to hear the truth from her lips.

"It wasn't like that—" she began.

"Is. It. *True?*"

She crumpled. Her shoulders folded in. Her chin dropped to her chest.

But her voice was clear, firm even.

"Yes."

Three letters that were a knife to his heart. But the pain, the absolute eviscerating quality of that word wasn't something he could deal with. Not right then.

Sucking in a breath and burying the hurt and anger deep down, burying it deeper than he'd ever hidden his emotions before, he merely said, "Okay."

Brit's head shot up, probably surprised by the even tone of his voice.

But he was barely holding it together, barely able to hold onto the calm front he was projecting for Susan.

It *hurt*. God, it hurt. He'd opened up to Brit and—

Stefan rotated to lock glares with Susan. "This"—he gestured between himself and Brit—"is done."

She opened her mouth, probably ready to protest or threaten him.

Stefan didn't give a shit. An icy numbness was soaking into him, sweeping away the anger, partitioning it away, and, blessedly, taking the pain alongside it.

"It's over," he said, "or I'm gone from the Gold."

Brit gasped.

That was the thing. The single bargaining chip that gave him the power in this situation.

Stefan had a clause in his contract, one that would allow him to demand a trade. Before this, he never would have enacted it, because of his mother. He wanted to be close to her, wanted her with the doctors she was comfortable.

He'd also been wholly committed to the team.

But now? With this?

He sure as hell wouldn't hesitate to pull the trigger.

Susan stammered for a moment, shaking her head, pressing her lips together, then finally sighing. "Fine."

"Go."

If Susan said anything further before she left, Stefan didn't hear it.

It was just he and Brit. In the entire universe, it was only the two of them. His battered heart gave a hard squeeze at the sight of her before he shoved the traitorous emotion back down where it belonged.

Normally, she was so bright, strong, and invulnerable. But in this moment, she was diminished. Small.

Or maybe that was just his opinion of her.

The betrayal from management was one thing. The betrayal from Brit was another issue entirely.

Stefan stared at her, felt his gut twist at the agony on her face, and the emotions he'd shoved down battered at the iron door in his mind, threatened to break through and surface. He wanted—

No.

He *couldn't* look at her, couldn't be in her presence. Not after this. Not after—

It took everything in him to keep his tone light.

"Well, that was fun," he told her. "See you at practice tomorrow."

"Stefan—"

He whirled away from the entreaty in her eyes, from the small part of his soul that refused to be caged, that wanted him to talk to her, to figure it out together.

To fight for them.

No.

Hurrying, he strode past the elevator, pushed into the corridor for the stairs, and walked.

He walked the streets of New York until the city got quiet. He walked until the shredded organ that had been his heart iced over.

It was only then that he went to the arena.

And he ran the stairs.

Up. Down. Up. Down.

Up.

Down.

FIFTY-THREE

Brit

IT WAS hell having Stefan in front of her. He wouldn't look at her, or at least not more than playing hockey together required.

But she needed to tuck her emotions away, shove them deep down and lock them the fuck up.

The puck didn't stay out of the net just because she was heartsick.

Using the flat of her stick, she pushed the extra buildup of snow into her goal, took a sip of water, then turned to ready for the faceoff.

The ref gave a sharp trill of his whistle, dropped the puck, and the game was on.

Brit watched them play through narrowed focus, shifting from side to side in her net as the players moved across the ice.

It was a tough game, with lots of shots, and she saw the breakaway forming even before her team did.

Stefan pinched—cutting hard to the net to intercept the Islanders' attempt at clearing their end of the ice. But in a rare moment of miscommunication, Max didn't slide back to cover for him.

Thunk. Stefan's shot was blocked, and it deflected out of the zone, one of the Islanders' forwards racing toward it, with her team chasing hard behind.

They wouldn't catch up.

Barely a second later, the Islanders' player was bearing down on her.

He deked—shifted the puck on his stick to try and fake her out . . . so much so that Brit had to restrain herself from rolling her eyes. The extra and unnecessary movements of that vulcanized disc of rubber as he carried it to the net were both showy and stupid.

No way would he get off a good shot now.

The player cut hard to the left, but she knew his game by then.

With a sharp thrust of her stick, she poked the puck away. It bounced into the corner where Max corralled it then passed it up to Blue. And just that quickly, play was tearing the other direction.

During intermission, Stefan glanced at her and said, "Good save." There was no warmth, no fluff or affection.

It was the most neutral praise she'd ever received.

"Thanks. I—"

Except Stefan had already turned away, and then Bernard came in to the room to discuss things the team needed to improve. Ten minutes later they were back on the ice.

They won, but victory had never tasted so empty.

Six weeks later, Julian broke his ankle, shattering the bones and tearing ligaments. It was a huge injury, probably career-ending.

Brit stepped in and carried the shaken team to a hard-fought victory.

And then seven straight more.

The wins put the Gold at the top of their division and second in the conference. For a team that had been the bottom of the barrel only the season before, it was huge progress.

The stands were full. The team was happy.

Brit was not.

She'd gotten everything she'd ever wanted, and yet . . . it felt empty.

A bunch of the team was going out tonight, and while she'd dutifully carted her butt out to all of the team events, even though she felt like sitting at home in her cozy, little apartment, watching *Pride and Prejudice* on repeat and gorging on mint chocolate-chip ice cream, this one she couldn't face.

Stefan was coming.

Things had been smooth between them. Polite. Cool and distant.

The night after he'd overheard her and Susan arguing, Brit had tried to apologize.

He'd replied, a charming smile on his lips, his eyes utterly aloof, *"Totally understandable, Brit. We all get pulled into things sometimes. No hard feelings."*

Then he turned his back on her and engaged Max in conversation.

She'd let that go, not wanting to draw him into a confrontation just before the game, but every single time she tried to talk to him, he'd had the same reaction.

Casual dismissal.

It would have been so much easier if he'd gotten angry, if

he'd yelled and screamed. This fucking polite conversation was going to be the death of her.

But she didn't know what to say, didn't think she had the right to be pissed off—not when she created the mess, not when she was the one in the wrong.

So she kept trying, attempting to glimpse any sign of the kind, caring man she'd known intimately for the best weeks of her life.

"Coming, Brit?" Blane called from across the locker room.

"Not tonight," she called back as she slipped into her sweats and a t-shirt.

"No?" Stewart asked as he undressed next to her.

Stefan had moved lockers, taking the space adjacent to Max's and bumping Stewart over near her. It would have been a logical move for Stefan—he and Max were D-partners, after all—except for the fact that he'd done it directly after New York.

The team wasn't blind. They'd seen the tension between her and Stefan before the game against the Islanders, and switching spots was like waving a very juvenile red flag.

Brit had gotten several sideways, sympathetic looks, a few *"Are you okays?"* but, other than that, her teammates had done very much the same thing as they had when she'd first started dating Stefan.

They'd ignored it.

Which she could kiss them all for. Because, even though they had to be gossiping about her and Stefan's obvious breakup, she hadn't heard a whisper.

To do so would've have been salt in an already open wound.

Stewart cleared his throat, and Brit blinked. "Sorry," she said. "No, I'm not going. Mandy wants to work on me, and then I need a little girl time."

He frowned, and she could almost see the wheels turning as he processed her words. "Is that code for crying?"

She laughed, and it sounded a little rusty. When was the last time she'd genuinely laughed? "Normally, no." She twisted her lips, shrugged. "Tonight? Maybe."

"It pains me to ask this," Mike said with a grimace, "but do you need to talk about it?"

"Hell no." Brit didn't need to hash out her mistakes for the thousandth time. She'd done that plenty on her own. "Sorry," she hurried to say when she saw his face cloud slightly. Could she have hurt his feelings? Mike was usually so secular that she would have thought it impossible. But he'd turned over a new leaf too, was probably feeling as fragile as she was. "I just want to forget for a little while, you know? I'm tired of thinking about it every waking minute."

"I get that." He bent to tie his shoe.

"Mike," she said.

His eyes found hers.

"Thanks."

A grunt paired with a shrug was her only response before he packed up and left, but it was enough to quiet the pain inside her.

At least for a few minutes.

She shoved her stuff into her bag then left it in her locker and went down the hall to PT.

Mandy waved her in. "You look miserable."

"Thanks." Brit snorted and lay on the table. "You're a good friend."

"The best," Mandy said, heavy on the sarcasm. "And if *you* were a good friend, you'd let me come over and binge on ice cream and bad reality TV."

"My place is small, and going out to dinner is easier," Brit said. "Plus, no clean up."

"That part is true, at least. But it's not the real reason you don't want me to come over."

She and Mandy had been out a few times. They'd laughed a lot and bonded over cooking shows and love for all things *Doctor Who,* but she hadn't realized Mandy had seen how much she'd been hurting.

Firm hands began working over the muscles of her shoulder, hard enough to make Brit grit her teeth. "Good friends don't let friends eat extra calories just for solidarity," she said, trying a different tack.

"Bullshit," Mandy said and hit a spot that made Brit hiss in pain. "That's half the reason to be friends with someone. Guiltless extra calories."

Brit sighed. She'd had weeks to shore up her defenses against the pain inside of her, to try and bury it deep. Not that it had worked, since both Mandy and Mike had seen right through her.

But apparently, no one was going to let her denial slide today.

She could only be thankful Dan was on assignment, that she and her brother had exchanged just a few emails because of that.

For once, the distance was a good thing, because Dan didn't know anything was wrong and hadn't come storming home to beat up Stefan.

The Gold needed their captain healthy and uninjured at this point in the season.

"I'm not ready to talk about it."

"That might be the first honest thing you've said tonight," Mandy muttered. "But seriously," she said, "when you're ready . . ."

"Noted." There was a moment of quiet. "Thanks."

"Anytime," Mandy said before chatting her up about all of the latest team and television gossip.

An hour later, her muscles sore, but much the better for it, Brit returned to the locker room.

Her phone buzzed, and she glanced down to see a number on the screen she would have never expected to see. Worry tore through her, and she scrambled to answer, her fingers trembling.

"Hello? Diane?"

"Could you come over?" Stefan's mother asked. "I tried Stefan, but he's not picking up, and it's my nurse's night off."

It wasn't even a question. "I'll be there as soon as I can." She started to say goodbye then hesitated. "Do I need to call an ambulance?"

"No, I'm just feeling a little shaky," Diane said. "And I don't think it's safe for me to be alone. There's a spare key under the bear statue on the porch."

"Okay, don't move. I'll be there soon."

Brit hung up, canceled on Mandy with a promise to explain later, and raced to her car. The plus with moving was that the media had backed off enough for her to drive again.

Two minutes later, she was out of the lot and en route to Stefan's house.

Fifteen minutes beyond that, she was at Stefan's front door, reaching under the statue for the spare key.

It wasn't two minutes after, she smelled a rat.

Diane was sitting at the kitchen table, two plates of delicious-smelling pasta in front of her.

"Hi, dear," she said when Brit hesitated in the doorway. "Come in. Sit down."

"You're not sick," Brit blurted, her heart in her throat. She shouldn't be here. Not like this. If Stefan came home . . .

Diane smoothed down the scarf tied over her hair. "Not sick," she said. "Sorry about the deception, but I didn't know how else to talk to you."

Brit took a step into the kitchen. Stopped. "If you're all right, then I really should go."

"I am all right," Diane said, "or at least physically. My treatment is finished. No more ER visits, and all the tests are clear so far. Only time will tell on that front, of course, but I feel better than I have in years." She shrugged. "That's something."

"Yes, it is." Brit bit her lip. "I'm so glad."

"Me too," Diane said, then chuckled when Brit's stomach growled loud enough to shake the house. "But enough about me. You've already come this far, why don't you at least eat?"

"I shouldn't."

But she walked to the table anyway and sat down, drawn by the wonderful smell of the pasta and maybe also a desire to alleviate some of the deeply rooted loneliness that had filled her since Stefan had found out about her deception.

The first bite of the pasta was heaven on her tongue, tangy and spicy and loaded with glorious carb after carb. "Oh, my God, this is incredible." She moaned between bites.

"Baked ziti," Diane said. "My specialty." She let Brit eat for a few minutes before saying, "You know, Stefan's never been good with sticking through the hard times, me and hockey aside. I love my son, and God knows, he's been so darned good to me, but the first sign of a bump in the road, and he cuts ties."

What had driven them apart was way more than a bump.

Try the freaking Grand Canyon.

But—

"What happened between us wasn't Stefan's fault," she said. "It's totally on me."

Diane smiled gently. "Nothing is one-hundred percent, sweetheart."

"Trust me when I say this one was."

Diane frowned, opened, and closed her mouth a few times before sighing. "I won't ask you to tell me, because that is something between the two of you," she said. "But I worry about him. He's unhappy."

"I know." Brit voice's cracked. "It's my fault. I'm sorry."

"Oh, honey." Smooth fingers grasped hers, squeezed gently. "I'm not trying to make you feel bad. It's just that Stefan . . . he's always been able to hide his emotions well. Even when his dad tried to take him, Stefan was calm and confident. Just said he wouldn't go, no matter what. But I've never seen him like this."

A knot of dread curled in Brit's gut.

"He put his fist through the wall in the study. Has been beating the punching bag in the garage to death." Diane shook her head. "*This* is different."

Brit dropped her forehead to her free hand and sighed, her heart hurting so much more than she would have ever thought possible. "Stefan's so cold anytime I talk to him. I don't know how to get through, how to make him understand that I'm so incredibly sorry."

"The thing about Stefan is that you just have to keep at it, keep battering at his walls. You have to almost force him to feel—"

The front door slammed open, and Brit's head shot up.

"Mom? Are you okay?"

"Tell me you didn't call him," Brit said.

"I didn't call him," Diane murmured. "I *texted* him."

Oh, for fuck's sake.

"Mom?"

Brit tried to pull her hand free. To stand and flee . . . somewhere. But Diane was surprisingly strong for a cancer patient.

"You're seriously devious."

"Sometimes." Diane smiled broadly. Then called, "In here."

"I got your message—"

Stefan stuttered to a stop in the doorway.

FIFTY-FOUR

"WHAT ARE YOU DOING HERE?" he bit out.

Well, there was the anger Brit had wanted.

"I called her," Diane said, standing and taking the empty plates to the sink. They made a soft *clink* against the cast iron, but Brit found that she couldn't keep her attention on the other woman.

Rather, it kept drifting back to Stefan, standing so stiffly in the doorway.

A soft hand on her shoulder made Brit jump, her heart in her throat. But just as quickly as it had come on, she pushed the tendrils of fear aside.

She wasn't that person any longer. And despite her cowardice of the last weeks, she wasn't the type to not fight for something she wanted.

Yeah, she had plenty of *she's-not-worthy* vibes bouncing around in her mind, but not fighting for Stefan, just giving up—

Now she saw that wasn't an option.

"Take a chance, sweetheart," Diane whispered as she moved toward the other room. "Batter at those walls."

Brit nodded.

"Stefan," she said, once they were alone, "we need to talk."

He sighed, walked across to the fridge, and pulled out a beer. His demeanor was still distant, but there was a softer edge to his words, as though the ice surrounding him had melted slightly. It gave her strength to push on when he asked, "What's there to talk about?"

"A whole fucking lot."

Pop. He removed the bottle top and threw it in the trash before taking a long swig of the beer. "Yeah, I guess there is."

"Look," she said. "What I did was all kinds of screwed up. I should have refused, and, barring that I should have at the very least told you what management—what *I* was doing. It's just—" She blew out a breath and swallowed down the tightness in her throat. "They had the pictures, Stefan. And then they threatened Bernard—"

"I know," Stefan interrupted. "Bernard told me."

"He t-told you?"

"Yup." He sat down across from her. "Why are you here, Brit?"

"Your mom—"

"I get that. But why stay?"

Her soul itched to round the table, to crawl into his lap and revel in the feel of his arms around her. Never had she felt safer, more whole, than just being held by him.

"I wanted to—"

Damn. Now her freaking eyes were getting all misty. She didn't cry. She was a badass hockey player. Tears weren't on the freaking menu.

"I wanted to make things right. I did wrong, I know that." She bit her lip. "I guess I was hoping . . . I just want another chance at us."

Stefan didn't look at her, just stared at the floor for a long, quiet moment. But when he did finally meet her eyes, her heart sank down to the floor.

"I don't think we can, baby." The endearment tore her insides to shreds. "What we had was something special, but now there's this thing, this *betrayal* between us, and I don't know how to get past it."

It was killing her to not touch him, so Brit stretched across the table, laid her hand atop his.

He pulled back.

Crack. She actually felt the fissure form right in the center of her heart.

"We just do it," she said, pressing her rejected hand to her chest in a feeble attempt at holding the broken pieces together. "One day at a time. It's not like I cheated. I made a bad mistake, but it was for all the right reasons."

"And what happens the next time someone threatens you with the pictures? Will you sleep with *them?* How far will you go to hide what happened?" He shook his head. "I can't be with someone who's got skeletons. Not like the ones you have. Not when they affect our life together."

She stood, paced the floor. "*Fuck,* Stefan," she said, finally finding her mad. "*Everyone* has skeletons. That's part of being in a relationship with someone. You accept their faults. But even *you* aren't perfect. The crap with your dad, that's a pretty big skeleton."

Brit knew she'd said the wrong thing the moment the words rolled off her tongue. It wasn't that they weren't the truth, but rather that this was an absurdly wrong time to say them.

The doorbell rang just as Stefan opened his mouth to reply, and she watched as the noise made drew him back into reality, erasing any warmth she might have gained with a deliberate, icy cold.

"I've got it," Diane called.

"You need to go."

Brit shivered at the frost in Stefan's tone, knew she'd pushed him too far.

Resigned, she nodded and started to leave the room. The door slamming shut with an abrupt cry from Diane made Brit hurry into the hall.

"Are you okay?" She rushed to the woman's side. Her face was pale, and, when she swayed, Brit led her to the couch before sitting beside her.

"Stef—" she began.

But he was already there, kneeling in front of his mother. "What is it?"

The doorbell rang again. Followed by a loud banging.

Stefan stood, and Diane grabbed at his hand. "Don't."

His face hardened. He pulled away, walked to the door, and flung it open.

An older man with salt-and-pepper hair and an expensive-looking business suit stood there. When he saw Stefan, a self-satisfied smirk curved his features.

"Your father wanted you to hear the good news first." The man thrust an envelope into Stefan's hand, turned, and left.

Stefan closed the door.

"Who was that?" Brit asked into the silent room.

"My ex-husband's right-hand man." Diane's voice was a little steadier. She pulled her hand free and stood. "I'm sorry. It just took me by surprise, seeing him after all these years."

Stefan tossed the envelope into a nearby trashcan.

"Aren't you going to"—Brit gestured toward the wastebasket—"you know . . ."

"No," he ground out. "I don't give two shits about what my father wants." He fixed Brit with a fierce gaze. "You need to go."

"I know." She rose and walked to the front door.

Diane cleared her throat when Brit reached the trashcan.

She glanced back over her shoulder.

Diane nodded at the envelope. "Read it."

Brit hesitated.

"Please."

She picked up the envelope.

"Mom—"

"Shh," Diane told Stefan. To Brit, "Open it."

With trembling fingers, Brit obliged her and tore back the flap. Inside was a legal document saying—

Holy shit.

"What is it?" Diane asked.

"Stefan's father bought the team."

FIFTY-FIVE

Stefan

STEFAN CROSSED the room and snatched the paper out of Brit's hands. He rapidly scanned the document, his gut sinking more and more with each word.

His father *had* bought the team.

Somehow his paternal sperm donor had managed to skirt all of the media outlets, to not let a single trace of a rumor out and . . . he'd bought the Gold.

"*Fuck!*" Stefan turned and slammed his fist into the wall. "Why the fuck can't he just leave us alone?"

Gentle fingers on his shoulder made him stiffen. His gaze snapped to Brit's. "Why are you still here?"

Those brown eyes widened with hurt, but the resultant slice of guilt didn't stop him. He pressed on. "Why, Brit? So you can get off on manipulating me some more? Why don't you fuck Blane instead? At least he's in love with you."

"*Stefan!*" His mother's voice held a tone he hadn't heard since he was a sixteen-year-old boy.

It made him see reason.

"Hey, I'm sorry—" No matter what she'd done, Brit didn't deserve to be treated like shit. He took a step in her direction.

She backed away.

Her bottom lip wobbled, but her chin was high, her shoulders squared. She looked over at his mother. "Call me anytime, Diane."

His mom rose from the couch, pulled Brit into a hug, and whispered something in her ear.

Red-hot envy inundated his nerves, and the ice around his emotions cracked and gave way. Regardless of everything, *he* wanted to be the one holding Brit, murmuring in her ear . . .

Well, now he'd gone and thoroughly blown any chance of that, wounding her time and again, rejecting her when she wanted to move forward.

Brit stepped out of his mother's arms and slid past him, obviously careful in her efforts to not touch him.

Stefan stopped her with a hand on her arm anyway. She stiffened but didn't pull back.

That was something, right?

When she flicked her eyes downward, he couldn't help but follow suit. Her arm looked so small encased in his fingers, so delicate and fragile.

Kind of like her expression.

"Brit," he said. "Please. Just—"

That spurred her into motion. With a tug, she extricated herself. "I've had enough for tonight, thank you." Cool, calm words that did nothing to hide the wealth of pain inside her heart.

Pain he'd caused.

He'd never even considered how guilty Brit must have felt through the whole relationship debacle, but if it was one iota of what he experienced in that moment, Stefan realized he might finally understand.

There had been occasional flashes of agony, of a deep, dark secret she was hiding from him, sometimes even during their happiest moments.

Feeling as he did then . . . well, it gave him clarity to what she'd gone through.

"Brit, I—" he said.

"That's enough." His mother's tone brokered no argument, but he might have still pushed the issue if not for the relief in Brit's expression at the interjection.

"Okay," he said and blew out a breath. "Just *okay*."

Stefan couldn't bear to watch as she left. Instead he went to the kitchen, grabbed another beer, and drank.

Then another. And another.

And another.

Sometime in the night, he made it to his bedroom and collapsed onto the mattress without bothering to strip.

It felt like ten whole minutes had passed when voices penetrated his consciousness.

"I don't care if he's sleeping—"

His door slammed into the wall with a bang. Stefan's eyes snapped open, and he groaned as a million stabbing knives jabbed at his brain.

"Wh—?"

A splash of water had him sputtering, but it also had him fully awake.

If he'd thought he couldn't feel any worse . . .

His father, Pierre Barie, was standing two feet away, an empty glass in his hand.

"You bastard," his mom spat. She rushed toward him and tripped on the rug.

Stefan lurched forward, but his father caught Diane before she fell.

"Let me go," she said and wriggled out of his grip. She

shoved at Pierre's shoulder. "How could you? After everything?" A rasping breath. "You barge in here and—" Her sob sounded as though it were torn from her.

Stefan was already moving. His mother hadn't cried when the doctors told her she had cancer. Not the first time. Nor the second. She hadn't even cried during the entire drawn-out court process of his teenaged years.

In fact, he'd never seen his mom cry, except while reading her trademark romance novels or watching sappy romantic movies.

But in less than two minutes, Pierre had achieved the feat.

Stefan's hands clenched into fists as he held his mother. She was crying hard, wrenching, tearing sobs that hurt his soul.

The pain. There was *so much pain* in them.

"Shh, mom," he said, holding her tighter, releasing his fists to stroke her back. "It's okay. We'll be all right. I'll just ask for a trade—"

She gasped in a breath, sobbed louder.

And he was getting frantic. Tears were one thing, but this hysterical crying was something else. She was going to make herself sick.

Stefan's father—no, *Pierre*—knelt next to them.

"Let me," he said.

Stefan snorted. "Just go. You've already done enough."

His mom cried harder.

"Shh . . . Mom. Come on, it'll be okay."

A firm hand on his shoulder had him glaring up at Pierre.

"You smell like you took a bath in a keg," his father said harshly. "Go shower and leave your mother to me—"

Stefan shifted, pulled his mom closer. "I'm not—"

"I've only seen her like this once before, son," Pierre said, "but I know what she needs."

The sound of Pierre's voice seemed to soothe his mom. She

quieted a little, slumped against Stefan, even as tears still continued to pour.

That slight calming was enough to make Stefan waver.

"Come on, son," Pierre coaxed. "Let me do this for her."

He was about to refuse, just on principal. But then Pierre put his hand on his mother's back, and she reached for him, turned to crawl into his embrace.

A jagged pulse of pain—of jealousy—lanced Stefan's heart before he managed to tuck it away. If his father was what his mother needed . . . he could suck it up.

Pierre ignored Stefan when he crossed to the dresser to grab some clothes and went into the bathroom to shower.

By the time he came back out, less than ten minutes later, his mother was sitting on the floor, her back against the mattress, her face red and splotchy.

But she wasn't crying.

She glanced up when Stefan came into the room, her eyes flicking between him and Pierre, who was holding up the far wall. His father looked totally together and distinguished, despite the wrinkled and tear-stained suit jacket.

"We need to talk," his mother said without preamble. "It's time you had the whole truth."

And that was when the bottom fell out of Stefan's world.

FIFTY-SIX

"YOUR SISTER DIED when she was two years old," his mother said.

Stefan staggered, barely made it to the mattress before his legs collapsed.

"I was newly pregnant with you, not even eight weeks along. I was so tired." His mother shook her head. "Pierre was traveling for business. I hadn't even told him the good news, wanted to do it in person."

Agony was stitched into every syllable of the words, and his subsequent pain was a punch to the gut. He wanted to take it from his mother, to help her—

She pressed on.

"Between Sophia's teething and the hormones, I was barely making it through the days. I was nauseous all the time, exhausted."

Stefan scrambled to comprehend, to understand. Because . . . he knew the other shoe was about to fall.

"Then I fell asleep one day while Sophia was napping—"

He sucked in a breath. Dear God, what had happened?

"She woke before I did and I guess I didn't hear her. Or maybe she didn't call out for me that day." Diane swallowed, her voice barely a whisper. "I don't know. I only remember hearing the crash and seeing her fall down the stairs." Her breathing hitched, but there were no more tears. "Sophia died in the hospital not even a week later. She'd hit her head, and the doctors couldn't get the swelling down."

Stefan sat very still, trying and failing to keep the images from his brain.

Of a child falling, his mother devastated, and his father—

"Where were you?" He turned, wished he could shoot fire from his eyes at Pierre. "During all of this—"

"Your father came back," Diane said. "As soon as I called him, he was on the next flight home. But the moment Sophia was gone, so was he." She paused. "I hadn't even told him about you."

Stefan flinched back, the words almost a physical blow to his senses.

His father hadn't known?

He hadn't abandoned Stefan—

No. Just his mother, who'd been ravaged by the death of her daughter.

The information didn't change his view of his father. Pierre was still a selfish, unfeeling bastard. "It doesn't matter. *He left.*"

His mom rose and sat next to Stefan on the bed. "Yes, your father left," she said, "I didn't know where he'd gone. There were no cell phones then, no Internet to track or emails. I tried leaving messages at the hotels I saw on our joint credit card statement, but then he stopped using the card." A pause. "And then I had you."

He stared into his mom's eyes, the hurt welling inside him, threatening to overtake everything.

"But why didn't you tell me?"

Diane stared down at her hands for a long moment. "There is really no good excuse except that it was so much easier for me to pack it all away. To box up the pain and never feel it again." His mother pressed a hand to her stomach. "It hurt so much to lose Sophia, but then you were there. My bright, sweet boy. And it was just the two of us."

She touched his cheek, and Stefan knew that he could never fault her for not telling him.

His mother had sacrificed so much for him, so to be hurt because she'd kept such a thing to herself? A private, shattering pain she'd been forced to endure on her own?

He could allow her that secret without a shred of anger or resentment.

"When your father didn't come back, I moved into a smaller place. I'd given the big stuff away—Sophia's furniture, clothes, the car seat and stroller," she said. "The rest I packed up . . . and I just never found the strength to open it again. It was so much easier when I didn't have to look at the reminders of how I'd failed her—"

Her voice broke, and Stefan bent to wrap her in his arms. "I'm so sorry, Mom."

She sniffed. "I'm the one who should be apologizing. I kept it from you."

He pulled back and put both hands on her shoulders, holding her in place until she met his eyes. "I understand why."

Her chin dipped down to her chest, and a long slow breath escaped her lips. "Thank you," she murmured.

"It's not your fault, Diane," Pierre said. Stefan stiffened. He hadn't heard his father come over, had forgotten he was in the room at all. "And I should be the one apologizing."

Stefan opened his mouth, ready to retort, but his father beat him to it.

"I'm sorry," Pierre said, a guileless expression on his face. "I failed as a parent . . . as a husband." He reached out, touched Diane's shoulder. "I have so many regrets when it comes to us. Yes, I was crazy with grief, but that's no excuse. What I did was unbelievably weak—both with S-Sophia and then later with Stefan."

Diane turned to face him, her eyes dry but the sorrow evident. "It's not your—"

Pierre shook his head. "I'm not looking for absolution or forgiveness."

"Then what?" Stefan said.

His anger toward his father wasn't red-hot any longer—more like a cool burn—but he sure as hell wasn't willing to just let this go. Putting aside that fact that Pierre had left his mother during her darkest moments, what he'd done when Stefan was a teenager—

For Christ's sake, it had almost ripped both of their lives to shreds.

"You can't go back," he told Pierre. "Not after all this. Too much time has gone by."

They all fell quiet, and Stefan could hear every damn breath, every freaking rustle of clothing. There was a tension swirling within him, tighter and tighter, until it threatened to burst.

"I don't want to go back," Pierre finally said. "I understand that we can't, that we may never have the kind of relationship we *might* have had. But . . . I would very much like to move forward."

Brit had said much the same thing, so much so that it was impossible for Stefan to ignore the similarities.

Except, he didn't want to move forward, dammit. He wanted to stay in his own peaceful world, to not have every buried memory uncovered and exposed to the world.

Yet when his mother said, "I'd like that, too," Stefan found he didn't have the strength to disagree with her.

THE NEXT MORNING, Stefan walked into the arena. They still had a few hours before their scheduled practice, but he'd seen Brit's car in the lot and hadn't been able to resist pulling in.

A few members of the media called at him for a picture, but Stefan ignored them. No doubt, he and Brit would make the news.

Their relationship was still going strong, at least if one believed the media.

Which clearly proved the press didn't know a damned thing.

There hadn't been any fallout, any reports of their breakup, partly because the team had been travelling a lot, and partly because Julian's injury had made it so the press was much more focused on Brit's skills and the Gold winning—actually *winning* games—than following them around and documenting *Brifan*—the honest-to-God term the media had dubbed for their coupledom.

Of course, if they found out the dirty details of their so-called relationship's inception . . .

Thankfully, that hadn't happened.

Instead, Susan had gotten her press. Brit had gotten her dream. And he—

He shook his head. He didn't know what he'd gotten.

His inner conscience called bullshit on that one.

Which was why he was at the arena in the first place. Because Brit was there.

He walked down the hall, barely noting the pictures and closed office doors as he passed by. There was nothing like the smell,—disinfectant, *IcyHot*, eau de Hockey. Nothing like the almost-revenant quiet.

It was as close to a religious experience as he got.

People had accused him many times of being distant. But Stefan wasn't that. He felt. He sympathized, raged, *hurt*.

But what he didn't do was punish himself, the last six weeks aside.

When things went to crap, he typically cut ties first. It made things easier, kept his heart more intact. Usually, it was less painful.

Not with Brit.

He'd said goodbye so many times in his life—to teammates, to coaches—left them behind while he'd gone ahead, enduring the cool slices of jealousy, of things changing in an agonizing, irrevocable way he couldn't control.

Keeping relationships superficial eased that transition.

But it was impossible to cut ties with Brit. He couldn't. She was a teammate and . . . the truth was he didn't want to.

Forget the deception. Fuck the lies. Brit had said she'd cared about him, and Stefan knew it was the truth. She'd trusted, showed him her weak spots, her soft, feminine side. He knew her well enough to recognize that those shared times hadn't been fake.

No matter what she'd told herself. No matter who had forced her hand.

Finally, he understood that their relationship had been real. *Special.*

And, idiot that he was, Stefan thought what he'd said the night before might have ruined that.

He had accused her of putting obstacles between them.

Well now, he'd thoroughly succeeded in topping that, both by insulting her and her relationship with Blane, and then by jabbing his fingers into the open wound that was all that remained of their relationship.

He sighed as he slipped past the locker room and into the arena.

The *crack* of sticks, plural, surprised him. Brit and Frankie were there, which he'd expected—she and the goalie coach usually did an extra practice together on non-game days.

So, no, that wasn't the surprise. What made his jaw drop open was that Stewart was on the ice.

He loosed a slap shot that Brit stopped handily then laughed when she ribbed him, "Next time put something on that, will you?"

Stewart laughing? Stewart spending extra time on the ice?

Since when?

Except . . . now that he thought of it, Stefan couldn't ignore the fact that Mike Stewart *had* been working hard to become part of the team. He hadn't missed a practice, had gone to more outside events than even Stefan.

He'd even seen Mike at a charity function, which the defenseman typically avoided like the plague.

Had he changed? Really, *actually* changed?

Frankie called, "That's good for now, Brit. Cool down and see Mandy so you're ready for this afternoon."

She skated off the ice, Frankie following suit. They both nodded at Stefan as they walked by, but there was a distance in Brit's eyes that made his gut sink . . .

Then twist into knots as Stewart stopped in front of him. "Hey," Mike said.

"Hey," Stefan responded.

And silence.

Stefan started to move away.

"I—uh, wanted to talk to you," Stewart blurted.

Stefan looked at him in surprise. "Talk?"

Stewart shrugged. "Yeah, I know," he said. "I'd joke about it being a girl thing, but I don't want Brit to kick my ass."

Stefan chuckled, and it felt rough, underused. But it also felt good. Really, *really* good to laugh after the last twenty-four hours of his life. "She probably would," he agreed. He waited a beat then asked, "What do you want to talk about?"

"I had some shit happening in my life," Stewart said. "Things that were really screwing with my head. They're better now, and my goal is do right by the team, but I wanted to say"—he hesitated—"I'm sorry. For all of it. The snark. The not trying. The general asshole-ness."

Tension Stefan hadn't even realized he was holding onto loosened, made it so he could breathe a little easier. If Stewart was saying that, making that big of a change . . . maybe he could too.

Mike glanced up, a slightly guilty look in his eyes. "And also, thanks for helping me with the ladder-drill-from-hell."

Stefan shrugged, feeling a little uncomfortable with the absence of Mike's snark. "I'd say it was my pleasure . . ."

"Yeah. No," Stewart said. "The words *my pleasure* should never come out of your mouth when referring to me."

Stefan snorted. "Yeah. Okay." He tilted his head in the direction of the hall. An idea had come to him suddenly, a way to make things right. "We good?"

"We're good," Stewart said. "Well, almost. There's one more thing."

"What's that?"

"I know where the pictures are." He fussed with the finger of his glove. "I want to get them for Brit."

Hope and respect swept to life inside of Stefan. He didn't ask how Stewart knew about the pictures when not another soul seemed to. That piece didn't matter. Brit's happiness was more important.

He nodded in agreement. "Yes. Along those lines, I've been thinking, and I have an idea."

Stefan had a number programmed into his phone that he hadn't used yet. He scrolled through his contacts, selected the name, and dialed.

It rang once before the man on the other side picked up.

"Dan," he told Brit's brother. "I need your help."

FIFTY-SEVEN

Brit

BRIT DROVE HOME from the afternoon practice wanting nothing more than a bath. Hours in Stefan's presence had grated, and his words from the previous evening were on repeat in her brain.

"Why don't you fuck him too?"

She stepped out of the stairwell and into the hall then promptly cursed under her breath.

Apparently, a bath wasn't in her immediate future.

Susan and a gorgeous blond woman—who looked vaguely familiar—were waiting outside her apartment door.

"Hello," she said, stopping in the hall and not bothering to unlock the door. She sure as hell didn't want Susan inside, and the bitchy pout on the other woman's face didn't particularly strike Brit as friendly.

"We need to talk. Now," Susan said without any of the usual pesky formalities, like *"Hello"* or *"Good to see you."*

"I think we've had all of the conversations we need to have," Brit said and tried to move past her.

"Not quite." Susan glanced around the hallway, gaze stopping pointedly on the five other doors dotting the walls. "And this isn't exactly one you want to have here."

"Fine," Brit snapped. "You can come in. But you'll say your piece and leave. I meant what I said before. I'm done." The blond woman snorted, and Brit glared at her. "Why are *you* here?"

"I'm here," the woman said, "because I'm critically important to your career. So invite me in and offer me a glass of wine."

For the love of all that was holy.

Brit unlocked the door and pushed it open. "Sit," she told them, gesturing to the cute little sofa she'd picked up at a used furniture store.

"This is . . . *cozy*," Susan said. "Jessica? Isn't it just darling?"

Brit ignored the jab. Her apartment had made her happy from the first moment she'd walked in. She'd painted the walls a cheerful blue, filled the space with mementos she'd gathered over the years.

It was delicate. It was feminine.

There wasn't a single detail of hockey.

Well, there were a few drawers crammed with awards she'd won over the years, but the rest of the space was hers alone. Just a woman carving out her own niche, reveling in a space that was hers alone.

Alone.

The word sent a wave of pain through her, but Brit dutifully shoved it away and walked into the kitchen.

She snagged three beers—because, if nothing else, her mom had engrained it in her to be polite to guests—and went back into the family room.

"Here," she said, handing them two of the beers. Susan gave the bottle a disgusted look and promptly set it on the coffee table then elbowed Blondie, who begrudgingly followed suit.

"You wanted to talk," Brit said, taking out her cell phone and setting it on the table, "so talk."

Susan and the woman glanced at each other then back to Brit. "I believe some introductions are in order. This is Jessica, my niece."

"I'd say it's nice to meet you . . ." Except Brit had no idea what this was about aside from it involving Susan. And that meant, it couldn't be good.

"Jessica is the reason that the Gold have gotten so much good press lately. She's a reporter for *The Herald*."

Brit didn't say anything. Didn't know *what* to say. Congrats? Thank you?

"But because of some . . . *conflicts* with her employer, she finds herself without a position."

"What kind of *conflicts*?"

Jessica rolled her eyes. "The kind where my boss is an asshole who accused me of sleeping with another reporter's source to steal the article from her."

Brit plunked down onto her pale-blue armchair, sinking into the comfy cushions. "Did you?"

"Of course I did," Jessica said without rancor. "That's how women get ahead in our fields. It's a necessary evil."

"No, it's not."

Or at least, it *shouldn't* be. No one should have to endure the secret shame, the guilt, the not-being-good-enough, just because they didn't own a pair.

Jessica sat up a little straighter, thrusting her chin and boobs into the stratosphere. "I'm going to write an exposé on the Gold and what they forced you to do—"

"Your aunt was the one who forced me to do it," Brit interrupted, her voice shrill with incredulity. "It was *her* idea."

Jessica smirked. "Mine, actually. My auntie here just supports my career. I needed a really good way to get back at

Stefan. What's better than painting him as the blackmailing bad guy?"

Brit's mind was spinning as it scrambled to keep up. *Jessica and Stefan? Stefan as a bad guy?*

"Blackmail?"

"Yes." Jessica smirked. "Some of the pictures I took of the two of you weren't *PG* enough for the traditional media, but I know of some websites that might like them—"

"Stefan is the best man I know," Brit said. "You can't do this to him."

"I can do what I want," Jessica sneered. "He refused—" She sniffed. "Never mind. I'm too good for him anyway."

Brit glanced around the room.

"What are you doing?" Susan snapped.

"Looking for the cameras, because I'm clearly on some scripted reality show. People don't act like this in real life." Her eyes flashed back to the pair. "You two cannot seriously be interested in ruining a man's life just because he turned you down for a date."

"This is not about a date," Susan said. "That's not important—"

Jessica opened her mouth. "It *is* impor—"

"Shut. Up." Susan shot her niece a dirty look. "This isn't about a date and it's not just about Stefan. We're going after what matters." The older woman's frown lines increased tenfold. "Men are scum. They take what they want and then throw you away when they're done."

"That's not true," Brit protested.

"Yeah?" Susan asked, cold cruelty filling her words. "So where is Stefan then?"

"That's not the—"

"Point?" Susan interrupted. "Brit. That's *exactly* the point.

We're going after the Gold. The board. Devon Carter. We're going to show we're not disposable. That they have to respect—"

"Auntie," Jessica interjected, probably wanting Susan to shut up just as much as Brit did.

"This is the time to fight." Susan said, waving her off. "For *all* women."

"Yes. Yes. Women's rights, blah, blah, blah." Jessica rolled her eyes. "But further that, this could be the story of the century. If we work together . . ."

It could be a huge story.

If Brit were going to be a part of it.

If she believed a word Susan was spouting.

Which she wasn't. Which she didn't.

"No one is going to believe Stefan acted on his own," she told Jessica. "Not after the scandal last season with Gordaine. Lightning doesn't strike the same place twice, and management —your aunt right alongside them—is going to take the fall."

It was that part Brit found hard to believe—Susan supporting this risk to herself. Then again, the older woman hadn't gotten as far as she had without knowing how to protect her own back.

"Definitely not," Jessica said. "Management is going to fall. But not my aunt. She's a victim, same as you, and has certain items to . . . *ensure* that fact."

Of course she did.

"Well, I'm sorry to tell you this"—no, actually, she wasn't —"but I will not be a part of this story. Write what you will, but I won't cooperate. And I definitely won't confirm anything."

Not like this. Not being forced into a situation where she knew the people on the other side of the lens, so to speak, didn't give a damn about her as a person and certainly didn't give a damn about the wrongs that had been committed.

No, if—*when*—Brit discussed this with the media, it would be on her terms with a person of *her* choosing.

"I don't know what Stefan sees in you," Jessica muttered. "You're not pretty and only mediocre at hockey. He could . . ."

Brit stopped listening. Because yeah, no. The person Brit poured her heart out to definitely wouldn't be the prissy bitch sitting across from her.

Susan stood. "I would encourage you to reconsider. This story is, pardon the pun, pure *gold*. A female player rises above the ranks, finds her way through horrible circumstances, only to gain a staunch supporter in a woman who fought her way up the management side." She paused, tapped her chin. "Devon will have to go, of course, and the rest of the board. But I have enough on them to make that happen."

Brit wondered why Susan hadn't mentioned Pierre's purchase of the team. Surely that would shake up things, management-wise, alter these carefully laid plans. But if Susan *didn't* know, Brit sure as hell wasn't going to tell her. She needed to hold on to as many cards as possible.

"I'm not doing this," Brit said, even though they were basically ignoring her as they discussed their grand plans to take over the world.

"Photographs," Susan and Jessica said in unison without turning to look at her.

For God's sake.

"Fuck the photographs," she told them, slamming her beer down hard enough on the table that some of it frothed over the top and splashed down the sides. Susan and Jessica turned, regarding her with calculating expressions, but Brit wasn't about to back down.

Hell. No.

"Print them or don't," she said. "Put them on a goddamned

billboard, for all I care. I'm done with giving them any power over me."

"Little late to get a conscience, don't you think?" Susan asked. "Maybe I need to arrange a trade . . ." It was a musing statement and full-to-the-brim with derision.

Even though Brit's stomach churned at the thought of being forced to leave the team, she knew that it was now or never.

If she didn't find her spine now, she might not. *Ever*.

"It's time for you to leave."

"I thought you told me that Stefan and Stewart both said they would activate their trade clauses if you released Brit?" Jessica asked.

Susan made a noise of disgust even as the terror gripping Brit's heart diminished slightly. She needed to remember she wasn't alone.

"Those clauses are the worst thing management ever allowed," Susan said as she grabbed Jessica's arm and yanked her niece to her feet. "And you need to learn the art of keeping your mouth shut."

At the door, she paused to look back at Brit. "I'll give you twenty-four hours to reconsider. Then Jessica is running the story. With *all* the pictures."

Brit swallowed but stood and squared her shoulders before walking across the room. Her voice was rock-steady. "I don't need twenty-four hours or minutes or seconds," she told the women. "I'm done being manipulated, so take your story and shove it up your—"

She slammed the door.

FIFTY-EIGHT

THEIR GAME the following night was one of the tough ones.

The thing about hockey was that sometimes the other team got the bounces, and there wasn't a damn thing anyone could do about it.

Tonight had been one of those games.

They'd lost 3-5, and only one of those goals had been something Brit should have stopped. Two had gone off defensemen, one had been on a missed offside call by the officials, and the last had been an empty netter when Bernard had pulled her in exchange for a sixth skater during the game's last minutes.

It was only one game, but Brit had a hard time shaking off the goal she should have stopped. She'd let it in just when her team had finally tied the game.

Totally demoralizing. Completely killed the momentum.

Post-game, she'd had her standing appointment with Mandy where she'd spent a few extra minutes chatting—okay, dawdling and avoiding the rest of the team—in the PT suite afterward.

But her delay had paid off, and the locker room was empty when she slipped back in to change.

At least, now she didn't have to make up an excuse to miss

the team dinner Stefan had planned for Blane's birthday. No one had been much in the mood for celebrating after the game, but she knew they'd warm up.

Brit didn't *want* to warm up.

She wanted to get her fucking blocker up to snuff.

The thing about professional players was that they could shoot, which meant they could exploit her weaknesses. And if the Gold were going to go all the way, she *couldn't* have a single one.

With a sigh, she grabbed her bag and slung it over her shoulder.

Brit was moping, she knew that. Just as she knew that by morning she would feel better. She'd hit the ice again, schedule some extra sessions with Frankie—though she was monopolizing his time already.

Wrinkling her nose—because she smelled like musty gym socks and B.O.—Brit turned to the door.

First order of business when she got home was a shower.

Except . . . she hesitated . . . did she really want to sit in her stink the entire way? Did she really want to continue to let the unreasonable fear rule the way she lived her life?

Why not just take a freaking shower?

And with that thought, Brit decided. It was time. She would take a damn shower.

Two strides brought her into the tiled space. A *creak,* and the water from one head was on. With a fortifying breath, she walked out, dropped her bag on the bench, and stripped.

By the time Brit had slipped her feet into her flip-flops and snagged a towel from the stack, her heart was pounding and a light sheen of sweat covered her body.

Every part of her, all of the nerves that had been wired to *fear* screamed at her to stop, to get dressed and go home.

She walked into the showers anyway.

Then jumped when the water nearly scalded her.

Some of the tension within her disappeared. She could do this.

After adjusting the temperature, Brit stepped into the spray and began washing.

The scent reached her as she was rinsing conditioner from her hair. Spicy. Masculine.

Stefan.

She was delusional and her longing was acute. So painful that it threatened to take her to her knees. How she wished things were different—

"Hey."

Her eyes flashed open. Stefan was there. Three feet away. Fully dressed and standing just outside the range of the water.

One side of his mouth was curved up, and his eyes were warm, exactly like they'd been two months before.

"You did it," he said.

"I—" She swallowed. She *had* done it. But even as she reveled in that, Brit was very aware of Stefan's eyes traveling down and heating to a molten shade of blue.

Just that quickly her heart was pounding for a completely different reason.

Her nipples tightened, her stomach quivered, and the space between her thighs ached.

"Stefan," she said. It was an invitation. A plea.

No matter what he'd said, how he'd hurt her and she him, her body still wanted his.

But her heart wanted his more.

"I didn't come here for this." He raked a hand through his hair. "Not that I don't want—" He stopped. "It's just that . . . I heard the water, saw your stuff, and I knew what it meant." His eyes locked with hers and glimmered intensely. "I'm so damned proud of you, Brit."

"What?" she asked. The water was dripping into her ears, obscuring her hearing. Because no way could he mean . . .

"I'm proud of you. What you've done with the team, with yourself. It makes me so damn ashamed that I wasn't as strong. I should have—"

"No," she said. "I'm the one—"

"It was a fucked up situation, sweetheart. A bad beginning to something I want more than my next breath." He took a step closer until the water licked at the toes of his boots.

"Be careful," she said. "You'll ruin your shoes."

Stefan grinned. "Who gives a damn about my shoes, Brit? I know I don't. Not when I have you in front of me."

Another step. Water splattered on his slacks, soaking them, encasing them around the wide breadth of muscles there. Then he came closer, and the water seeped into his shirt.

"I want you," he said.

Good God, did she ever want him back. The need was a fire within her, a burn only he could extinguish.

He was inches away, and her fingers cramped with the urge to touch him.

So she did.

It was as if the contact shattered something in him—the distance, the last wall around his heart. The moment her hands touched his skin, he was a flurry of activity.

He kissed and stroked, caressed and touched her in all the places that ached—her throat, her breasts, her stomach and thighs . . .

In between.

It was too much and not enough. The sensations coursed through her, drove her higher until she was desperate for release—

But that wasn't the part of Stefan she wanted.

"No more," she gasped, yanking up on his hair.

He stood and plastered her against his chest, his mouth on her throat, then her ear. Warm puffs of air punctuated his words. "No condom."

"Then be thankful I'm on the pill," she said.

Stefan pulled back, the desire in his eyes a physical caress to her system. "Please tell me you're not joking."

"Serious as a breakaway," she told him.

"God," he said. "I love you so much."

She barely had time to process that before his pants were down, and she was pinned to the wall. The tiles were an ice-cold shock.

A heartbeat later, he was inside her, his body flush against hers, every inch—both inside and out—rock hard.

The cold was forgotten. The past, the fears, the deceit—it all disappeared.

Brit lost herself in the moment, in the hard strokes and hot kisses, and when she tumbled over the edge, her words followed suit. "I love you too."

Stefan held her close and slanted his mouth across hers in the most tender kiss imaginable, and Brit knew she'd never look at those showers in quite the same way again.

And that was totally fine with her.

FIFTY-NINE

Stefan

STEFAN GRABBED Brit's elbow when her legs proved a little unsteady, then cranked the water off, and wrapped her in her towel.

He grimaced as he zipped up his pants. His clothes were soaked, having moved into the uncomfortably tight stage.

"Why am I always ending up with wet pants around you?"

Brit laughed, but the sound wasn't as carefree as he'd expected or had hoped.

He closed the distance between them and cupped her face in his palms. "You okay? Was it too much? Did I—"

"No." She sniffed. "It was perfect."

Then why was she looking as though someone ran over her dog?

"It's just that I almost ruined this." Her eyes dropped to the floor, and her voice was decidedly watery.

Stefan's heart grew a full size. It seemed impossible that Brit made him feel so much, but every moment in her presence, he felt more.

Loved her more.

He snagged her chin, forced her to meet his gaze, dead on. "And that's the last time that I want to hear you say that. We *both* made mistakes, and we won't ever move forward if we keep looking back." His fingers slid to the back of her head, wove into her hair, and he kissed her.

Because he couldn't *not* kiss her, because her mouth was irresistible, and—most important—because the feel of her lips against his was everything. "I want this, Brit. Us. When I'm with you, I feel whole." He blew out a breath. "I don't want to spend another moment not feeling whole."

"But what if we fight?" she asked. "We were together once, and it nearly ruined both of us. What if next time it affects the team? This whole thing could be a recipe for disaster."

"Could be," he said. "But I think we and the team have been playing pretty damned good, fighting or not." He flashed her a smile and stepped back. "I think we'll have more to worry about when we're both limp and satiated."

She snorted. "*Satiated*, really?"

"Yup. I might not have gone to college, but I can pull out a big word every now and then."

Brit bent to pick up one of her flip-flops that had apparently fallen off her foot and slipped it on. "I'm impressed."

"You should be. Now come here. I've got something to give you."

What he'd been planning to give her before he'd been distracted by the sight of her naked in the shower.

His pants got tighter at the memory, more so when Brit walked over and snuggled up to him.

"Is it a present?" she asked. "I like presents."

"Kind of," he said and walked over to his bag. "Just so you know, I didn't do this alone. Dan and Stewart helped."

She paled as he handed her the envelope.

"I didn't look, and neither did Stewart. I think Dan only looked so much as he had to for the investigation."

"Investigation?" Her hands clenched, wrinkled the brown paper. "My brother *looked*?"

"Turns out that a lot of funds have gone missing from the Gold's coffers, enough that the IRS noticed and alerted the FBI."

"Dan?"

Stefan knew what she was asking. Had her brother known when he'd come to visit months before?

"No, Dan didn't know. It wasn't his case." Stefan paused. "But it turned out he knew the FBI team investigating. When I called him a few days ago, he talked to his buddy and found out about it. He was able to cash in a few favors, so the original and digital copies of your pictures were *lost*."

Brit's eyes were suspiciously glossy. "You did all that?"

"I didn't do anything." He touched her check.

"You called." She bit her lip. "Thank you."

"It was nothing."

"Not to me."

They sat in quiet for a moment. "So what about your dad? Why did he decide to buy the Gold?"

"Apparently, he's been wanting to buy an NHL team. He thinks it's a good investment—or at least that's what my mother says. Devon was so panicked to hide the tax mess he caved when my father put in an offer."

"Your mother—"

"I don't know." He clenched his jaw, tried not to put into his voice how much the notion infuriated him. "They've talked some. I think they're trying to put the past aside."

"That's good," Brit said. "Your mom deserves to be happy."

"Be reasonable, why don't you?" he said then, "And yes, she does."

He stifled a sigh and took Brit's hand. The envelope crinkled, and she glanced down as though surprised to still find it in her fingers, then released a shaky breath.

"Oh, God." She sank to the bench, dropped the folder into her lap, and put her head in her hands.

Stefan sat next to her. "It's okay. It's *finally* okay."

Releasing her head, she asked, "How did Stewart know?"

"Overheard Susan and Jessica talking. Apparently, he has some lock-picking skills, and you know your brother is as good as any hacker."

"I didn't even know he'd finished his assignment."

"He was just heading back to the States when I called."

Brit nodded, her eyes back on the envelope. A moment passed before she opened the small metal brads and pulled out the pictures.

Stefan looked away.

"No," she said. "This is it. The thing I was most ashamed of and"—she flipped to the next and the next until she'd looked through the entire stack—"as I'm seeing them now . . . I wonder what I was so afraid of. They're bad. Terrible, even. But they're also not any reflection on *me*." She turned to him. "How could I have ever thought otherwise?"

"Because you're human." He stroked a finger down her cheek, the skin slightly flushed but still as soft as silk. "And something was done to you without your permission. It was unacceptable, and when you went to the people who should have had your back, they didn't. What's the saying? 'You can't cure normal'?"

Brit rolled her eyes. "I'm hardly normal."

"No," he said. "You're so much more. Which is a big part of why I love you."

She smiled and rested her head on his shoulder, pressing the wet cotton of his shirt into his skin. "I don't think I'll ever get tired of hearing that."

Fingers trailed through her now-damp hair to the delicate skin of her shoulder as he joked, "You could say it back, you know."

He felt more than saw her smile. "Yeah, I could. I love you, Stefan."

Brit shoved the pictures back into the envelope and set it on the bench then rotated to face him. "You want to know when I knew we had something different?" Her expression had gentled, those brown eyes melting with affection.

"When?"

"From the beginning."

Stefan laughed, and her cheeks were tinged with the slightest hint of pink.

"The attraction was always there," she continued, "but seeing you react to the team, your tenderness when I freaked out on the stairs . . . well, I"—her lips curved—"I've got a weakness for men who protect my crease."

He chuckled. "Couldn't resist, could you?"

"No." She reached up, cupped his cheek. "Bad hockey puns aside. You get me, Stefan. And if you'll take me, I'm yours."

His arms wrapped around her waist and held her tight. *This is right.* She was right. "Only if you promise to take me in return."

"As if that were ever in question." One side of her mouth slid up. "I feel like I should be promising something like, '*In sickness or injury, in the event of a trade or penalty shot.*'"

Stefan laughed, pressed a kiss to her ear, her throat, her lips. "Proof positive that goalies are weird."

The notion was a common one. Who signed up to have hard cylinders of rubber shot at them at speeds faster than the typical car traveled?

The woman he loved did.

"So biased," she said. "And I'm not weird. I'm quirky. Quirky is cute. Weird is . . . just weird."

"Noted."

"Also, I have something that should help Dan with his investigation." She reached into her bag and pulled out her cell phone.

A few taps on the screen then Susan and Jessica's voices poured out of the speakers. *"What's better than painting him as the blackmailing bad guy. . . Men are scum . . . We're going after the Gold. The board. Devon Carter . . ."*

"How—" Stefan shook his head.

Brit smiled. "Jessica and Susan decided to pay a house call, but apparently they also didn't know cell phones could record their scheming." She shrugged. "Or maybe they just thought me too dumb to think of it."

"God, I *love* you." He pulled her close. So close that the towel slipped, and her breasts pressed against his chest, until her scent wrapped around his very being and soothed all the ragged edges.

He bent and sealed his mouth to hers, fell headlong into the swell of love.

Things wouldn't be easy, wouldn't be perfect.

But they had the sport. Had the team.

And each other. They definitely had each other.

Which was how he knew they would be okay.

SIXTY

Six Months Later

"PIERRE WANTS to see you in his office," Max told Stefan as he came out of the shower after the first day of training camp.

His gut got a little tense, but it no longer churned at the mere mention of his father's name.

They were working toward something that might resemble a friendship someday. It wouldn't ever be the father-son relationship he'd dreamed of as a child, but Stefan also no longer possessed a soul deep fury at the man who'd fathered him.

Brit had been a big part of that.

She'd never told him he should forgive his father, but she had facilitated opportunities for them to begin building bridges —weekly dinners when they were in town, the occasional team outing.

Another reason he loved her more every day.

It was getting easier to be around Pierre, and while the past wouldn't just disappear, Stefan found it wasn't quite so hard to shove it back where it belonged.

"Want me to wait for you?" Brit asked when he sat down

next to her. He'd promptly shoved Stewart out of *his* spot after he'd patched up things with her last season.

Her face was freshly scrubbed, her blond hair back in its usual ponytail. He wanted to kiss her.

So he did.

Then flipped off the room at large when somebody wolf-whistled.

"No, go on," he told her once they'd broken apart. "I know it's your night for dinner with Mandy. I'll fend for myself."

"Or grab the guys and go out," she teased.

"Or that." He laughed and stole another kiss. "See you tonight."

His eyes trailed her as she grabbed her bag then headed over to the PT suite. She was gorgeous as ever, maybe even more beautiful because the secrets and pain that had once weighed her down were gone.

Last season, she'd led the team to the third round of the playoffs before they'd lost to their conference rival, the Minnesota Wild. She'd been capable and strong, but the team had gotten tired after having gone to seven games in each of the previous two rounds.

Despite the elimination, she still ended up with the second best GAA—goals against average—in the league and had endeared herself to hockey fans for life with her goaltending acrobatics.

Stefan still didn't know how she managed to anticipate the play so well, how she seemed to instinctively *know* where the players would shoot.

It was thoroughly impressive, and her skill at her job was just another thing he loved about her.

"Whipped, dude," Stewart said. But there was no smirk in his tone, only amusement.

Mike had done as promised. He'd checked the attitude at

the door, worked hard as hell, and as thus, had become one of the Gold's biggest assets.

Stefan was happy to have him on the team.

He turned to Mike and narrowed his eyes. "Dinner. Text me, and I'll meet you and the guys after I talk to Pierre."

Two minutes later, he was walking into his father's office.

Pierre had dismissed the entire board—well, with the help of Dan, Brit's recording, and the rest of the FBI, they'd *resigned* . . . then promptly been indicted on charges of money laundering and embezzling.

Susan and company would be enjoying all of the comforts of a prison cell for many years.

Once the board was out of the picture, Pierre had hired a new GM, appointed a new board, and things were in much better shape, management-wise.

Stefan had half-expected his father to be at the rink every day, making snide remarks and generally making a mess of things.

He hadn't.

Pierre travelled often for his various businesses, and though he seemed to be in touch with the pulse of the team and checked in often, his father hadn't been a nuisance.

Despite everything, he might even be starting to tolerate—okay, *like*—the guy. With Brit in his life, everything from the past seemed very much in the past, and the anger . . . well, the anger was getting very hard to drum up.

"You wanted to see me?" Stefan asked once he was through the office door.

"Yes. Want to sit?" Pierre indicated an empty chair in front of his desk. "It'll only take a moment."

There was a note of something in Pierre's voice. Nervousness?

"Okay." Stefan sat. "What's up?"

Pierre straightened a stack of papers, opened and closed the drawer.

Definitely nervous.

Was it about the team? A trade? *Brit?*

"I'll just get straight down to it," Pierre said. "I want your blessing to court your mother."

Stefan's fist shot out before he'd even comprehended what had happened. It collided against his father's jaw with a loud *crack.*

Pierre's head whipped back, and Stefan felt a moment of horror at what he'd done.

Then his father grinned, and the pang eased. "I guess that is up for interpretation?"

Stefan didn't reply, only glared. What had he been thinking? *Like* his father? Fuck no. He was going to kill the bastard.

"Look," Pierre said. "I did wrong by your mother and you. So damned wrong." He rubbed his jaw, the red mark from Stefan's fist large and spreading by the moment. "But the thing about getting older, about working hard and getting everything you thought you ever wanted is that it feels empty without someone to share it with."

Unfortunately, Stefan understood that feeling very clearly.

Pierre watched him, eyes serious now, all signs of the previous grin wiped away. "I'd like to have an opportunity to change that."

Stefan thought about what his father was saying, knew how lonely and miserable he'd been without Brit. He couldn't give his blessing. It was too soon for that, but—

"It's really up to Mom," he told Pierre. "If she says yes, I won't stand in your way."

A flicker of emotion crossed his father's face. "Thank you."

"Don't thank me. Just don't hurt her again, and we'll be okay. You so much as make her cry and . . ."

Pierre nodded, was quiet for a moment before he said, "I'd like a chance with you too."

That wasn't so easy. Part of Stefan wanted it, had *always* wanted it. The rest wasn't so willing. "We'll see."

"Tough crowd," Pierre quipped.

"Can you blame me?"

"No," his father said, voice filled to the brim with remorse. "No, I can't."

Stefan wanted to tell his father to fuck off, to leave him and his mother alone. But it had been *six* months since Pierre had reentered their lives. Six months of building tentative bridges and not being a total asshole.

So, with a mental shrug, Stefan gave into the part of him that wanted to see where things went with his father. If nothing else, the last months had taught him that sometimes it didn't hurt to take a risk with his heart. "The guys and I are going to dinner. Want to come with?"

Pierre's eyes were suspiciously shiny. He cleared his throat, looked away. "I'd like that very much."

As they walked out together, Stefan thought that, for the first time in a long time, happily-ever-afters might actually be a reality.

EPILOGUE

Sara

THE LIGHT WAS PERFECT . . . until it wasn't.

Sara glared up at the large, brick-wall style shadow that was marring her perfect view.

Did the person not understand just how *freaking* long she'd had to wait for the moon to peek out from behind the fog, to gild the rotunda at the Palace of Fine Arts and reflect off the water in perfect symmetry?

She clutched her pencil—the same one that had been sketching furiously just seconds before—and leaned to the left, trying to get one more glimpse of the scene, to commit it to memory before it was . . .

Gone.

Son of a—

"I know you."

The male voice was chocolate ice cream with hot fudge and marshmallow fluff, warm sand sifting between her toes, the perfect ending to a dramatic rom-com all rolled into one.

The hairs on her nape rose, and she shivered, wanting to snuggle into the sound, to pull it close like a cuddly sweatshirt—

At least until alarm flared to life, and she remembered she was totally alone.

Suddenly, skulking around the Marina District in the middle of the night seemed like a horrible idea.

Her sketchbook fell to the ground, the book light that had been clipped to the top making a sickening crack as it hit the concrete and went out. She blinked, trying to get her eyes to adjust, but darkness descended as fog swallowed the moon back up. She gripped her pencil like a knife and held it threateningly . . . or at least as threateningly as a pencil can be held. "Back off."

Her attempt at a growl, a warning.

And not a very scary one at that, if the man's reaction was anything to go by.

A soft chuckle was the only thing she heard before the pencil was plucked from her fingers. Sara opened her mouth to scream, but instead of jumping her like she'd half-expected, he sank into a crouch and handed the pencil back.

"You shouldn't be out here by yourself," he said.

"Noted," Sara muttered and shoved it into her pocket before bending to grab her sketchbook and light. "And you shouldn't ruin a perfect setup."

A flash of white teeth penetrated the darkness. "Noted," he said and put a palm to his knee, as though to push himself to standing.

Her eyes dropped. They'd adjusted enough to see his hands. And those hands were *gorgeous*. Long, lean fingers and neatly trimmed nails with enough character to make them interesting. She flipped to a blank page of her sketchbook, flicked the switch on the light, and spread his fingers on her thigh. The contrast, the shadows, the scars on his knuckles. His hand was the perfect juxtaposition and she *had* to get it on paper.

"Umm—"

"Shh." Her pencil flew across the page. It made a soft scratching sound as she worked, outlining, shading in the image, blending and building until his hand was captured on paper.

She didn't know how long she worked, just that when she'd finished, her neck ached and her legs were stiff and . . . a strange man had his hand on her thigh.

Her breath caught, and she looked up.

He was beautiful. Oddly familiar with his face half-illuminated in the lamplight, eyes as dark as ink, several days of scruff on his cheeks and chin, nose just slightly askew, as though it had been broken a time or two. And was that a bruise just above his right cheekbone?

Sara didn't have a chance to look closer.

His fingers flexed on her thigh, and every one of her thoughts beelined straight for that particular body part. She was in jeans, so it wasn't like he was touching her skin. But he might as well have been.

The warmth of his palm seeped through the thick material, made her quads flex. He was huge, his hand spanning the width of her thigh easily, and just the kind of man she liked. Big and strong, tall and wide-shouldered. Here was a man who could do all the clichés: protect her, shelter her, weather proverbial storms.

"You done?" The soft question held just the slightest hint of amusement, except there was a bite to the humor, as though that piece of his personality hadn't been used in a good long time.

No. She wanted to sketch his face, flip his hand over and draw the lines of his palm, but she'd submitted enough to her artist-crazy for the evening. And her hand was sore.

"Yeah," she said, ignoring the slightly breathless quality to her voice and standing.

Sketchbook into her pack, light off and into her pocket, stiff and aching hip, ribs, and shoulder from sitting too long on the cold, hard ground. Yup. All was as it should be.

The man stood as well. His size on the ground hadn't done his real breadth justice.

He. Was. Ginormous.

Okay, so she was petite, barely five feet three, but this man towered over her.

Yet she didn't feel scared. Embarrassed, maybe, that she'd hijacked his hand for—she pulled out her phone and glanced at the time—an hour and a half. But definitely not scared.

And she'd focus on that at a later time. For now, she should probably make an escape before she looked even more crazy cakes.

"Sorry I messed up your sketch," he rumbled.

She nibbled on the side of her mouth, biting back a smile. "Sorry I stole your hand for so long."

He shrugged. "My mom's an artist. I get it."

Well, there went her battle with the smile. Her lips twitched and her teeth came out of hiding. If there was one thing that Sara had, it was her smile. It had been her trademark in her competition days.

Which were long over.

Her mouth flattened out, the grin slipping away. Time to go, time to forget, to move on, to rebuild. "Thanks," she said and extended a hand.

Then winced and dropped it when her ribs cried out in protest.

"You okay?" he asked, head tilting, eyes studying her.

"Fine." And out popped her new smile. The fake one. Careful of her aching side, she shrugged into her backpack. "I've got to go." She turned, ponytail flapping through the hair to land on her opposite shoulder.

"That—" He touched her arm. "Wait. I *know* I know you."

She froze. That was the second time he'd said that, and now they were getting into dangerous territory. Recognition meant . . . no. She couldn't.

There had been a time when *everyone* had known her. Her face on Wheaties boxes, her smile promoting toothpaste and credit cards alike.

That wasn't her life any longer.

"Thanks again. Bye." She started to hurry away.

"Wait." A hand dropped on to her shoulder, thwarting her escape, and she hissed in pain.

"Sorry," he said, but he didn't release her. Instead, he shifted his grip from her aching shoulder down to her elbow and when she didn't protest, he exerted gentle pressure until Sara was facing him again. "It's just that know I *know* you."

No. This wasn't happening.

"You're Sara Jetty."

Her body went tense.

Oh God. This was *so* happening.

"It's me." He touched his chest like she didn't know he was talking about himself, and even as she was finally recognizing the color of his eyes, the familiar curve of his lips and line of his jaw, he said the worst thing ever, "Mike Stewart."

Oh *shit.*

—Get Backhand, book 2 of the Gold Hockey series now available

GOLD HOCKEY SERIES

Blocked

Backhand

Boarding

Benched

Breakaway

Breakout

Checked

GOLD HOCKEY

Did you miss any of the Gold Hockey books?
Find information about the full series here.
Or keep reading for a sneak peek into each of the books below!

Blocked

Gold Hockey Book #1

Get your copy at books2read.com/Blocked

Brit

THE FIRST QUESTION Brit always got when people found out she played ice hockey was *"Do you have all of your teeth?"*

The second was *"Do you, you know, look at the guys in the locker room?"*

The first she could deal with easily—flash a smile of her full set of chompers, no gaps in sight. The second was more problematic. Especially since it was typically accompanied by a smug smile or a coy wink.

Of course she looked. *Everybody* looked once. Everyone

snuck a glance, made a judgment that was quickly filed away and shoved deep down into the recesses of their mind.

And she meant *way* down.

Because, dammit, she was there to play hockey, not assess her teammates' six packs. If she wanted to get her man candy fix, she could just go on social media. There were shirtless guys for days filling her feed.

But that wasn't the answer the media wanted.

Who cared about locker room dynamics? Who gave a damn whether or not she, as a typical heterosexual woman, found her fellow players attractive?

Yet for some inane reason, it *did* matter to people.

Brit wasn't stupid. The press wanted a story. A scandal. They were desperate for her to fall for one of her teammates—or better yet the captain from their rival team—and have an affair that was worthy of a romantic comedy.

She'd just gotten very good at keeping her love life—as nonexistent as it was—to herself, gotten very good at not reacting in any perceptible way to the insinuations.

So when the reporter asked her the same set of questions for the thousandth time in her twenty-six years, she grinned—showing off those teeth—and commented with a sweetly innocent "Could've sworn you were going to ask me about the coed showers." She waited for the room-at-large to laugh then said, "Next question, please."

–Get your copy at books2read.com/Blocked

Backhand

Gold Hockey Book #2

Get your copy at books2read.com/Backhand

Sara

"Sorry I messed up your sketch," he rumbled.

She nibbled on the side of her mouth, biting back a smile. "Sorry I stole your hand for so long."

He shrugged. "My mom's an artist. I get it."

Well, there went her battle with the smile. Her lips twitched and her teeth came out of hiding. If there was one thing that Sara had, it was her smile. It had been her trademark in her competition days.

Which were long over.

Her mouth flattened out, the grin slipping away. Time to go, time to forget, to move on, to rebuild. "Thanks," she said and extended a hand.

Then winced and dropped it when her ribs cried out in protest.

"You okay?" he asked, head tilting, eyes studying her.

"Fine." And out popped her new smile. The fake one. Careful of her aching side, she shrugged into her backpack. "I've got to go." She turned, ponytail flapping through the hair to land on her opposite shoulder.

"That—" He touched her arm. "Wait. I *know* I know you."

She froze. That was the second time he'd said that, and now they were getting into dangerous territory. Recognition meant . . . no. She couldn't.

There had been a time when *everyone* had known her. Her face on Wheaties boxes, her smile promoting toothpaste and credit cards alike.

That wasn't her life any longer.

"Thanks again. Bye." She started to hurry away.

"Wait." A hand dropped on to her shoulder, thwarting her escape, and she hissed in pain.

"Sorry," he said, but he didn't release her. Instead, he shifted his grip from her aching shoulder down to her elbow and when she didn't protest, he exerted gentle pressure until Sara was facing him again. "It's just that know I *know* you."

No. This wasn't happening.

"You're Sara Jetty."

Her body went tense.

Oh God. This was *so* happening.

"It's me." He touched his chest like she didn't know he was talking about himself, and even as she was finally recognizing the color of his eyes, the familiar curve of his lips and line of his jaw, he said the worst thing ever, "Mike Stewart."

Oh *shit.*

—Get your copy at books2read.com/Backhand

Boarding

Gold Hockey Book #3

Get your copy at books2read.com/Boarding

HOCKEY PLAYERS HAD the *best* asses.

No pancake bottoms, these men—and *women*—could fill out a pair of jeans. She wanted to squeeze it, to nibble it, bounce a dime—

Mandy dropped her chin to her chest, losing sight of the Sorting Hat cupcakes she'd been pondering.

Blane with his yummy ass had a unique way of distracting her.

No, it wasn't even distraction, per se. He had *always* been able to get under her skin.

And that was very, very bad for her.

"Ugh," she said, tossing her phone onto her desk and standing, knowing that she wouldn't be able to sit still now.

Nope, she needed about forty laps in the pool and a good hard fu—

Run, her mind blurted, almost yelling at the mental voice of her inner devil. *A good hard run.*

Unfortunately, the cajoling tone wasn't completely drowned out. *Some sexy horizontal time with Blane would be more fun—*

But the rest of the enticing words were lost as the roar of the crowd suddenly penetrated through the layers of concrete. Her stomach twisted. Mandy could tell, even before her eyes made it to the television, that it wasn't in celebration of a goal or a good hit either.

This was fury, a collective of outrage.

She was on her feet the moment she saw the prone form lying so still face down on the ice.

Her gut twisted when she spotted the curving line of a numeral two on the back of the player's jersey.

"Not him," she said and the words were familiar, a sentiment she had whispered, had *prayed* a thousand times before. She needed the camera angle to shift, for her to be able to see more clearly *who* was hurt. "Not him."

Then Dr. Carter was on the ice and the player moved slightly, rolling away from the camera, giving a full shot of his back and the matching twos adorning his jersey.

Fuck. Not him. Not Blane.

And that was when she saw the pool of blood.

—Get your copy at books2read.com/Boarding

Benched

Gold Hockey Book #4

Get your copy at books2read.com/Benched

Max

He started up the car, listening and chiming in at the right places as Brayden talked all things video game.

But his mind was unfortunately stuck on the fact that women were not to be trusted.

He snorted. Brit—the Gold's goalie and the first female in the NHL—and Mandy—the team's head trainer—would smack him around for that sentiment, so he silently amended it to: *most* women were not to be trusted.

There. Better, see?

Somehow, he didn't think they'd see.

He parked in the school's lot, walked Brayden in, and received the appropriate amount of scorn from the secretary for being thirty minutes late to school, then bent to hug Brayden.

"I'll pick you up today," he said.

Brayden smiled and hugged him tightly. Then he whispered something in his ear that hit Max harder than a two-by-four to the temple.

"If you got me a new mom, we wouldn't be late for school."

"Wh-what?" Max stammered.

"Please, Dad? Can you?"

And with that mind fuck of an ask, Brayden gave him one more squeeze and pushed through the door to the playground, calling, "Love you!" over his shoulder.

Then he was gone, and Max was standing in the office of his son's school struggling to comprehend if he had actually just heard what he'd heard.

A new mom?

Fuck his life.

—Get your copy at books2read.com/Benched

Breakaway

Gold Hockey Book #5

Get your copy at books2read.com/BreakawayGold

Blue

"Thanks for the ride."

"Try not to go out and get a fresh bimbo to ride tonight. I hear STIs on are the rise in the city."

Blue sighed, turned back to face her. "Really?"

She shrugged, smirk teasing the edges of her mouth, drawing his focus to the lushness of her lips. "Just watching out for Max's teammate."

He rolled his eyes. "Not hardly."

"Okay, how about I'm trying to prevent you from spreading STIs to the female populace."

"I'm clean, and I'm smart," he told her. "Condoms all the way."

"Ew."

Except there was something about the way she said it that made Blue stiffen and take notice. Because . . . he stared into her eyes, watched as the pale blue darkened to royal, saw her lips part, and her suck in a breath.

Holy shit.

"You're attracted to me."

Her jaw dropped. "No fucking way," she said, too quickly, pink dancing on the edges of her cheekbones. "You're delusional."

Blue got close.

Real close.

Anna licked her lips.

And fuck it all, he kissed that luscious mouth.

—Breakaway, www.books2read.com/BreakawayGold

Breakout

Gold Hockey Book #6

Get your copy at books2read.com/Breakout

PR-Rebecca

A fucking perfect hockey fairy tale.

Shaking her head, because she knew firsthand that fairy tales didn't exist outside of rom-coms and occasionally between alpha sports heroes and their chosen mates, Rebecca slipped through the corridor and stepped onto the Gold's bench.

Lots of dudes in suits—of both the boardroom *and* the hockey variety—were hugging.

On the ice. Near the goals. On the bench.

It was a proverbial hug-fest.

And she was the cynical bitch who couldn't enjoy the fact that the team she was with had just won the biggest hockey prize of them all.

"I knew you'd be like this."

Rebecca turned her focus from Brit, who was skating with the huge silver cup, to the man—no, to the *boy* because no matter how pretty and yummy he was, Kevin was still a decade younger than her—leaning oh so casually against the boards.

"Nice goal," she told him.

A shrug. "Blue made a nice pass."

And dammit, the fact that he wasn't an arrogant son of a bitch made her like him more.

She nodded at the cup. "You should go have your turn."

"I'll get mine," he said with another shrug.

She frowned, honestly confused. "You don't want—"

Suddenly he was in front of her on the bench, towering over her even though she was wearing her four-inch power heels. "You know what I want?"

Rebecca couldn't speak. Her breath had whooshed out of her in the presence of all that sweaty, hockey god-ness. Fuck he was pretty and gorgeous and . . . so fucking masculine that her thighs actually clenched together.

She wanted to climb him like a stripper pole.

"Do you?" he asked again when her words wouldn't come. "Want to know what I want?"

She nodded.

He bent, lips to her ear. "You, babe," he whispered. "I. Want. You."

Then he straightened and jumped back onto the ice, leaving her gaping after him like she had less than two brain cells in her skull.

The worst part?

She wanted him, too.

Had wanted him since the moment she'd laid eyes on the sexy as sin hockey god.

"Trouble," she murmured. "I'm in *so* much fucking trouble."

—Breakout, www.books2read.com/breakout

Checked

Gold Hockey Book #7

Get your copy at books2read.com/Checked

"Rebecca."

She kept walking.

She might work with Gabe, but she sure as heck wasn't on speaking terms with him. He'd dismissed her work, ignored her contribution to the team. He'd made her feel small and unimportant and—

She kept walking.

"*Rebecca*."

Not happening. Her car was in sight, thank fuck. She beeped the locks, reached for the handle.

He caught her arm.

"Baby—"

"I am *not* your baby, and you don't get to touch me." She ripped herself free, started muttering as she reached for the handle of her car again. "You don't even like me."

He stepped close, real close. Not touching her, not pushing the boundary she'd set, and yet he still got really freaking close. Her breath caught, her chin lifted, her pulse picked up. "That. Is. Where. You're. Wrong."

She froze.

"What?"

His mouth dropped to her ear, still not touching, but near enough that she could feel his hot breath.

"I like you, Rebecca. Too fucking much."

Then he turned and strode away.

—Checked, coming March 29th, 2020, www.books2read.com/Checked

ABOUT THE AUTHOR

USA Today bestselling author, Elise Faber, loves chocolate, Star Wars, Harry Potter, and hockey (the order depending on the day and how well her team -- the Sharks! -- are playing). She and her husband also play as much hockey as they can squeeze into their schedules, so much so that their typical date night is spent on the ice. Elise is the mom to two exuberant boys and lives in Northern California. Connect with her in her Facebook group, the Fabinators or find more information about her books at www.elisefaber.com.

facebook.com/elisefaberauthor

amazon.com/author/elisefaber

bookbub.com/profile/elise-faber

instagram.com/elisefaber

goodreads.com/elisefaber

pinterest.com/elisefaberwrite

ALSO BY ELISE FABER

Roosevelt Ranch Series (all stand alone, series complete)

Disaster at Roosevelt Ranch

Heartbreak at Roosevelt Ranch

Collision at Roosevelt Ranch

Regret at Roosevelt Ranch

Desire at Roosevelt Ranch

Billionaire's Club (all stand alone)

Bad Night Stand

Bad Breakup

Bad Husband

Bad Hookup

Bad Divorce

Bad Fiancé

Bad Boyfriend (Jan 19th 2020)

Gold Hockey (all stand alone)

Blocked

Backhand

Boarding

Benched

Breakaway

Breakout

Checked (March 29th, 2020)

Chauvinist Stories

Bitch (Feb 16th, 2020)

Cougar (March 1st, 2020)

Whore (March 15th, 2020)

Life Sucks Series (all stand alone)

Train Wreck

Phoenix Series

Phoenix Rising

Dark Phoenix

Phoenix Freed

Phoenix: LexTal Chronicles (rereleasing soon, stand alone, Phoenix world)

From Ashes

KTS Series

Fire and Ice (Hurt Anthology, stand alone)

Made in the USA
Columbia, SC
01 May 2022

59771710R00221